Lynette Rees is a RONE award-nominated author and former writing therapist, tutor and mentor.

She has written in many genres and has seen huge success with her self-published books. *The Workhouse Waif* hit the Amazon Kindle bestseller list and was No. 1 in 'Victorian Historical Romance'. She now publishes orphan sagas with Quercus Books in the UK.

Also by Lynette Rees

The Matchgirl
A Daughter's Promise
The Cobbler's Wife

The Workhouse Waif

Lynette Rees

Quercus

First self-published in 2017 by Lynette Rees

This edition first published in 2019 by

Quercus Editions Ltd
Carmelite House
50 Victoria Embankment
London EC4Y 0DZ

An Hachette UK company

A CIP catalogue record for this book is available
from the British Library

PAPERBACK ISBN 9 781 52940 0 663
EBOOK ISBN 978 1 78747 2 884

Cover design © Head Design

www.quercusbooks.co.uk

Typeset by Jouve (UK), Milton Keynes

Printed and bound in Great Britain by Clays Ltd, Elcograf S.p.A.

This book is dedicated to my lovely family. I am so grateful for your support. Thank you all!

Merthyr Tydfil, 1867

Chapter One

In her shabby dress, pinafore and scuffed leather hobnail boots, eleven-year-old Megan Hopkins skipped down the road. The thick material of the dress scratched at her skin, but for once, it was the furthest thing from her mind. Matron had entrusted her to go shopping in the marketplace as the Board of Guardians was due to meet later that day. She rarely ventured into Merthyr town and she was excited. She swung her wicker basket back and forth as she skipped, humming softly to herself. Completely in her own world, she stopped to tie up her bootlace, and as she crouched to the floor, the most beautiful, melodious voice she had ever heard drifted to her consciousness. She stood there for a while to listen to the song and wondered where it was coming from, and who it might be. It sounded like it was coming from the Temperance Hall.

Walking in the opposite direction to the marketplace she made her way over and read the poster, which was attached firmly to the front of the building: 'Appearing tonight, Miss Kathleen O'Hara, the voice of an angel . . .'

She was quickly pulled out of her reverie as the sharp, cold sensation of water hit her. It was a young woman with a – now – empty bucket, from which she had sloshed a whole load of dirty water onto the pavement, and also onto Megan.

The bottom of the woman's dress was tucked into the top of her bloomers and Megan wondered if she should tell her, but then the woman glared and said, 'Whatcha doing there, get on with yer. Don't want any waifs and strays around 'ere!'

Waifs and strays? That woman didn't look too fine herself. Sarky, silly cuss.

Megan drew her woollen shawl tightly around her shoulders as if it would somehow afford protection and made off for the outdoor market. That young woman didn't know how lucky she was, and clearly didn't appreciate good music. If she, herself, worked at the Temperance Hall as a cleaner, she'd have a high old time watching the rehearsals and would never have such a sour face on her. Maybe if she got the chance she'd try singing on the stage herself.

Megan had been living at the workhouse since the age of seven. Her family had fallen on hard times when her father was killed in a pit accident, and without any other options to help them get by, her widowed mother had brought her and her five siblings to the workhouse. She had vague memories of their happy little home – it was small but it was theirs – in the neighbouring village of Troedyrhiw, just on the banks of the River Taff. It had been noisy but lively: her younger brothers, bursting back and forth playing choo-choo trains, her sisters cradling their wooden dolls and her elder brother Tom trying to help their mother by chopping up sticks for firewood in the yard. It had been a happy home and she missed it dearly.

Both her parents had been hard workers. Her dad, Neville Hopkins, would return from work, his face slick and grimy with coal dust, yet he held his broad shoulders erect. He was strong and fit and he could carry a sack of coal for miles – it was said he was the strongest man in the whole of Troedyrhiw. Her mam had been so proud of him, as had she, always boasting to the other kids in the neighbourhood about her strong and brave father. She always looked forward to him coming home from work, his smile as he lowered his head to duck beneath the wooden door frame and his pearly white teeth that stood out against his dust-specked face. He'd often drop his metal snap tin on the table with a clatter and hoist one or two of them up onto his shoulders. Then Mam would fill a tin bath with hot water she'd boiled from the multitude of pans on the stove.

Outside in the backyard, he'd scrub the coal dust from his skin. Then they'd sit down to an evening meal of either lamb cawl or beef pie and potatoes. Sometimes, if they had enough money, there'd be an apple pie and custard for afters or some of her mother's Teisen Lap, which was a sort of sponge fruit cake. Megan's mouth watered at the thought of such wholesome food. All she got at the workhouse these days was a grey tasteless gruel for breakfast, and bread and cheese or a thin watery soup the rest of the time. They'd be graced with the occasional meal which was supposedly meat and potatoes, but rations were meagre and oftentimes the meat full of fat and gristle. She would usually go to bed with her stomach still growling with hunger.

When the family had first arrived at the workhouse, Megan had been dismayed that the family was to be split up. Her mother had to go into the adult women's quarters, Megan was sent to stay with girls aged seven to fifteen years old, and similarly, her brother Tom was to go with the boys of the same age. Their remaining siblings, Alfie, Harry, Lizzie and May, had been sent to the under-seven section. They rarely saw one another, but Megan took comfort in the fact that the little ones were all together. Alfie and Harry were non-identical twins, and like chalk and cheese, they were, Alfie being the most robust of the two. Lizzie had a mane of red curly hair and May was dark-haired like Megan; both of them were as shy as anything, and she often hoped that they weren't finding the conditions of the workhouse too overwhelming.

And that left Tom, her older brother, who had been lucky enough to be boarded out from the workhouse to a family in Twynyrodyn. The Evans family were good to him by all accounts, and he was expected to work in the shop they owned. Tom delivered goods to customers using a pony-drawn cart, which he'd been taught to use by Mr Evans. They lived on Twyn Hill which was breakneck steep, so some nearby deliveries had to be made on foot, which was easy for Tom when he was walking downhill, but walking back was hard going for him sometimes. He was young and fit, yet still he came back red-faced, huffing and puffing. When he visited the workhouse, he brought Megan and her siblings ha'penny sugar twists or Bentley's Chocolate Drops, but he had to be discreet as he would undoubtedly be punished if he were found out.

Megan stopped off at a stall in the town to buy two large loaves of crusty bread, a pat of cheese and a jar of pickles, as requested by Matron Langley. Nothing was too good for the Board of Guardians – they dined like kings and queens whilst the workhouse inmates ate very meagre meals – and Cook was busy baking a selection of cakes and roasting a goose for them.

Megan loved the hustle and bustle of the marketplace, with all its vibrant colours and smells. She was in a world of her own until she turned and spotted a young lad of around her own age loitering near a fruit stall. His arms and legs were thin and gangly, and his tattered jacket and trousers had seen far better days. His flat cap was so big it almost covered his eyes. She wondered what he was up to as he was looking very suspicious; he didn't look the sort who would have much money of his own to purchase anything. There was no adult with him either.

Curious, she moved in closer and eyed him closely. She watched open-mouthed as he slipped a shiny red apple into his jacket pocket, and then another and another. She couldn't believe the cheek of the lad! She'd never dream of doing anything like that. It wasn't the way she'd been brought up, to thieve off people. He turned and caught her eye and, wilfully, she gave him a hard stare and shook her head, before turning to the stallholder to catch his attention. As if realising he might be caught, the boy grabbed all the apples he could carry in his arms and elbowed her out of the way as he dashed off.

'Oi! Stop that boy at once!' the stallholder shouted to the group of people nearby.

Megan turned to watch the young lad scarpering off. He was headed in the direction of St Tydfil's Parish Church, leaving a trail of dropped apples in his wake. Before she realised what she was doing, she dropped her basket on the ground and flew after him, her arms and legs taking on a life of their own. She ran so fast she felt as if her heart were about to burst out of her chest. Sensing the outrage of the baying crowd behind her, she knew she had to catch the boy before they caught him.

When she reached the boy she yanked at the back of the collar on his jacket and he fell backwards on top of her so they were both in a heap on the ground.

'Gerroff!' he shouted and made to get up.

'I'm trying to help you!' she said gruffly, cross because he'd misunderstood. She didn't want him to get into trouble, and looking at his thin frame she had felt sorry for him. 'Look, come this way with me, I know where we can hide.'

He nodded and helped her onto her feet. She let out a long breath as she steadied herself.

They were behind the Three Salmons Inn, and to the right of them there was a gap in the wrought-iron railings which led into the church grounds. There, they could both hide behind a large oak tree until the coast was clear.

They quickly crept over, and from the safety of the tree watched a crowd of people run past.

Megan giggled and soon the lad was giggling too. 'What's your name?' he asked, wide-eyed and blinking in expectation.

'Megan. Megan Hopkins. And yours?'

'Griff. Griff Rhys Morgan.' He wiped his runny nose on the back of his sleeve.

Megan rolled her eyes in disgust. 'Yuck, mun. Doing that. You should use a handkerchief.'

'Oooh, hark at you, quite the lady, aren't you? I ain't got one, have I?'

'*Haven't* got one,' Megan corrected. 'Why did you steal those apples?'

'Cos, I'm blooming starving.' As if suddenly remembering, he lifted one of the few he had left, shined it first on the knee of his well-worn trousers and took a bite.

'You ought to be careful, though. I heard of one lad who

stole some pies a lady had left on her windowsill to cool, and he ended up going before the judge and jury.'

'Pah!' Griff scoffed. 'Won't happen to me, I'm too quick for them all.'

Megan tossed back her curls. 'Are you now? Well, I managed to catch you didn't I?'

He frowned and nodded. 'Suppose so . . .'

He inspected the apple as if examining it for worms.

'In any case, that poor boy I told you about ended up in Australia.'

'Australia?' He gulped.

She nodded. 'Yes, it's miles and miles away. The furthest place you could ever get to. He was transported with all the other boys and girls who'd been up to mischief in the town. They can do you for the slightest thing, you know. One lad was sent there for nicking just one loaf of bread.' She paused. 'Though I can see as how you're hungry.'

Griff stared into space, digesting all Megan had just said. 'I didn't realise that could happen. I often run around with the Rodneys.'

'Rodneys?'

'Aye, they're a bunch of boys who live in the China district where I live, see. I stay there with me Uncle Berwyn. My parents died and he gave me board and lodgings. He's been kind to me but he lost his job at the ironworks because of his drinking and he's not been the same man since.'

'Oh dear.' Megan settled herself down on a granite tomb-stone, forgetting why she was there in the first place. Somehow she felt drawn to Griff and she didn't know why.

He finished his apple and tossed the stump on a mossy verge, then promptly offered her one. Should she take it? They were stolen goods but she was hungry too. She took it from his outstretched hand, and he smiled at her. It was great to be free of the workhouse for a while, she thought as she chomped on the rosy red apple, tasting its sweet flavour. It tasted far better than anything she got in the workhouse. At night, she had dreams of eating with her family in the days when Mam had made sticky sponge puddings covered in strawberry jam, and her mouth watered at the mere memory of it. She drew on those happy memories whenever she felt sad or lonely.

'So where do you live?' Griff asked when they'd both finished eating, breaking into her thoughts.

'At the workhouse. Been there a few years now. My dad died and my mam and brothers and sisters had to go there too.'

He gazed at her quizzically. 'What's it like in there? I often wonder.'

She thought for a moment because no one had ever asked her that question before, then said, honestly, 'Well, the Master and Matron run a tight ship and they're firm but fair. Kind enough to me, but some inmates there, I stay away from. Some scare me. I've heard them weeping and wailing during the night.'

Griff's eyes widened. 'I don't think I'd like it in there myself.' He shivered.

'Well let's hope you never have to go in there. There's a Board of Guardians meeting this afternoon and—'

'What's wrong? Your face 'as turned white as a corpse.'

'My basket! I was shopping for Matron and I dropped it when I ran after you!' Now she was going to be in trouble; she'd spent most of the money Matron had given her and she had no basket to take back with her to the workhouse. That meant no bread or cheese or pickles. She was going to arrive empty-handed and that wouldn't do at all. She'd be in trouble for sure, and that didn't bode well, especially as one person at the workhouse in particular had it in for her.

Chapter Two

'I'll come with you, we'll find your basket together,' Griff offered, reaching out to touch her arm in reassurance.

'No, you lie low here. People will remember what you look like. We don't want no Bobbies catching you and sending you to Australia. It's a long way and you'll never see your Rodney friends nor your Uncle Berwyn ever again.'

Griff grimaced. 'All right, but I hope you find your basket and don't get into any trouble because of me.'

Megan wished she could be sure of that but she wasn't. Miss Hamilton could mete out the punishment of her choice, and if it wasn't the swish of the birch she could be made to work for a full twenty-four hours in the laundry room. It was like torture: not being allowed to have any sleep, nor any food, only water.

'It's my own silly fault,' she said with tears in her eyes. 'Look, it will be dark soon. Stay here until you're sure you're safe and then go home. And stay away from the market for a while in case they remember you.'

'I will, for sure.' Suddenly he leant forward and pecked a swift kiss on her cheek, taking her by surprise. 'Thank you, my lady!' He tipped his Dai cap.

Megan's cheeks flamed hot. No one had ever called her a lady before, and no young lad had ever kissed her either, not including the times her young brothers did on the rare occasions she got to bump into them at the workhouse.

'I'd better go,' she said, the panic rising in her throat.

'If you ever need me and can't find me, go to the Vulcan Inn. My Uncle Berwyn is always in there, he's more at home there than in his own house . . .' He hesitated. 'I know it's not a place for a young lady like yourself, but the barmaid, Florrie, is a helpful sort. She'll help you find my uncle.'

'Very well.' She nodded, looking at him one last time, and then ran in the direction of the marketplace. It was getting late and they would be packing up their stalls now.

She'd dropped her basket near the fruit and veg stall, and as she arrived, puffing and panting, she had to elbow past a few stragglers who were after last-minute items, hoping to bag a bargain.

'Excuse me, ma'am,' she asked one lady. 'Have you seen a wicker basket on the ground? I lost it earlier . . .'

The woman shook her head and carried on walking.

Next, she tried a man in a top hat. 'Excuse me, sir, have you seen my wicker basket? I drop—'

But the man dismissed her with the wave of his hand. Why would anyone want to help a workhouse girl? Going by her appearance, they probably thought she wanted to pick their pockets. She guessed he had a nice fat wallet in his jacket pocket, but, unlike Griff, it wasn't her style. She liked to earn her keep, not steal from others.

Dismayed, she searched around for the basket but it was nowhere to be seen. She didn't dare tell the stallholder of her plight as he might think she was associated with Griff, and that wouldn't do at all. She didn't want to get transported to Australia either, with all those other young villains. The only thing she could do was go back and tell the truth: she'd lost everything; or she could pretend someone had accosted her and stolen everything – though she didn't feel good about doing that at all.

She began to sob, scared of the punishment she would get for this. Matron and Miss Hamilton would be so cross with her.

'What's the matter with you, child?' She heard a soft feminine voice enquire. It had an Irish lilt, which wasn't surprising as there were many Irish people in Merthyr. They came to work in the ironworks and the accent was familiar to her. There were even some who had fallen on hard times at the workhouse. But this voice was entirely different, and Megan knew immediately that this was a voice she wanted to hear again.

She looked up to see the most beautiful lady she'd ever seen in her life. Even though it was beginning to get dark, she could make out the faint glimmer of sparkling emerald eyes and the woman's auburn hair cascading in waves upon her shoulders. She was wearing a green velvet gown and cape, which gave her a kind of elevated presence amongst the other people in the street, giving her an altogether regal quality. Megan noticed several passers-by stopping in their tracks to whisper and stare.

Megan stopped sobbing long enough to answer the beautiful lady. 'Please, miss, something happened earlier. I had to chase after someone and dropped my basket as it was so heavy. I'm from the workhouse, see, and I was shopping for Matron. There's a Board of Guardians meeting later . . .' Her bottom lip quivered in distress.

The lady brought a lace-edged handkerchief out of her reticule and bent down to dab at Megan's eyes. 'Now there's nothing we can't sort out . . .' She smelled of soap and lavender. 'What was in the basket all together?'

'Two loaves of bread, a lump of cheese and a jar of pickles.' She huffed out the words as she was so short of breath from the rushing and the crying.

'Come with me,' the lady said kindly. She approached the same stall where Megan had earlier bought the goods and

Megan followed meekly behind. She spoke to the stallholder in a murmur and Megan couldn't quite make out their words, but when she turned back to her the lady said, 'Now, I've managed to get us a good deal.' She handed a large wedge of cheese wrapped in a muslin cloth to Megan. It was even bigger than the one Megan herself had bought earlier. She also handed her a jar of pickles and held two loaves of bread herself. 'I'll take you back to the Temperance Hall with me. There's an old wicker basket there we use as one of the props . . .'

Realisation dawned on Megan. 'So you are the lady whose voice I heard earlier, singing inside the theatre?'

'Yes, that was me. I was rehearsing for tonight. If you had more time I'd take you in to show you around but I know how keen you are to return.'

Megan nodded. 'I really don't know what to tell Matron or Miss Hamilton.'

'You must tell them you bumped into me, Kathleen O'Hara, and I needed your help as I'd fallen in the street. They will know who I am, and if they come here to enquire whether it 'tis the truth, I shall back you up. T'ain't right that a young lady like yourself should be punished for going back late. At least you now have the items you lost.'

'And it's all thanks to you, miss,' Megan said, in awe of the beautiful lady stood before her.

'Come on then, let's get to the Temperance Hall to fetch

that wicker basket and pack those goods inside it, then you can return to the workhouse.'

'I don't know how I can repay you, miss,' Megan said sadly.

'Don't worry about that, child. Maybe you can return the favour to me in some other way some day.'

Megan left the lady feeling that maybe all would be well, after all; the wicker basket even looked the same as the one she had lost. No doubt, someone would have whipped that up as soon as it touched the ground. There were many people starving in Merthyr Tydfil.

When she returned to the workhouse, the dark, foreboding building made her stomach lurch. It was then she realised that she had never been allowed out of its confines on her own during the hours of darkness before. That would be another strike against her.

Bill Harris, the porter, was at the lodge and she was relieved to see him stood on the doorstep as she returned. He was a friendly face and he lived in Troedyrhiw, on the street next to her childhood home in fact, so was familiar with her family. 'Hello, young Megan. What's the matter with you, *cariad*?'

'Oh, Mr Harris, I'm in big trouble. I was supposed to get back sooner than this. Cook sent me to buy some food for the Guardians' meeting and I lost my basket.'

He stared at her a moment under the gaslight. 'Hmm, I think you still have your basket, Megan, on your arm.'

'No, sorry, this is another. A kind lady who is a singer at

the Temperance Hall found it for me and helped buy more food so I don't get in any bother. But I'm scared Miss Hamilton will see me sneaking in.'

'Hang on, we'll get you in this way. Over here . . .' He led her to another entrance she'd never used before and unlocked the heavy wooden door with a key he had on a chain in the pocket of his jacket. 'Take care and mind as you go,' he warned as he departed.

'Thanks, Mr Harris.' She bustled off down the dimly lit corridor and, after passing a couple of rooms she didn't recognise, found herself at the foot of a flight of stairs opposite the entrance to the kitchen.

Breathless with anxiety, she entered the steamy kitchen to find Cook in a stew as the kitchen maids clattered around. There were saucepans of food on the boil and frying pans on the stove. 'Come on, girl, where the heck have you been? The bread, cheese and pickles should have been laid out ages ago!' She dipped her hand into the basket she had placed on the scrubbed pine table, and Megan held her breath. But then Cook's face broke out into a smile. 'You've done well here, girl. That stallholder 'as given yer a lot for your pennies.' She unwrapped the muslin cloth and examined the cheese, giving it a long, hard sniff. 'Hey, what's going on here? This is best quality stuff, would of cost yer a fortune.' She studied Megan through narrow-slitted eyes.

'Must have been because he was putting away his stall,'

Megan explained shiftily, hoping Cook believed her story. 'Maybe he was selling things cheaper than usual.'

'Aye, maybe he felt sorry for you and all.' Cook wasn't Welsh. She was from somewhere in the north of England, so far away that Megan had never heard of it. Her bark was sometimes worse than her bite. 'Well, you're forgiven, girl. Now go and hang your shawl up and wash your hands and face, so Miss Hamilton won't realise you've only just got back. Then for your time and trouble, I'll give you a small crust of this bread and cheese.' She winked at Megan which made her smile.

She hung up her shawl and went to wash her face and hands in the big stone bosh just off the kitchen. She was just about to return when she felt someone roughly grab the neck of her dress from behind, almost choking her.

'And where do you think you're going?' an unmistakable voice barked at her, causing her to gulp as the woman released her from her grip.

Realising what had happened, Cook stepped forward, stepping between Megan and the supervisor. 'It's orright, Miss Hamilton. The girl's with me. She's been helping me in the kitchen since she returned from Merthyr market. See, she buttered all those rounds of bread.'

Miss Hamilton, who was a tall, spindly woman with beady black eyes, and salt-and-pepper-coloured hair scraped back so tight there wasn't a tress out of place, roughly pushed

Megan away as she inspected the plates of bread and butter, the keys on the chatelaine around her waist jangling away. 'Hmm, wouldn't take long to butter those slices, would it? And why didn't she turn up for prayers in the chapel?' She peered over her round spectacles at Megan. The woman was a tyrant who most at the workhouse feared, particularly Megan, as she seemed to have it in for her in particular. She couldn't do anything right in her eyes and she didn't under-stand why that was. She never seemed to punish her friend Eira for anything at all.

Megan's heart hammered. 'I forgot as I was so busy, Miss Hamilton . . .'

'Forgot? You forgot that every day between six and seven in the evening we have prayers in the chapel?'

'And the girl had washed pots before that. She's been a great help,' Cook chipped in.

'Well, she wasn't assigned here, so next time get permis-sion for it, Mrs Woodley.'

Cook nodded, her cheeks flushing, and Megan hoped upon hope Miss Hamilton would go on her way, but she was having none of it.

'Let me see those hands, Megan.'

Megan held them out for inspection. Freshly washed, they were nice and clean.

'Both sides,' Miss Hamilton ordered.

Megan turned them over.

'Get on your way to prayers and then I want you upstairs cleaning the corridors.'

'Yes, ma'am,' Megan said, shooting a glance at Mrs Woodley.

When Miss Hamilton had departed, Cook whispered, 'Well, you've got away with it this time, but you might not be so lucky the next. Do take care, Megan my love.'

Megan nodded. 'Thanks for covering for me, Mrs Woodley.'

The woman smiled with tears in her eyes. She was a kindly soul. 'When it's safe for you after you've mopped those floors, come back and I'll have left that bread and cheese for you hidden under the sink.'

Megan nodded. 'Thanks, Mrs Woodley.'

Then she left the kitchen for the chapel to say her prayers, shortly before flying up the flight of stairs to the next landing where she would scrub the floors. She filled a metal bucket with hot water and soapy suds, and thought about how she was missing supper. She didn't mind too much as she'd had that tasty apple, something she hadn't eaten in years, and Cook had been so nice to promise her some food as well.

Mopping the floors was a job she hated doing, but some-how meeting Griff today made the task seem less laborious. She went over and over in her mind the things they'd said and done and the feelings inside her they had evoked, particularly when he'd kissed her cheek. She just had to see him again. She wondered what he was doing right now and if he was safe. Did he even have a bed for the night?

I hope you're all right, Griff, and the police haven't caught up with you. I'd hate it if they sent you to the other side of the world just for nicking some apples because you were starving.

Now she'd found a new friend, she didn't want to lose him.

Chapter Three

Griff felt that sickening feeling in the pit of his stomach when he arrived back home, the lurch that made his palms sweat and his teeth chatter with fear. The China district of Merthyr wasn't the best part of the town to live in, with all its undesirables – pickpockets, pimps, prostitutes . . . But it wasn't any of those he feared today; it was his own Uncle Berwyn. Berwyn had taken care of him over the past few years, but in recent months he had taken to the drink, following the deaths of his wife and unborn child, and then later, the loss of his job at the ironworks.

When he was sober he was fine, but in drink he became a demon. It never used to be that way.

Griff's hand shook as he pushed open the wooden front door with its peeling paint and entered the damp hovel inside. He let out a sigh of relief. His uncle was nowhere to be seen, which could only mean one thing: he was in some alehouse somewhere getting drunk again. But still, now he might have the house to himself for a while. The reason he'd gone out to pilfer from the market in the first place was because he was starving. For weeks there hadn't been any decent food in the house. There were even days when his uncle hadn't bothered to come home at all. Sometimes he was out for days and nights at a time, and Griff had to make do with any old scraps he could find, even the mouldy old cheese and bread that was so hard he had to soak it in water before he could chew it. The rats in the alley got better pickings than he did. Why had things changed so much?

Images of his aunt's smiling face were beginning to fade away. All that was left now was a house that was not a home.

One thing Uncle Berwyn had always ensured in the past was that there was a good meal on the table, but that was no longer to be. It was as if his grief meant nothing to him, nor anyone or anything else for that matter, other than his next pint of beer.

Griff's thoughts turned to Megan. She was a pretty little thing with her long eyelashes and deep brown eyes, and he loved her curly dark hair, too. She was a real doll, and her cheeks had gone rosy red when he'd teased her. He liked that bashful side to her.

He'd never been friends with a girl before, only the boys from the gang he ran around with – and now he'd realised he was better off keeping away from them in case he got carted off to Australia. Exhausted, he fell asleep on the thick rag rug in front of the embers of the fire and drifted off into a contented sleep.

He was awoken by the front door being yanked open, bringing with it a sharp autumn draught. A voice was bellowing at him and he felt someone kicking at him so hard it hurt. 'Gerrup, you lazy little upstart!'

He shook as he pulled himself up on his haunches. His Uncle Berwyn towered over him. The smell of beer fumes churned away at Griff's guts.

'I . . . I'm sorry, Uncle. I fell asleep . . .' He trembled as his stomach rolled over and now he wished he hadn't eaten those apples – he felt as if he might throw them up at any given time.

His uncle reached down and yanked him up by the collar. 'You little swine, you've let the fire go out an' all! It's freezing in here. Now go and get some coal and bank it up, you little bastard! Why the hell I took you on after my sister died, I'll never know. You're no use to me, you lazy article! Do some work for once. Go and get some bloody coal from the *cwtch*, now, this very minute!'

'But we ain't got any coal, Uncle. Remember we used the last of it a couple of days ago?'

'Then you are just going to have to thieve some from somewhere, aren't you?' He kept his hand firmly on Griff's collar and shook him so hard his teeth chattered. Then he dragged him from the hearth and pinned him against the wall, his one hand so tightly wrapped around his neck that Griff could hardly breathe. His uncle's eyes were bulging and spittle flew out of the corners of his mouth. His bad breath made Griff gag and he fought to stop himself from vomiting. That would cause a beating, that was for sure. The tears were now threatening to stream down his face.

For days, they'd managed to make do with pieces of old driftwood Griff had collected from down by the riverbank. What was he going to do now his uncle wanted coal? He didn't want to steal from any of their neighbours as they were struggling to survive themselves. He closed his eyes. He half wished his uncle would put him out of his misery right now. He'd be better off that way, he thought bitterly. But instead, he loosened his grip and let Griff slide onto to the hard, cold flagstone floor. It hurt like hell as he had little flesh on his bones, but he held back the tears. There had been too many bumps and bruises lately, but he knew if he cried then he'd get even worse.

'What's for supper?' his uncle growled.

'Th—there's nothing left in the house, but I got a couple of apples I nicked from a market stall earlier . . .' He dipped his hands into his pockets and presented his uncle with both apples.

Berwyn grabbed them from him and inspected them under the light of a candle on the windowsill. 'Not good enough. Next time bring something better than that or your backside will be so red raw from my belt you won't be able to sit down for weeks. Understood?'

Griff nodded. 'Yes, sir.'

'Now get out of here and don't come back until you've got me something tasty to eat like a nice pork pie and some bread and cheese. Forget about the coal tonight, you can get that tomorrow.'

Griff watched as his uncle threw himself down on the old horsehair sofa and promptly fell asleep. He was snoring heavily within minutes. Griff was beginning to hate the man with a vengeance and wished he could run away. Life in Merthyr was tough, and for some like himself, it was particularly hard.

Later, when all the lights were out for the night, Megan tried to sleep on her hard mattress pallet but was failing. She gazed up at the stars from the dormitory window. The rest of the girls were fast asleep, some letting out gentle snores as they lay there oblivious to her insomnia.

It was an odd thing to think about, but this time last night she didn't even know of Griff's very existence, and now all she could do was think about him and wonder about his life. She'd never dare go to the district known as China to try to find him. Mrs Woodley had warned her about that place; it was teeming with pimps and prostitutes. And when Megan had asked what a pimp or prostitute was, the woman had given her a knowing look, tapped the side of her nose and replied, 'Yer'll find out soon enough, girlie. Let's just say they're not nice people. You recognise a prostitute by the clothes she wears – garish colours – and she'll probably rouge her cheeks and wear lots of scent.'

Well, thankfully, that didn't sound like The Lady, Kathleen O'Hara. She was a lady of refinement. And to think that Griff had called her, little Megan Hopkins, a lady too! That must mean she could one day become a star like Miss O'Hara herself. She'd wear the finest satin gown in either emerald green or maybe cornflower blue and she'd have her hair piled up on top of her head with a diamond hairslide in place. In her hand she'd carry one of those flowered fans to hide her face from the audience if she felt demure, then she'd whip it away and smile at them as she sang with a voice of an angel. She quietly hummed a tune whilst the other girls slept. One day maybe she'd have the confidence to sing on the stage too, and be a lady like Miss O'Hara. She'd earn pots of money too, and she'd forget all about the poor life of drudgery she used to live. She'd be inundated with bouquets of flowers from all her admirers, and everyone would treat her like a star instead of a workhouse lackey.

It was a long while before she fell asleep and when she did, she slept soundly, only to be rudely awakened by Miss Hamilton. Opening her groggy eyes, she could see the woman glaring at her as she watched her in her bed. 'Get up, girl!'

She pulled her roughly out of her bed by her hair. Megan had to stop herself from crying out in pain, so as not to anger the woman further. 'The others are washed and dressed and on their way to breakfast. As you're late, you can do without.' She released her from her grip and Megan stood by the side of her bed rubbing her head.

She could have wept. Why hadn't any of the others roused her to warn her she had slept late? It wasn't like them to leave her there – not that she usually overslept. She got herself washed and dressed, and cursed herself for having missed two meals in a row. But then she remembered the bread and cheese Cook had left out for her under the sink.

The kitchen was hectic when she entered. There were two kitchen maids busy stirring the pots of gruel, whilst Cook prepared fried bacon for the Master, Matron and rest of the staff. Megan's stomach growled from the smell of the rashers sizzling in the large cast iron pan and she eyed another pan of fried eggs, with nice sunny-coloured yolks. It was ages since she'd eaten anything like that.

Cook glanced at her, unsurprised by her presence in the kitchen. 'Have you eaten that bread and cheese I left out for you yet?'

'No, Mrs Woodley.'

'Go and get it quickly and eat it in the washroom so Miss Hamilton can't see you, girl. Here, take this too.' She handed Megan some pieces of cooked bacon rind. Megan glanced around to ensure Miss Hamilton wasn't nearby, and slipped the hot greasy rind into her pinafore pocket. She then scoured beneath the sink for the bread and cheese, which thankfully was still there, wrapped in muslin. Scurrying to the washroom, she held them close, eagerly awaiting the moment when she could devour the meagre portions. She stuffed them into her mouth as quickly as she could, for fear that Miss Hamilton found her. It wasn't ideal, but it was delicious all the same.

When she returned to the kitchen, Cook poured some buttermilk into a cup for her. 'Here, drink this quickly and be off with you. I usually use it for cooking scones and such, but you look as though you need feeding up, to me. You're outgrowing your strength, girlie.' She handed her the cup and Megan thanked her, then downed it as quickly as possible, wiping away her milky moustache with the back of her hand.

Cook smiled at her, then ruffled her hair. 'Be on your way, Megan, before that old crone comes in and catches you,' she warned.

She nodded and left the kitchen. She now had a full belly, which was more than Miss Hamilton would allow, and promised herself she would say a prayer for Cook that night for her kind generosity. It made a lot of difference having someone like her around looking out for her. She knew her mam would be very grateful for it too.

As Megan set about her chores later that morning, she cornered Eira Bevan, who was one of the girls from her dorm and a very good friend. 'Why did you lot leave me to sleep in this morning?' she accused, with more than an air of impatience.

Eira's bottom lip quivered. 'It wasn't any of our doing, Megan. It was Miss Hamilton – she told us we were to allow you to sleep as you needed it. I thought maybe it was because you were up cleaning the corridor last night. I thought she was showing you a kindness.'

'A kindness?' Megan said. 'Since when has *Mrs High-and-Mighty* ever done anyone a kindness? She used it against me this morning, told me I was late and dragged me by my hair out of bed, then said I was to go without breakfast.'

'Oh Meg, I'm so sorry. If only I'd realised. That woman is an evil witch. So now you're starving, I suppose?'

'Well, thankfully, Mrs Woodley saved me a bit of bread and cheese from last night and she gave me a cup of buttermilk. But Miss Hamilton seems to have it in for me lately and I've no idea why.'

'Keep your head down,' Eira advised in hushed tones. And almost as if on cue, the sound of Miss Hamilton's voice filled the corridor. 'Here, quick, take my sweeping brush and make it look as though you're busy doing something or she's going to get mad at you.'

Gratefully, Megan took the brush from Eira's grasp as the girl went off to clear the grate in the staff restroom.

Miss Hamilton walked past but did not make any eye

contact with Megan, just sniffed loudly as she went along her way, the set of keys still jangling from a belt on her dress. She was exactly like a jailer, Megan thought.

Pity I can't put her into a prison cell, lock the door and throw away the key! She laughed to herself at the thought of Miss Hamilton rattling the bars whilst screaming for help. Wouldn't that be a kind of justice, though?

As she continued sweeping, a group of young boys passed by in a long line with their teacher heading for the schoolroom. She searched their faces for two she recognised: her twin brothers, Alfie and Harry. They were now eight years old and she didn't want to get them in any trouble, nor herself, so she just winked at them as they passed on by. They each carried a slate under their arms and smiled at her when they saw her standing there, before turning their heads back to follow the teacher. They knew only too well how strict the workhouse regime was.

She badly needed to see her mother, but the last two times she'd attempted to get into the women's dormitory she'd been denied access. She feared something was wrong. She had not set eyes on her mother for almost two weeks now and it troubled her so. She had planned on asking to see her, but knew Miss Hamilton would never allow it. In fact the more she'd ask, the less chance of getting to see her there would be. The supervisor seemed to take great delight in dashing Megan's hopes. She was going to have to try to slip away from her duties and sneak in there herself when no one was around to catch her.

Later, when Megan's chores had been completed and she'd had that day's lessons at the girls' school, she walked into the exercise yard where Gwendolyn Morris was taking some exercise with the other women. They stood gossiping against the wall. Gwennie, as she was known, was in the middle of telling the ladies something funny about Master Langley. She stopped mid-flow when she saw Megan.

At the sight of her, the other women drifted away, leaving Megan standing with Gwennie against the wall. They sensed the need for their privacy; it wasn't often the young girls and adult women were allowed to be in the same place at the same time.

'Oh, *cariad*,' Gwennie began, 'you've come to ask about your mam again, haven't you?'

Why is Gwennie acting so strangely? Megan thought. She had a strange look in her eye as if she pitied her.

Megan nodded. There was a lump in her throat that threatened to choke her and her eyes misted with the unshed tears she'd been determined not to give in to. 'Why haven't I seen her around and why am I being prevented from going to see her?'

Gwennie stooped, so she was at eye-level with Megan. Then, looking around so as not to be overheard, she said,

'It's women's troubles. She needs to rest in bed. That's why you can't see her, Megan. Now go back before they discover you're missing, there's a good girl.'

Somehow Megan wasn't satisfied with that answer. She could tell something was amiss, though she wasn't sure what that something was. *Women's troubles.* What did that even mean? She turned and ran in the direction of the dining room. It was lunchtime and she didn't want to fall foul of Miss Hamilton again. Though to be honest she'd lost her appetite as she still hadn't received a satisfactory answer about her mother's welfare. What was it they weren't telling her?

Someone had to know the truth and she intended on finding out.

Lunch was supposed to be a mutton and vegetable soup but she hardly saw any meat in it at all, though the liquid itself was tasty. Cook could only do her best with the ingredients provided, she supposed. She'd told Megan once that they only gave workhouse paupers small portions so as not to get them too fit in case there was a rebellion. And in light of this, Megan was shocked to see how thin some of the men around her father's age had become: their clothing hung off them, and where once had been broad shoulders and chests strong as oxen, there was now emaciated and pale bone, the prominent sight of ribs sticking out. All that and still they were expected to break rocks and crush bones on a daily basis. (The bones were used as some kind of fertiliser, she'd been told.) Eira had told her she'd once heard a story of how sometimes the men became so hungry that they tried to pick bits of meat off the bone and became ill as the bones weren't all that fresh. Megan hoped they were animal bones and not human ones, but you just never knew in places like this.

Not many lived long lives in the workhouse. Some died before their time, and some – like her brother, Tom – had much better lives outside of it. The Evanses had really taken a shine to him. They had no children of their own and treated him like a surrogate son. There was even news that they were thinking of taking two of the younger children to live with them, but it was undecided which two yet. It wouldn't be Megan, that was for sure, and she was glad of it. She could handle herself, but her younger sisters, for instance, weren't made to withstand the conditions of the workhouse. But whatever happened, whichever were chosen, if any, they would have much better lives out there.

In the dining room that evening Eira looked at her across the wooden table as she supped her soup from a large spoon. 'What's the matter, Megan?'

'I'm concerned about my mam. I haven't seen her for about a fortnight and when I asked a woman from the same block, she told me my mam had "women's troubles" and was on bed rest. But I don't really know what "women's troubles" are. And in any case, I feel it's not the real truth. They're all keeping something from me, I just know it. They look at me with pity in their eyes.'

Eira frowned. 'Well, one of the older girls in our dorm had women's troubles and she said it was because she had just become a woman.'

That didn't make sense at all to Megan. Wasn't her mam already a woman? She carried on eating her soup, dipping in a small hunk of bread. 'I just don't get it at all.' Megan sighed.

'Never mind,' Eira whispered. 'We'll find some way to get you over there to see your mother.'

Megan forced a smile. She'd just die if she never saw her mother's kind, lighthearted face again. It was the very thing that kept her going, in here.

As she was returning to her chores, walking silently along the corridor, she became aware of a figure behind her. Turning, she noticed it was Miss Hamilton.

'Where are you off to, girl?' the woman demanded to know.

'I've . . . er . . . just finished my lunch and now I'm due to help in the laundry room.'

As if dissatisfied with Megan giving such a straightforward answer, the woman grabbed hold of Megan's arm and twisted it behind her back. 'I've never liked you nor your kind!' she sneered, all the while putting more pressure on Megan's arm, causing her to yelp out in pain.

It hurt so much and as the woman dug her fingers into her flesh, she was worried she might bruise. The supervisor had rough-handled her before but never as bad as this. She seemed to take delight in Megan's pain and her eyes gleamed. Megan realised if she screamed or shouted it could make things worse for her. No way did she want the woman to break her and make her cry. Also, the corridor was deserted, so it wasn't even as if there were anyone around who might help her.

So instead, wincing, she said, 'I'm sorry if I've upset you, ma'am. Why don't you like me?' It was a forward question to ask the supervisor, but Megan figured she had nothing to lose.

'Because you're the devil's spawn. You come from bad blood!' she spat out, her beady eyes boring a hole into her flesh as she twisted Megan's arm even tighter behind her back. 'Dirty little workhouse girl.'

Megan gasped. 'Don't you dare speak about my family like that!' She booted Miss Hamilton hard in the shin, causing the woman to relax her grip on Megan.

Taken aback by the way Megan had spoken to her, she let her go and then flung her to one side. Megan's back fell against the tiled wall, robbing her of her breath. She wanted to cry so much but she didn't dare. In any case, she wasn't going to show the witch that she'd got at her. There was a strong streak in Megan that she'd had to develop over the years after having to look out for her brothers and sisters, and particularly now that Tom was no longer at the workhouse, the need was even stronger. She remained firm and resolute that she would be brave for the sake of the little ones.

'For your impudence, you are to remain in the laundry room without food or water for the next eight hours!' Miss Hamilton commanded, whilst rubbing at her leg where Megan had kicked her. 'Understood?'

There was no point in arguing, it would only make things worse, so Megan nodded. 'Yes, ma'am.'

It was no use. Even if the woman hadn't despised her before, she was going to really despise her now after what she'd done. But how dare she speak about her family like that? They were good people. All the neighbours in Troedyrhiw had respected her parents, particularly her father. He'd been like the local hero.

Shaking with anger, Miss Hamilton wagged her index finger at Megan and said, 'I shall inform Mrs Crossley you are to stay there for the duration of the day and you are not allowed even one little break. And if I catch you even talking to anyone else, there shall be hell to pay!' She stared hard at Megan, the whites of her eyes bulging. Megan felt like she was looking into the eyes of Satan himself.

She dragged Megan down the corridor by her ear lobe, her keys still jangling. Megan pulled back on the heels of her boots, trying to stand her ground, but the woman was too strong for her.

I hate this horrible woman. She's doing her best to give me a hard time here. But what could she do? Having to slog away in the laundry room was now going to stop her from locating her mother.

She had once thought of complaining to Master Langley but he seemed to be in cahoots with Miss Hamilton, and if he didn't believe her, she'd get a severe thrashing, that was for sure. Or even worse, she might be moved to the Cardiff workhouse and have to leave her brothers and sisters behind. It just wasn't worth taking the risk.

As Miss Hamilton dragged her along the corridor into the laundry room, in amongst the steam and sweat, Megan could see several young women piling clothing into big, bubbling copper vats of hot water. They didn't meet her eye as they scrubbed away with thick bars of lye soap on corrugated wash boards. They knew it was best not to get involved when someone was being mistreated. It was fair. It was one of the rules of the workhouse: look out for yourself and yourself only. The room was hot and uncomfortable and it felt airless to Megan. She really didn't want to be here at all.

'Let me go!' Megan shouted at Miss Hamilton who now had her by the hair, tugging at it so tightly that Megan was now on tiptoes.

'What's going on here?' Mrs Crossley asked. She could tell the supervisor was being particularly rough on Megan and she didn't like to see that sort of thing in her laundry. This was her domain.

The supervisor glowered at the laundress over the top of her spectacles. 'This cheeky little madam needs to be taught a lesson. She's to work here for the next few hours and she's not to be allowed a break for her impudence. She answered me back and kicked me on the shin.'

Mrs Crossley sucked in a breath between her teeth and tutted as she shook her head. 'Leave her to me!' she said. 'I'll sort out the little upstart!' She grabbed hold of the collar of Megan's dress and dragged her over to one of the sinks.

'Come here, you good-for-nothing workhouse brat. I'll work you like a packhorse in here, my girl!'

Miss Hamilton slapped the palms of her hands together. 'Thank you, Mrs Crossley. It'll do her good to wash all those clothes. Cleanliness is next to godliness! It'll teach the little madam a good lesson!'

'Don't worry, Miss Hamilton. I'll ensure I teach her the ways of the laundry room!'

Oh no, Mrs Crossley is going to take it out on me too! Megan trembled with fear. She'd expected it from the supervisor but not Mrs Crossley. They were both as bad as each other.

When the supervisor had departed, Mrs Crossley released her grip on Megan. Then in a softer tone of voice said, 'Sorry, I had to do that, Megan, to make out I'm on her side. Now tell me, what happened? Don't worry, I shan't harm you, you're quite safe in here with me.'

A sense of relief washed over Megan as she let out a long breath. 'She attacked me in the corridor, Mrs Crossley.' She sniffed. Her arm was still aching from the altercation.

'Well I never.' Mrs Crossley shook her head. 'She's really got it in for you, Megan. Cook had told me all about it, but I never quite believed her. But now, after seeing that, I wonder why . . .'

'She says I'm from bad blood and all. But my family are good people.' Her eyes began to water with tears.

'There, there, child. Don't you fret, you'll be all right here with us. What did she tell you about what you had to do here?'

'She sent me here to work a full eight-hour shift and I'm to talk to no one and to have neither food nor water.'

'Pardon?' Mrs Crossley asked, as if she could scarcely believe her own ears.

'I'm being punished, ma'am.'

'She said you kicked her. Is this true, Megan?'

'I was only walking along the corridor when she accosted me. I was on my way here anyhow. I wasn't cheeky or anything. Then she got nasty with me over something to do with my mother and father, so I spoke out of turn. I couldn't keep quiet about it. I know I shouldn't have kicked her but she was really hurting me.'

'Let me look at you.' She took hold of Megan's arm. 'Roll up your sleeves a moment.'

Megan did as instructed, rolling them up to above her elbow.

Mrs Crossley stood back as if she couldn't quite believe her eyes as she inspected both of Megan's arms. 'What on earth has that woman done to you? Your arms are red and sore. I can even see the marks where she's dug her fingers into your flesh . . .'

Megan shook her head. 'Please don't tell anyone. Miss Hamilton will punish me ten times worse otherwise.'

'I've a good mind to speak to Matron Langley about this,' she said, the emotion evident in her voice.

'No, please don't. Matron believes everything Miss Hamilton says and so does the Master.'

'But this is a travesty!' Then, catching sight of Megan's defeated demeanour, she said in a softer tone, 'What I'll do is say nothing for now but if it ever happens again, then I'm straight to Matron's room. Now, I won't have you working hard for eight hours with no food or water. She won't know if I feed you and give you little breaks. We'll just watch we don't get caught.' She winked at Megan.

Most of the members of staff employed at the workhouse were firm but fair, but Miss Hamilton was not to be trusted. Megan feared what the woman would do next.

Chapter Four

Griff thought hard about how he could please his uncle by getting some coal for the fire. If he could do that, then maybe he wouldn't get beaten up so much. But he just couldn't bring himself to steal from the neighbours – even though he could easily sneak in, or jump over their walls to get to their coal *cwtches*, they had very little, too. So he decided the best plan might be to steal from the pubs in the town. They made enough money from people like his uncle, so surely they wouldn't miss a few lumps of coal here and there?

At the back of the Vulcan Inn he'd noticed there was a ton of coal just delivered, but there was one problem: the owner had a dog called Scamp and he sometimes left him out in the yard. He'd need to nick something from the market to distract him with, maybe a pork pie or a piece of cooked meat. He didn't much like the idea of thieving from anyone after what Megan had said, and of course, he didn't want to let her down, but if this saved him from getting a beating, then so be it.

He spied some cooked ham at one of the market stalls manned by a very elderly owner. He would have felt bad about swiping a little meat for the dog, but there was something about her that made him feel like she wouldn't miss it. The elderly woman was chatting to a female customer and, oh, how she loved to yak on! The customer was trying to stifle a yawn as the woman prattled on about her son who had opened a china shop in Pontmorlais, boasting about his new house and wife and how they were going to buy her a house as well. The woman couldn't keep her gob shut, but luckily for him, it meant that he was able to slip a couple of pieces of cured ham into his pocket. He'd keep one for his uncle's tea and the other he'd share with that damned pub dog.

Griff congratulated himself on a job well done as he walked back to the house. He planned to return to the pub for the coal when it was darker and he desperately hoped that his peace offering would satisfy his uncle.

But surprisingly, his uncle was in a fine mood when he returned. For one thing he looked well spruced up. He wasn't drunk or anything. He was sober and steady on his feet. Even the grime had been washed off his face, his hair was combed and he was wearing a clean white shirt and his best tweed jacket. What was going on here?

'I've brought you some ham for your tea, Uncle Berwyn!' Griff announced, thinking his uncle would be pleased.

'I'll have it later, I'm going out on a bit of business, Griff, and I won't be back until much later. Tell you what, you keep it for yourself.' He smiled, which made Griff feel a little ill at ease. It had been a long time since his uncle had smiled at him or had a kind word to say.

'Thanks, Uncle. I'm going to get some co—' He was just about to tell his uncle about how he planned on nicking some coal from the back of the pub, but his uncle was already out of the door. Whatever it was he'd got dressed up for, it must have been important. It had put him in a good mood, too, which was something he hadn't seen in a long while.

Griff should have been happy that he didn't get a hiding that evening, but he had a niggling feeling that something was up. Still, he decided to leave the slice of ham for his uncle anyhow, so he placed it on a clean plate in the pantry to keep it cool. He ate half the remaining slice with a piece of stale bread and when the sun had gone down, he left in search of that silly mutt. If it wasn't for that dog he could have got over that wall easily and made away with the coal. He crept away from the house with an old sack tucked under his arm to carry the coal. By the time he arrived at the pub he could hear the sounds of raucous laughter inside and smell the beery fumes wafting towards him. It flipped his stomach over with fear, as it reminded him of his uncle, and all the times he had come back in that state and beaten him.

He checked no one was watching and then scaled the old stone wall which led into the backyard. From his grasp on the wall he could peer over, and the light from the pub gave him enough light to see what he was doing. And, sure enough, Scamp was there gazing up at him. He gave a low growl from where he sat in the shadows, a menacing sound that gave him the jitters. *Please don't bark*, he prayed.

Griff dropped a small piece of meat over the wall and the dog ran to get it. He wolfed it down like there was no tomorrow. The poor thing was as hungry as he was, and for a moment he felt compassion towards the hound.

But he had a job to do, so shiftily he placed one leg over the top of the wall, then another, until finally he was seated on top with his legs dangling over into the yard.

Scamp looked at him with curiosity and cocked his head on one side.

'Ssh, boy, I've got something for you!' And he dropped another piece of meat onto the ground. Again, the dog wolfed it down and looked up, waiting for the next piece.

Griff dropped to the ground, landing in a crouched position, making a small thud. He didn't think it was loud enough for anyone inside to notice, but immediately the dog came over to him and started sniffing his face. What if he bit him? But instead, Scamp licked Griff's face.

He was actually quite a cute thing, and he hugged the dog to him. Feeling his warmth against his body comforted him. It had been a long while since he'd hugged anyone or anything.

'Now, I'm just going to take some of that coal, you hear me? Now don't you go barking, see . . .'

Scamp wagged his tail as he watched Griff place several lumps of coal into the old sack. He wasn't about to raise suspicion by taking too much, oh no; he'd learned when stealing not to overdo it as then he'd get caught. If only he'd taken his own advice when he'd got greedy with those apples.

When he'd filled the sack half full, he patted the little dog on the head and then turned to scale the wall. It wasn't so easy to climb from this side and he now had the sack of coal, too. There was only one thing for it; he was going to have to leave through the pub itself.

He swallowed. Oh well, if he was going to end up transported to Australia for his efforts, then so be it. Life couldn't get much harder than living with that uncle of his in Merthyr, could it?

He prayed that the pub's back door would be unlocked as, gingerly, he pressed down on the handle, which was a little stiff. But he gave it a hard nudge to find it opened slightly. Scamp was now at his heels, and he hissed at him to go away. The little dog whimpered and ran off to his makeshift bed in the corner of the yard, made of rags and old newspaper, circling around and around until finally he sat down. He was beginning to feel a great deal of sympathy for the poor dog, whose life seemed to be just as wretched as his own.

Taking a chance, he pushed the pub door open wide. It

was a room housing lots of kegs of beer and old wooden crates. Thankfully it was dark and so noisy inside the pub that no one noticed the young lad with the sack on his back walk through and out of the side door. Safely in the alleyway, and immeasurably pleased with himself, he strode briskly away in the direction of home. He thought he'd got away with it, too, until in the darkness of the alleyway he bumped into someone with a familiar voice.

'Griff, where are you off to?'

He blinked until his eyes came into focus and he made out the outline of Florrie, the barmaid, who knew him well from all the times he'd gone looking for his uncle in the pub. It looked like she was on her way to the pub, so, thinking on his feet, he said, 'I just popped into the pub to see if I could find Uncle Berwyn, but no luck.' Now he hoped that his uncle wasn't in the pub when she arrived or else she'd think it very odd indeed.

To his relief she replied, 'No, he's not in there. I passed him earlier and he was in company with someone.'

'Someone?' The sack of coal was heavy on his back and he didn't want to lay it down on the ground for fear she would guess what it was.

Florrie hesitated before replying. 'Yes, you get along now, Griff. It's too dark for a young lad to be walking the streets. Get off home with you.' It was obvious she didn't wish to elaborate on who Griff's uncle was with. Maybe it was his elder sister, Dorothy. That would be it, and maybe that's why he tidied himself up – he wanted to impress her and ask for a loan. They'd lost touch since Griff's mother, their sister, had died.

Well at least the house would be warm, for a change, when his uncle got home.

'Bye, Florrie,' Griff shouted as he walked away before she could ask any questions about the sack on his back. In the distance, he heard Scamp bark and smiled to himself. That little dog wasn't so bad after all.

The work in the laundry room seemed never ending and Megan was frustrated. It was hot and uncomfortable and now her hands felt red raw from the soap and soda crystals. If she never saw another bed sheet or undergarment again it would be enough for her. Some were highly soiled and they had to soak those garments in cold salted water, then boil them up in a big copper pan. If you weren't careful you could scald yourself, and all.

Everywhere she looked there were women and girls with the same dull expressions on their faces from the monotony of it all. Their red faces were a mass of perspiration from the heat and gruelling hard work. Some were scrubbing shirts and dresses on washboards, others were pegging out clothes on long indoor washing lines, and others were folding or ironing.

There was steam everywhere, but at least it was warm in here and Mrs Crossley was kind-hearted to work for.

Mrs Crossley looked at her with pity in her eyes. 'Look, Megan, you need a break now.'

Megan grimaced. 'But I can't, Miss Hamilton will kill me if she catches me . . .' She prodded a sheet with a pair of tongs, and stood back from the boiling pan for fear the bubbling water should scald her.

Mrs Crossley dipped her hand into her apron pocket and passed Megan something wrapped in a piece of muslin. 'It's a piece of bread and ham from Cook,' she said. 'Go over there and hide away in that store cupboard for a while whilst you eat it. Cook is bringing you some buttermilk to drink. You need feeding up, my girl. You're all skin and bone. There's nothing to you.' She shook her head as she walked away, leaving Megan with a feeling that not every member of staff in the workhouse was bad. But she just couldn't relax as she nibbled on her food since she feared every footstep she heard outside the door was Miss Hamilton's, readying herself to string her up from the neck for breaking workhouse rules. The food stuck in her throat as fear spoiled the experience for her. She was thankful when one of the laundresses passed her the cup of buttermilk from Cook as it made the food easier to swallow.

The laundry girls were kind enough. They were all older than her and she asked some of them if they knew how her mother was, but they either claimed not to know her or they just weren't saying. They must have known, though, as they lived in the women's section of the workhouse. They were trying to protect her from something, but what?

'Megan,' Mrs Crossley said later, when Megan felt she could hardly remain standing on her feet, that tired she was.

Megan turned from the sink where she'd been rubbing a shirt on the washboard. 'Yes, Mrs Crossley?'

'I've been thinking ... As soon as you're old enough, which shouldn't be too long, if you get the chance to be boarded out, you should go. It would do you good to get away from this place.'

Megan smiled and nodded. She had every intention of leaving these walls behind forever and that's exactly what she was going to do.

The following day, Megan was pleased she was awake with the lark like the other girls and she got herself washed and tidied up ready for breakfast.

She'd got back late the previous night and all the other girls in the dormitory had been fast asleep. Megan had fallen down upon her bed fully clothed and hadn't even had the energy to undress herself properly. Her poor hands were cracked and sore from being immersed in hot soapy water for hours on end and she had been too tired to even worry about what the morning would bring.

After all that work and all that worry, in any event Miss Hamilton hadn't even returned to check on her once. She'd been a bag of nerves and all for nothing. But now, in the cold light of day, she wasn't sure whether her penance had been enough, or if Miss Hamilton had more in store for her.

When she finally entered the dorm Megan was surprised that the woman did not reprimand her, yet she had a sly, knowing smile on her face, which still managed to unnerve her. It was almost a smirk, as if she held some secret to herself. It gave Megan such an odd feeling that she couldn't get it out of her mind.

After breakfast, Megan managed to perform her usual tasks and was about to head to the schoolroom, when Miss Hamilton approached her. 'Megan,' she said in a sickly sweet voice, 'your mother has been asking to see you. Go along now at once to the women's quarters. You have my permission to miss school for a visit of no longer than twenty minutes.'

Megan couldn't believe her ears. Why was Miss Hamilton no longer angry with her? Maybe she'd changed her mind about the whole situation and had a heart after all. She couldn't wait to see her mother. She'd tell her all about how she'd met Griff and how the kids were doing well in the schoolroom, how Tom was loving working for the family at their shop in Twyn. But she wouldn't tell her about Miss Hamilton. There was no use in worrying her. Puzzled, but pleased, Megan headed off for the women's quarters.

When she arrived, she found Gwennie standing near the dormitory door, her head lowered. She looked up as Megan approached. 'You can't go in there, *bach*, what are you doing here?' Her eyes were full of concern.

Megan paused for a moment, before replying. 'Miss Hamilton said I was to come here and could stay for a full twenty minutes.'

Gwennie shook her head. 'There must be some sort of mistake, *cariad.*' Her eyes looked pained and sorrowful. Something was wrong, she just knew it.

'But I have to see my mother, I simply must.' Megan balled her hands into fists. If someone was to prevent her seeing her mother now that she had permission, she would scream the place down.

Megan heard approaching footsteps and turned to see Miss Hamilton stood behind her. She must have followed her over to the block. 'Let her see her mother!' she said sharply, addressing Gwennie.

Gwennie knew better than to argue with the ogre and slowly pushed open the door.

Megan approached the door and from the doorway she could see her mother lying on the bed, covered in a grey woollen blanket. Her eyes were closed and her skin was pale and sallow, like wax. Her once luxurious chestnut-coloured hair, now peppered with grey, clung to her face and looked long and unkempt, fanned out over the pillow. As Megan drew closer, she sensed something was wrong, and then thought maybe her mother was fast asleep. She reached out her hand to touch her mother's face, and traced the outline of her soft cheek with her fingertips. It felt icy cold. Realisation swept over her as a feeling of dread seeped into her veins. It was exactly how her father had felt to her touch in his coffin: stone cold, his limbs rigid and stiff. All life had left his body.

Megan's lower lip quivered and she turned to look at Gwennie and Miss Hamilton in utter disbelief. Gwennie couldn't make eye contact and Miss Hamilton just sniffed and said, 'Well, now you're truly an orphan, Megan. I doubt you'll ever escape this place!' Then she turned on her heel and departed, leaving Megan numb with shock. No wonder she'd been so nice to her earlier on – it was all part of her plan to inflict even more pain on her. It was the worst thing she could do to hurt her. It had been the woman's intention all along. How could she be so cruel?

Gwennie held out her arms and cradled Megan to her bosom. She felt as though her heart would break. When she'd cried as much as she could, she pulled away and asked, 'What happened to my mother?'

Gwennie hesitated before saying, 'She really did try to hang on for as long as she could, and Miss Hamilton promised her yesterday that she would bring all her children to her, but it never happened.'

A sharp shard of pain sliced Megan's heart in two. To think

she had never got to spend time with her mother, and all the while she'd been sent to work in that laundry room, with the old witch Hamilton knowing full well what was happening. Her mother had but hours left to live, hours when Megan could and should have been at her bedside holding her hand. It was all too much.

'I hate that old witch!' Megan shouted. 'She made sure I wasn't around yesterday. I was sent to wash clothes for eight hours as a punishment for back-chatting her after something awful she said about my parents!' She let out a long, piercing scream which echoed off the stone walls. She couldn't seem to stop.

She didn't know how long she had been standing there screaming when Gwennie slapped Megan's cheek hard, making her recoil backwards. 'Sorry, Megan. I don't want things to get any worse for you if Miss Hamilton hears you. I had to do it.' She pulled Megan roughly towards her and cradled her like she would a young child. 'Ssh!' Gwennie soothed. 'We don't want her to hear you, else she'll punish you even more for it.' She dipped her hand into her pinafore pocket and handed Megan a cotton handkerchief. 'Take it, it is clean. It's fresh from the laundry.'

Megan nodded and dabbed away at her swollen and watery eyes, then blew her nose. Now she would have to give the news to her younger brothers and sisters. How would they take it? And what about Tom, too? He'd be devastated. He had been so close to his mother.

'Thank you.' Megan was grateful for the woman's concern and support and understood why she'd chosen to slap her. That scream had felt like it was coming from someplace else, not from Megan herself.

'I know this is difficult for you, *cariad*, but let me tell you your mother passed away peacefully. If I were you, I'd spend a little time with her before they take her body away. Miss Hamilton doesn't allow the bodies to rest for long at the workhouse before getting them over to the chapel. Once they've been pronounced dead by the doctor, she gets the undertaker over as quick as a flash. I don't like it myself – I feel the soul needs time to leave the body . . .'

'My brother Tom . . .' Megan said. 'He needs to be here.'

Gwennie shook her head doubtfully. 'I don't suppose they'll get hold of him if he's out on orders. You'll have to be the brave one for all of your brothers and sisters now, Megan.'

Nodding, she realised the truth behind the words and knelt beside the bed where her mother lay. She took her pallid hand as the tears rolled down her cheeks. She wasn't even aware of how long she remained there, staring at her mother's gentle face. She'd lost a lot of weight since they'd been in the workhouse, and that, along with bearing six children and enduring her husband's death, had taken its toll.

'Come along now, *cariad*,' Gwennie soothed. 'You'll have to return to your quarters, we have to wash and change your mam before the undertaker gets here. The doctor was called to pronounce her dead before you arrived, so they'll be ready to take her to the chapel . . .'

Megan gulped. Could this really be happening to her? It didn't make sense. Just last month her mother had seemed fine, though if she thought back on it, she seemed a little tired and had complained of a slight backache.

She dreaded telling her siblings, imagining the distress on their faces. They were too young to understand, but Tom would, only too well, and he too would be angry at how their mother's illness had been kept from them.

Now that Tom was no longer at the workhouse she'd have to be the one to look after the little ones. She'd have to be both mother and father to them all.

The day of the burial was a grey day, shrouded by heavy mist. They were led over to the workhouse chapel by Bill, the porter, who shook his head sadly. 'I'm sorry for all you children. Your mother was a lovely woman. She always had a kind word for me and I remember your father, of course, he was my butty underground.'

Megan's ears pricked up. 'I never realised you knew my father well,' she said with some surprise.

'Oh aye, I used to work down the pit with him till I suffered a knee injury. I got better but vowed I would never return. It was a pity he hadn't taken my advice, too. Sorry, I shouldn't be talking to you like this.'

'No, it's all right,' Tom said. 'We're happy to hear anything about him at all. It feels like a lifetime since he was still here.'

'He was a good man, and all,' Bill continued, 'a hard worker who looked out for his family. You were all his world and he worshipped the ground your mother walked on.'

A lump stuck in her throat. Of course she'd realised how close her parents were, but to hear it from someone else tugged at her heartstrings.

'Strongest man I ever knew,' Bill continued fondly. 'He was also a good fellow to work with, watched your back for you.' Then, turning to the children, he said, 'This is going to be a difficult day for you all. Tom, you're now head of this family. Watch out for your brothers and sisters.'

Tom nodded. 'I will, Mr Harris. I'm boarded out to a shopkeeper and his wife in Twynyrodyn, so now I'm earning a bit of money for myself. And I hope that soon Megan can get away from here too. Maybe work as a maid somewhere or something like that . . .' He hesitated as he looked at his younger brothers and sisters. Alfie and Harry were doing their best to remain strong in front of Bill, but Lizzie and May were whimpering, hanging on to Megan's skirts. She really feared for all of them. It also made her wonder whether she should leave them at the mercy of someone like Miss Hamilton if she took a job outside the workhouse. What if she left and then Miss Hamilton turned on them as a way to wreak her vengeance on the family? She just couldn't bear that to happen.

The chapel service was quite short, with the small wooden coffin placed at the altar and a few flowers scattered around in glass vases. Some of the staff members were in attendance and some of the inmates too, including Gwennie. Miss Hamilton was nowhere to be seen and Megan sighed a breath of relief.

After they'd sung the hymn 'Abide with Me', Megan turned to Tom, who was stood at her side. 'How long can you stay?'

He shook his head. 'Sorry, Meg. I have to get back as soon as possible. Mr and Mrs Evans are short-handed in the shop. In any case, once this service is over, no one will be hanging around, will they? Miss Hamilton will expect you back scrubbing floors or in the laundry room, and the younger ones will be expected to return to their schoolroom studies. Life goes on at the workhouse; it doesn't come to a stop just because our mam died.'

Megan knew that what her brother said was perfectly true. It didn't come to a standstill, but for her it had. Her world had collapsed around her. There would be no get-together back at the house, as happened in many Welsh families following a funeral. It was usual for the women to remain at the house when the burial took place, with only the men in attendance. Then there'd be a spread laid on back at the house, usually a few sandwiches, maybe a ham would be cooked and some homemade Welsh cakes and a fruit cake. Sadly, there was no real send-off for their mam, only a sparse service at the work-house chapel.

When the service came to a close, and she and Tom took a long last look at their mother's coffin, they left the small chapel in silence, stunned that it had ever happened at all. The woman who had been there for them through thick and thin no longer existed in this world. A silent tear coursed its way down Megan's cheek. She quickly wiped it away; she didn't want the little ones to catch her crying, nor give Miss Hamilton the satisfaction of breaking down, today of all days. The woman could break her physically but she would never break her spirit. She'd show her. One day she'd leave the workhouse far behind and make a success of her life.

The rest of the day went by so slowly. People were especially kind to Megan. Eira offered to help her mop the floors and black-lead the grate in Matron's room, but Megan refused all offers of help. She needed to keep busy – it stopped her from thinking too much. She still wondered what had really taken her mother. Surely 'women's troubles' couldn't do that? Could they?

She needed a friend right now and although she had Eira, they couldn't really speak as freely as she would have liked. In the workhouse the walls most definitely had ears. She decided that the following day she would ask if she could help in the kitchen. That way, if any errands were needed running over the town, Cook might send her and she could seek out Griff. If she could get word to his Uncle Berwyn in the Vulcan she might find him to speak to. Griff would understand how she was feeling. He'd lost both parents too.

She was just finishing off black-leading the grate in Matron's room, and was down on her knees wiping her blackened hands on a clean cloth, when Matron Langley herself walked in. She didn't notice Megan.

'I tell you, it will be so much better when we return to Hereford,' she was saying to her husband. 'The new Master and Matron are to arrive here next month.'

Surely her ears were deceiving her? If Master and Matron Langley were going back home, who were this new pair taking over?

Her husband huffed out a breath. 'Hmm, I've heard he's a hard taskmaster, this one. He ran a workhouse in Carmarthen. He takes no prisoners. Though appears to have left under some sort of cloud.'

'Whatever do you mean?' Matron asked.

Megan stiffened, feeling the hairs on the back of her neck bristle with fear. She was just wondering how she could hide herself before the Matron saw her, but it was too late.

'Oh, Megan, I didn't see you there. What did you just hear?' Matron's eyes widened.

Megan shook her head. 'Nothing at all, ma'am.'

'Good. And please keep it that way.' She shot Megan a

knowing look. 'Anything you should happen to accidentally hear in this room is to remain private. Understood?'

Megan nodded meekly. She was never going to find out the circumstances of the new Master's departure now. She was so upset to hear the Langleys were leaving. With that, on top of her mother's death, she felt her whole world was collapsing around her. It just wasn't fair. Of all the things she could say about the Langleys, they were firm but fair. She couldn't abide the thought of new people taking over.

Megan stood, head lowered, gazing at Master Langley's shiny black leather shoes.

Then, in a gentle tone of voice, the Master said, 'You shouldn't be working today, Megan. Your mother's funeral was only this morning. You can return to your quarters if you wish.'

'Please, sir,' she said. 'I'd much rather work. it stops me from thinking so much.'

The Master drew in a breath and let it out again, then extracted a gold watch on a chain from his top waistcoat pocket. 'Good heavens, I'll be late. I'm supposed to meet someone from the Board of Guardians at the railway station. I'd better be going. The cab driver will be waiting.' He excused himself, and then turned to Megan. 'Sorry to hear about your mother. You do whatever you wish today.' Then he left the room, leaving her with his wife.

Waiting to be dismissed, Megan was surprised when Matron Langley told her to be seated. She glanced around the room as if Matron were speaking to someone else. It just wasn't done – her, a pauper, sitting in the Matron's room – but she sat on the seat nevertheless.

'Now what I'm going to tell you is for your own good,' Matron began. 'Soon, you are going to have to be boarded out just like your brother is now. What would you like to do, Megan? Would you like to become a parlourmaid? Work in a shop? Become a seamstress? What in particular?'

Megan drew in a long breath and then let it back out again. 'I think I'd like to work in a tea shop, Matron. You know, one of those that serves up fancy sandwiches and cakes.'

Matron smiled. 'I know what you mean, child, though I don't think there would be that many vacancies around for a young girl to work in one of those. You're more likely to earn work as a parlourmaid, but I can look into it for you before I leave.'

Megan thanked Matron Langley and left the room. It was comforting to know that she had some people behind her in the workhouse, even if that time was limited.

Chapter Five

Megan walked into the steamy kitchen seeking out Cook, but she was nowhere to be seen.

'Where's Mrs Woodley?' Megan asked one of the kitchen maids, Alicia, who stood at the scullery sink washing up. Her sleeves were rolled up above her elbows, and her arms were soaked in the soapy suds as she splashed around scrubbing at the dishes.

Alicia stopped what she was doing, turned and smiled. 'Good morning, Megan. I'm afraid Mrs Woodley isn't well today, she's resting in bed. She has a fever.'

'Oh, I hope she'll be all right.' Megan didn't like to think of Cook being unwell.

'She's a strong woman. I'm sure she'll overcome whatever it is that's ailing her,' Alicia said brightly. 'So, you've been sent over here to help out this morning, have you?' She wiped her wet hands on her pinafore.

Megan nodded eagerly. 'Yes, for most of the day, in fact.'

'Well, that's good. We could do with an extra pair of hands now Cook is off her feet. If you can finish these dishes I can get on with making the soup for dinner.'

Megan nodded and went to fetch an apron from where they hung behind the door, all the time wondering if she'd get a chance to escape to the town.

She found her chance when all the dishes had been washed and Alicia began to complain she needed more vegetables for the soup as it tasted too bland. Some of the vegetables had rotted in the sacks they were stored in due to damp conditions. Alicia had saved the best, chopping off the black bits, but her cooking skills fell far short of Mrs Woodley's.

'The market's in town today . . .' Megan offered. 'How about I take a walk over there and pick up some carrots and onions?'

The young woman immediately cheered up. 'Thank the Saints you arrived here today, Megan.'

Megan nodded and smiled. 'Anything else I can get when I'm out?'

Alicia dipped into her pinafore pocket and handed Megan a coin. 'Buy us a ha'penny bun from the cake stall. We can share it with a cup of tea later on.'

Megan beamed. Not only might she get to see Griff, she was being rewarded for her ingenuity, too.

Griff had occupied her thoughts a lot lately and even though she was still grieving for her mother, she couldn't wait to see him again. She didn't know what it was about him but she was happy and content in his company. There was an understanding between them of what it felt like to be orphaned.

The cake stall was her favourite in the marketplace. It was run by Mrs Mathias, who baked wonderful delicacies such as iced buns and custard tarts. The woman also ran a fancy cake shop in the town, which is what had given Megan the idea of working at a tea shop in the first place. She'd have a word with the woman, and then if she liked the idea she could send her to see Matron Langley before she left for Hereford.

When Megan got to the High Street she made her way to the Vulcan Inn. The side door was heaving with men – most looked like ironworkers and colliers like her dad, no doubt blowing off steam after a hard night's graft. Some were spilling out into the alleyway, pewter tankards in hand, and she jostled her way past them. The pubs seemed to be open all hours in the town. A couple of the men inside the pub eyed her with interest as she scanned the flagstone-floored room, with its long wooden bar. All she could see were men and even young boys, supping pints and smoking pipes. Yuck, she hated the smell. Fancy that, young boys in a place like this. She guessed maybe they were workers, too, as it wasn't unusual for young lads to go underground from the age of ten in these parts – she'd even heard of children, both boys and girls, working from the age of six at the ironworks. At least these lads had jobs to keep food in their bellies, though why they'd waste it on alcohol and tobacco was beyond her thinking.

Her eyes were drawn to a young woman in the corner speaking animatedly to a group of men. This must be the barmaid Griff had told her about. Megan studied her carefully. She was wearing a long maroon dress, so low cut she could see the woman's breasts spilling out over the top. It wasn't decent, in her book. Over her dress she wore a soiled apron and had a white mob cap on her head. Her hair was such a vibrant shade of flame red that Megan admired it from afar. In her hand, the barmaid carried a round metal tray as if she had just delivered drinks to the men. For a young woman, she seemed to be very popular with them all, but at the same time seemed to be dealing well with their high jinks, slapping their hands away if they got too close to her.

Megan walked up to her and tapped her on the shoulder. 'Excuse me, miss.'

The barmaid turned and shot her a surprised smile. 'Now, what's a young girl like you doing in a place like this?' She looked at Megan for the longest time, waiting for an answer.

'I'm searching for a man called Berwyn. He's my friend's uncle. I need to find their house,' she explained.

'Ah, you're talking about young Griff?'

Megan nodded. 'Yes, that's him.'

'I'm sorry, I haven't seen Berwyn for a few days, not since he's taken to spooning with that lady friend of his.'

Megan wasn't sure what 'spooning' meant. 'Could you show me where he lives, please?'

The woman smiled and shook her head. 'I'm sorry, *cariad*. I'm too busy here at the moment to come with you, and you don't want to go wandering round that area on your own, believe me!'

'Florrie, over here, another pint, darling!' A man in the corner beckoned, and Florrie left her side to see to him. Dispirited and head down, Megan made her way out of the pub, pushing past groups of men as she departed. Thankfully none of them touched her or got in her way.

But just as she was leaving the alleyway, a tall man in a shabby long tailcoat and battered top hat grabbed her by the arm so forcefully she almost dropped the basket she was carrying. 'Say, miss, how old are you?'

'Almost twelve,' she said, trying to not allow the fear to seep through into her voice.

'Hmm, nice and young and good-looking too. Want to make some money?' He twirled his thick black moustache. If he cleaned himself up and wore nice clothing, she guessed he might be considered quite handsome. Though there was something about him that warned her not to hang around.

She blinked several times. It sounded too good to be true that she could make some money, and wouldn't it help her brothers and sisters? It could help them get out of the workhouse now their mother was no longer alive.

'How?'

'If you go over to the wash-house in China and tell them Twm Sion Watkin sent you, they'll give you a job.'

The mention of a wash-house immediately put Megan off. She'd had enough of the laundry at the workhouse the other day, and her inner voice seemed to warn her he was bad news, a man most people feared. But he put his arm around her waist and drew her closer to him. She could smell his beery breath and unwashed skin. 'Please, sir. I don't need to go to the wash-house. I'm from the workhouse and I'm not even supposed to be in here. I'll get into trouble, please let me go!'

'Oh, I'll get you into trouble all right, a fine-looking young lass like you . . .' He had a glint in his eyes as if he were the wicked wolf in *Red Riding Hood*. She'd read about it in a book once and it had scared her half to death. Her father had had to reassure her there were no wolves sleeping beneath her bed at night nor prowling around Gethin Woods for months afterwards.

'Please, I want to go now . . .' she protested, looking around for someone to come to her assistance.

Still he held on to her tighter and tried to turn her around to lead her away. 'Come with me and you won't want to go back to no workhouse. I know a way you can earn me lots of money.'

'No, please. Help! Help someone!' she cried out. But no one listened, it was too noisy inside the pub.

'Come along now, lovely. I promise it's worth your time,' the man urged as he held her even tighter in his grasp.

There was nothing else for it. She screamed as loud as she could, high pitched and alarming. 'Help! Police! Help!'

A man at the side door of the pub heard her and then a group of men came rushing out. They looked at one another and walked towards the man in a threatening manner. These were ironworkers and colliers who grafted with pick axes, shovels and the like all day long, so they were very fit and muscular. It was as if time stood still, a stand-off between the man and the group.

Megan gulped. What would happen now? She closed her eyes and then opened them once more to see a woman shouting him off. "Ere, leave that gal alone, you big brute Twm Sion Watkin!' the barmaid, Florrie, said.

The men walked even closer to the bully, who shook his head and scuttled off down the alley.

Megan blinked at Florrie in surprise. 'Who was he?'

'Let's just say he's not someone you'd like to know. He's a pimp, *cariad*. You need to keep away from people like him.'

A pimp? So that's what a pimp looked like. She remembered Mrs Woodley's words. 'So is he something to do with a prost-a-something?'

'Prostitute?'

'Yes, that's the word. What are they?'

'"Nymphs of the pave" we sometimes call them. Bad

ladies who do wicked things for money. Now I'd get out of 'ere if I were you, it's not safe.' Florrie shook down her dress as if shaking off the man's evil presence.

'But I need to find my friend Griff,' she protested, her chin jutting out with determination.

The barmaid's face softened. 'I know the lad well – he comes in here often enough to take his uncle home when he's in a state.'

'Any idea where he could be right now?'

'He runs around with a lot of bad lads called the Rodneys. They're a bunch of barefooted urchins. Some people don't like them as they think they're a load of pickpockets. But they're just starving, bless 'em. Some like Griff, got no mothers or fathers and have fallen into bad ways. Two of them are due to go to court and my guess is they'll end up transported to Australia. It's not right, those kids are blooming starving.'

'They'd be better off in the workhouse where I am,' Megan said softly, remembering Griff's recent theft of apples.

'Maybe,' the barmaid said, 'but it's become a way of life for them. They know no other. China is a dangerous place for a young lady like yourself to be. Please don't go looking for Griff's house on your own, will you?' She gave Megan a stern glance. 'I'll take you there myself, if you like, I'm due to finish soon enough. I know where he lives as I had to help him get his uncle home once.'

Megan beamed. 'That would be grand. I'll just go and get my shopping from the marketplace and meet you back here.'

'No, I'll come with you right away,' she said. 'If you go walking through there with a basket full of goods, you're likely to get jumped. Some are starving half to death. They'll knock you to the floor for a crust of bread.'

Megan took heed of the barmaid's cautionary words. 'Very well, and thank you, miss. I don't have a lot of time to spare as I'll be missed from the workhouse and the food I need to buy is for dinner time.'

'Don't worry, it shan't take us long. I'll just pop back inside and tell the landlord I'm due to finish.'

She was as good as her word and some minutes later they were stood outside a small, dilapidated, grimy house in a narrow alleyway. The houses seemed to be on top of one another and the stench made Megan want to heave.

'That'll be the open canals of people's waste,' Florrie began. 'They throw it all out into the street and it finds its way into the River Taff. People blamed it all for the cholera outbreaks that killed all those folk . . .'

Megan had heard about that; some at the workhouse had died, but luckily most had been segregated to the infirmary where they were isolated from the other inmates. Else it could have been far worse.

'This is Griff's house,' she said, then tapped on the door. The house was a small affair that looked to Megan like a one-up one-down sort of building. It stood in amongst the others in a higgledy-piggledy fashion. The windowpane was smashed upstairs and stuffed full of old newspaper, to keep the heat in, she guessed. The thick coating of dust on the windows made her think they hadn't seen a washcloth in years. It looked as if the walls might once have been whitewashed but had since turned black with mould and green moss over time. To Megan it looked as if it were unoccupied. Surely this must be the wrong house, there had to be some mistake?

But then she heard the angry shouts from inside, and the ramshackle wooden door with its peeling paint swung open. Griff stood there, blinking. His eyes widened as if he were astonished to see her on the doorstep. He looked thinner since the last time she'd seen him and the dark rings beneath his eyes made him appear gaunt and skeletal. Her heart went out to the lad. 'Megan, is it really you?' he asked.

She nodded. 'Of course it is. Are you all right, Griff? Have you been ill or something?'

He shook his head. 'I'm all right. Just not had a lot to eat lately.'

She shook her head and reached out to touch his shoulder. 'I don't have long as I've been sent from the workhouse kitchen to pick up some shopping. Would you like to come with me and we can walk and talk along the way?'

He nodded enthusiastically. 'I'll just tell my uncle I'm going out then. All that shouting was him. He's in a bad mood as he has no money to buy booze.' He looked at the barmaid, who gave a knowing smile.

'Well, I'll be off then,' she said, turning back in the direction they'd arrived, leaving Megan and Griff staring at one another.

She heard him shouting to his uncle that he was going out for a while and some muffled shouts in return. She was so glad she didn't have to live with an uncle who was permanently drunk, and she got the impression that Griff was more than happy to leave that little scene behind.

'Come along then, m'lady,' Griff said with a cheeky grin as they set off for the marketplace, chit-chatting on the way.

Griff suddenly stopped in his tracks. 'What's the matter, Megan?' he asked.

'It's my mother. She died, and the funeral was only the day before yesterday, so now I'm an orphan, just like you, Griff. I can't believe she's no longer here with us. I wasn't allowed to see her for ages at the workhouse, she was in a different block, and when I finally did, she had already slipped away . . .' She swallowed, fighting hard to hold back the tears that were threatening to trickle down her cheeks. Why did life have to be so unfair? What had she and her brothers and sisters done to deserve this? They'd already lost their father.

'I'm so sorry to hear that, Megan, but what happened?'

'I don't know really. I hadn't seen her for a couple of weeks. I wasn't allowed to, even though I tried. Then Miss Hamilton, the supervisor, suddenly sent for me and didn't tell me she'd died, so I walked into the room, seeing her on the bed, cold as ice. It was an awful sh–sh–shock.' But before she could stop herself, the emotion that had been building up began to spill over as her body began to wrack with grief. Huge sobs shook her shoulders, and Griff hugged her to him. She felt safe and secure in his arms as he held her tight. It was nice to be hugged by someone after all that treatment she'd had of late from Miss Hamilton. She wished he could hold her close forever.

'But you'll never be alone, I'll always be around for you, Megan,' he soothed, until finally she stopped crying and pulled away, wiping her tears on the back of her shawl. If only she had a handkerchief right now, like the lady at the Temperance Hall used.

She let out a long breath. 'Thank you so much, Griff. My big brother Tom watches out for me too, but he's not at the workhouse anymore, now that he's boarded out to a shopkeeper and his wife at Twynyrodyn. Mr and Mrs Evans are going to take on two of the younger children soon, but I don't know which ones. I was hoping they either take both girls or both younger boys as it will be awful for them to be split up in the workhouse.'

Griff looked thoughtful for a moment. 'Ah, you say that, but I think whoever they might choose will have a much better life. Pity Mr and Mrs Evans can't take you all.'

Megan lowered her head and shook it sadly. 'I was thinking that myself, but maybe they can't afford to. I think they actually want to adopt two of the younger children – if they took us all, there would be six extra mouths to feed.'

'I suppose so,' Griff said, digging his hands in his jacket pockets. 'Wish they'd take me too, so I could escape that uncle of mine.' He laughed. Megan knew he didn't really mean it. She could tell he really loved his Uncle Berwyn. He just wished he could lay off the booze.

'Tell me about your parents, Griff. You've not said much about them.' Megan was really curious as, so far, he'd hardly mentioned them.

He looked at the ground as if he were fighting to bring an image of them both to mind. Then he let out a long, shuddering breath. 'It seems so long ago, it feels it never happened at all, but I do remember something about them taking me to the park and us all sitting around a table at home eating together. My father died first, he got killed in an accident at the Cyfarthfa Ironworks, he was badly burned I'm told. Uncle Berwyn told me that my mother, his sister, died of a broken heart. I never knew quite what happened, only that she fell into the River Taff and drowned. No one knows whether it was an accident or not. He's been looking after me ever since, but I'm not even sure for how long.'

Megan couldn't believe that there was someone who was in the same position as herself, but at least he still had his uncle. She and her brothers and sisters had no family left at all, only one another.

Bringing the awful incident from earlier to mind, she said, 'Griff, I bumped into Twm Sion Watkin earlier . . .'

Griff's face paled. 'Stay well away from him, Megan, whatever you do, or he'll have you working at the wash-house and then you might end up at the house next door.'

'Florrie warned me and he did ask if I wanted to work at the wash-house. He said I was good-looking. I don't understand, what happens at the wash-houses, Griff? Why does he want me to work at the one in China and what happens in the house next door?'

Griff's eyes darkened. 'Believe me, Megan. You just don't want to know. They are places where bad men go. They've been the ruin of many a young woman.'

Megan didn't quite understand what he meant, but at least her instinct was right. That Twm Sion Watkin was a bad person and although she'd worked in the laundry at the workhouse, she'd never consider working in that wash-house in China.

'I can't even believe that man thought I was good-looking . . .' Her cheeks flushed as she spoke.

Griff smiled. 'Well, he wasn't wrong there. That's why I told you to contact me through my uncle or the barmaid; you don't want to visit China on your own or you might never come out from there again. Believe me, I know.' Protectively he put his arm around her shoulders and she liked the feeling. He was her protector.

Chapter Six

Griff helped Megan pack her shopping into the wicker basket.

'Gosh, I'd forgotten this basket belongs to the Temperance Hall,' Megan said, looking at him. 'The Lady gave it to me.'

'Which lady?' Griff's eyes widened.

'The lady who sings on the stage with the voice of an angel . . .' she said dreamily.

'Don't think I know of her.' Griff sniffed and wiped his nose on the back of his sleeve.

'Yuck!' Megan shook her head. 'You should use a hand-kerchief.'

'I don't have one, sorry. My mother always had beautiful lace handkerchiefs when she was alive, but my Uncle Berwyn doesn't have any and I ain't got enough money to buy one.'

Taking pity on him, she said, 'Well, I suppose it's not your fault. I'll see if I can sneak a couple out of the workhouse for you.'

'Wouldn't that be stealing, though?'

She realised he was accusing her of the very thing she had recently accused him of, though she had partaken of the spoils. 'No, I don't think so, because if you were really down and out, you'd end up in the workhouse anyway.'

It sort of made sense to Griff. 'I'm hungry,' he complained, rubbing his stomach in a circular motion.

She only had onions and carrots in her basket but still needed to go to the cake stall anyhow for a ha'penny bun. When they arrived, Mrs Mathias was busy serving a little lady who wore a frilled bonnet. She often slipped Megan a little something extra and her mouth salivated with hunger. As she handed the woman the halfpenny for the bun, Mrs Mathias handed her a brown paper bag. 'Some broken biscuits for you as well, *cariad*,' she said. 'No extra charge.'

Megan beamed. 'Thank you so much, Mrs Mathias.'

'You need a bit more meat on your bones. They're not feeding you enough at the workhouse.'

Megan carefully put the bun and the biscuits in her basket and then said to Mrs Mathias, 'Please, would you consider me working in your tea room sometime? Matron says I can go out to work soon but she seems to think I'd be best off as someone's parlourmaid or seamstress, but I'd love to work in a tea room.'

Mrs Mathias smiled. 'I have enough people serving in the shop, but I suppose I could do with a young girl to mind the stall here, so I could stay at the shop longer and bake more. I'm not so sure though, Megan. You're quite young and all you've ever known is the workhouse. You don't have much experience of these matters. I need someone fit and capable to run things here. Some of the customers will try it on with you, like. They might try to take advantage because you're so young.'

Megan's heart sank. 'Please, Mrs Mathias,' she urged. 'I have all sorts of experience at the workhouse. I've helped Cook in the kitchen, lots of times. And I can assure you after being in that place I've learned how to fend for myself. I'm a hard worker too and what I don't know I can always learn! I can write and add up and take away sums of money too!'

'Oh, I don't know, you're very persuasive. Maybe I could give you a chance. Only one, mind . . .' Mrs Mathias eyes still looked doubtful, but she had a smile upon her face.

Megan gazed at the woman in expectation. 'Please could you have a word with Matron Langley, Mrs Mathias? And soon too? She's leaving for Hereford and someone else is going to take her place.'

Peggy Mathias chuckled. 'My word you are keen, child. I'm right on to it, as soon as I pack away my stall I shall call at the workhouse to have a word with her, but I can't promise any-thing, mind you, Megan. Maybe Matron won't allow it, so don't get your hopes up too high. I don't want you to be sorely disappointed.'

Megan understood. Her small hopes of getting away from that place even for part of a day was all she needed, her chance for a bit of freedom. 'Just ask her, please, Mrs Mathias?'

'I will, don't trouble yourself, *bach*. I shall do my level best for you.' She glanced sideways at Griff. 'And who is this, might I ask?'

'He's my friend.'

Peggy narrowed her eyes suspiciously. 'There was a boy who looked just like you who ran through the market the other day. He made off with an armful of apples. Blinking good hiding he needs!'

'Terrible,' Megan said, feeling a little annoyed that she needed to cover for Griff. If anyone found out it was him, then he would surely be in trouble. As it was, no one knew for sure who the boy was. 'So many boys though look like Griff, especially from the China area. They are so poor, that's why they nick things. They're starving half to death.'

'I appreciate that, young Megan, but they could go in the workhouse and not steal off honest people like me who are trying to earn a living.' She folded her arms and pursed her lips.

'It's not always that easy,' Megan was quick to reply. 'Some still have families where the adults are wastrels who don't know what's best for them.'

Mrs Mathias, who was a portly woman, huffed and then lost her train of thought as a customer summoned her. 'I'll speak to you again soon, Megan. I'm too busy right now.' She turned her head to deal with the customer, and for a brief moment, Megan feared she wouldn't bother to see the Matron at all.

'Cor, you got me out of a sticky situation there, Megan,' Griff enthused as they walked away.

Megan shook her head and looked heavenward for a moment. 'Well, maybe, but if it happens again, Mrs Mathias will recognise you now.'

'It won't,' he promised. 'Cross my heart and hope to die. I don't want to end up transported. Two of the Rodneys have been locked up. They were my friends. I don't want to end up on a big ship going to Australia and never get to see you nor my Uncle Berwyn ever again. He's hard work for me sometimes when he's drunk for days . . . but he's the only family that bothers with me and, to be fair, he only raises his hand in drink, so I do my best to keep out of his way during those times.'

'Well, that's a good thing then,' Megan said thoughtfully. 'Florrie mentioned he was "spooning" with someone, but I don't know what that means. Do you? What made him take to the drink in the first place?'

Griff blinked in surprise. 'It means "courting", I suppose. That makes sense now if Uncle Berwyn's cleaned himself up and not as drunk as he used to be.'

'You haven't answered my question: why does he drink, though?'

Griff sighed heavily. 'It's a sad story, but he was very happily married at one time, but his wife, my Auntie Ginnie, died in childbirth. So he lost the two of them at the same time . . .' His voice trailed away.

'That's so sad, Griff.' She touched his shoulder with great affection, and for a moment felt like hugging him tightly, but there were so many people in the marketplace she feared they'd be seen and it would be reported back to Matron at the workhouse.

Outside relationships and inside ones were both frowned upon. There was a good reason why men and women were kept apart in the workhouse. Some babies had been born out of wedlock and they didn't want any more mouths to feed. Megan realised she wasn't as yet quite a woman; her friend Eira had become a woman only a couple of months ago and Megan had noticed a big change in her. She had developed breasts and every few days out of the month suffered bad stomach cramps, which meant she had to ask for special sanitary wear to use in her bloomers. She couldn't just throw the rags away; she was made to wash them, dry them and use them again. Being a woman seemed a real nuisance to Megan. Eira had told her that women had to be careful once their courses began because if they had relations with someone of the opposite sex it meant they could now have a baby. Megan was going to ensure that would never happen to her.

'Shouldn't you be getting back to the workhouse, Megan?' Griff asked.

'Cripes, I was so far away in my thoughts there, I forgot this stuff is needed for the soup! I'd better dash!'

'I'll walk you there,' Griff said. 'I can carry your basket for you.'

'Best not, in case anyone from the workhouse sees, but any chance I get to escape from that place, I'll let you know!' She handed him the small paper bag of broken biscuits, taking one for herself, then blew him a kiss and watched his face flush beet red. Then she turned on her heel and scarpered back to the only home she had now: the workhouse.

When she entered the kitchen, the first thing Megan felt was a cuff around the face. Smarting from the stinging blow, she turned to her side to see Miss Hamilton rooted to the spot. She massaged her sore cheek, her lower lip quivering in terror, fearing the old crone would hit her again.

'You, girl, shall be punished severely for this!' she shouted, raising her hand ready to bring it down for another blow to the face.

Megan dropped her basket to the floor, lowered her head and put her hands on top of her head to brace herself. She waited, but the blow didn't come. She dropped her hands to her side and looked up to see Matron Langley standing with a look of strong disapproval on her face. 'There'll be no need for that, Miss Hamilton,' she said sharply. 'Alicia informed me earlier the girl was out on an errand.'

'But she was gone for a full hour,' Miss Hamilton said, through gritted teeth.

'There might well have been good reason for that.' Matron scowled.

Miss Hamilton huffed out a breath, glared at Megan, turned on her heel and walked out of the kitchen. As soon as she'd gone, Megan began to sob. Without showing any emotion in front of the kitchen staff, Matron led her to her office.

'Please sit down, Megan,' she ordered. Megan sniffed but had stopped sobbing. 'Look, I can see that woman has it in for you and unfortunately, there's not a lot I can do as the new Master and Matron will be here soon. I don't really have any grounds to sack her, unless of course, you tell me differently.'

Megan thought for a moment and remembered the times Miss Hamilton had made her work long hours in the laundry room without food or drink, or made her mop the corridors all times of the day and night, particularly when she'd been fast asleep and dragged from her bed. But she realised the woman might be called in front of the Board of Guardians who could well take her side, which would leave Mcgan in a worse position if the woman was humiliated. It could even make the newspapers.

'No, Matron Langley. I don't think you have any grounds to sack her. I was out a little longer than I should have been.'

'Oh, and why was that, child?' Matron peered at her over her round spectacles.

'Because I was in talks with Peggy Mathias who owns the tea rooms in Merthyr. She has a stall in the marketplace.'

Matron raised her brows. 'My word, that was very forward-thinking of you, young lady. You certainly don't let the grass grow under your feet, Megan Hopkins, I'll give you that much. And what did she say?'

'She said there was no vacancy at the tea room for me at the moment but she could give me a job on her cake stall. It would mean long hours, though . . .'

'That should be all right, Megan. Send her to see me, will you?'

'To be honest, Matron, I already told her she should come to see you. She might show up here later on.'

Matron smiled warmly. 'That was very bold, Megan. I like that.'

Once dismissed, Megan made her way back to the kitchen where Alicia was waiting for her with a scowl on her face. 'You ain't doing yourself no favours,' she said. 'Miss Hamilton called in here several times to check where you were. I didn't know what to say. It shouldn't have taken you that long to fetch a few onions and a bunch of carrots!'

'I know, but I had to do some business with the lady who

owns the cake stall. Matron knows all about it,' she said with some satisfaction at how grown-up she sounded. Alicia looked at her wide-eyed.

'Megan Hopkins . . . you do amaze me,' she said, and then her face broke out into a smile. 'Come on. Let's share that ha'penny bun with a cup of tea.'

Chapter Seven

And so it was arranged that Megan should work on the cake stall five days a week. She was thrilled. She realised her wages were to be sent to the workhouse but had struck a deal with Mrs Mathias that she pretend she was paid very low wages, and the remainder was kept for Megan herself. Mrs Mathias said she'd store the money safely at home for her in case it got confiscated by the workhouse staff. Any time Megan wanted any of her secret earnings, she only had to ask. Plus, there was the added bonus of her eating anything that wasn't good enough to sell at the stall, like with the burnt buns or bread; she'd pick the charred bits off and eat the rest as if there were nothing wrong with it at all. Sometimes she'd get stale leftovers from the tea room, too, and all would go immediately into mouth or pocket. And she always kept some for Griff. Mrs Mathias's baked goods were to die for. When Megan awoke starving in the middle of the night at the workhouse, she'd conjure up the smell of the cinnamon in a baked apple pie, or the taste of the creamy custard in an iced slice, or the jam and cream in a Victoria sponge, so delicious that the mere vision made her stomach growl. She was one of the lucky ones to try these tempting treats. She appreciated that there were many at the workhouse who hadn't tasted anything so fine for years since their fortunes changed for the worse. The one day of the year they could all enjoy a good nosh-up was Christmas Day itself, when the guardians put on a special meal, usually a beef roast dinner followed by plum pudding. She so wished the grub could be like that every day of the year.

Megan started on the stall early on a Monday morning – it was perishingly cold and very dark when she had to leave for the bakery in Plymouth Street to pick up her wares. The bakers were just unloading the bread – some of it was still warm to the touch. She took in the delicious aroma as her stomach grumbled with hunger. She'd left the workhouse too early for breakfast, though Cook had said she could always leave out something for her if needs be. But truth be told, she didn't feel like eating first thing and Mrs Mathias promised she could have a teacake or something else whilst she worked and a tin mug of tea from one of the market stalls. Sometimes if it was a particularly cold day, she bought herself a hot jacket potato to hold between her hands or a mug of hot pea soup to warm them up – she'd never starve working in the market, that was for sure. The other stallholders were so kind to her and watched her back.

Megan observed at close quarters as Mrs Mathias wrapped the loaves of bread in clean muslin cloths and laid them inside different-sized wicker baskets as carefully as if they were newborn babes, along with the cakes and buns, on the back of a wooden handcart which bore the name *Mathias Family Baker and Tea Room*. Once on board, Megan had the task of pushing the heavy cart from Plymouth Street to the open marketplace in Merthyr town. It was hard work, but far better than being at the workhouse, where she'd be scrubbing floors on her hands and knees or rubbing soiled bed sheets on washboards with lye soap, making her hands crack and sting for days on end.

The first day working for Mrs Mathias thrilled her. She'd hardly set up the stall when they were inundated with early bird customers. Peggy said she'd go with her every morning of that week to help her set up and stay for an hour or so, and the following week Megan would have to go it alone.

The first morning went by very quickly, and by the time Peggy returned to her little tea room just down the road, Megan was like an old hand on the stall. Having lived at the workhouse for the past four years, she had got used to the things people tried to get away with and was sharp if someone tried it on with her. She might have been almost twelve years old, but she had a wealth of experience and common sense.

Griff turned up later that afternoon and cocked her a grin as he could see how well she was coping. He stood there, hands dug deep into his tattered trouser pockets, cheeks ruddied from the cold north wind.

'I've kept a couple of stale buns leftover from the weekend for you, Griff,' she whispered behind the back of her hand.

'Thanks. Cor, you're doing really well by the looks of it, proper little sales lady you are, I've been listening to your patter.'

Megan beamed. 'Aye, well, I'm going to have my own tea room some day, Griff, and you can help me to run it. I did want to be singer on stage like The Lady, but I'd much rather have my own shop instead.' She handed him the two buns into his grimy palms. He took one and put it into his jacket pocket and immediately munched hungrily on the other.

'I'd like that,' he said, after swallowing a large morsel. ''Ere, you won't get into trouble for giving me those buns, will you?'

'No, not at all,' she said confidently. 'Mrs Mathias told me I was to have them. I've had my share, she gave me three in all.'

Griff's face fell. 'I'm robbing you of yours,' he said sadly.

She shook her head. 'No, not at all, Mrs Mathias is giving me a couple of meat pies later too.'

His face lit up.

Megan was the happiest she'd been in years working at the market stall. She always ensured she had some broken biscuits, stale buns or even a meat pie for her brothers and sisters to share, as well as the odd tasty morsel for Griff. But she had to take care when smuggling the items back to the work-house. She'd found a place to hide them, wrapped in a cloth in a vent in one of the walls, but it soon attracted rodents. Their scampering over the floorboards at night had put paid to that idea, especially as sometimes it would be days before she could get the food to her brothers and sisters. And every time she passed something on to them there was the chance she'd get caught red-handed and punished. So eventually, the leftovers were reserved for herself and Griff. Tom didn't need any; he was well fed with his new family in Twyn. It was better than giving it to the mice and rats, which is how it most often felt.

One day, Tom turned up at her stall as she was handing over change and a bagful of buns to a customer. She looked up to see him grinning at her.

'What's going on?' she asked.

'Mr and Mrs Evans have decided to take on Harry and Alfie. They're to move into their home next week!'

'Oh, that's great news, they've chosen at last!' She was so pleased for her brothers, but at the same time feared for her two sisters. Alfie and Harry were quite strong little boys who could hold their own, but her sisters were timid sorts who could be taken advantage of.

'Yes.' He nodded enthusiastically. 'I think the reason was

that the boys will be able to handle more manual stuff like lifting heavy tea chests. I think Mrs Evans would have liked to take a boy and girl as she's never had a daughter, but Mr Evans said it would be cruel to split up either sisters or brothers.'

'Well, I agree with him!' Megan said, as she began to pack away her stall, covering the leftover buns and bread in muslin cloths and loading them into the cart.

'Here, let me help you with that,' Tom said. With her brother's help, the stall was soon packed away back into the handcart.

'Here you are,' Megan said brightly, handing her brother a leftover sticky bun.

His face broke out into a huge smile. She didn't give him much from the stall these days. He really was becoming very muscular from all the lifting of sacks of potatoes and other heavy goods at the shop. And the constant hefting of goods onto the cart for deliveries, and all the walking up and down Twyn Hill, kept him fit and well.

Tom accompanied Megan towards the lower end of the town, pushing the handcart over the cobbled ground whilst she walked alongside him. He described his employer as 'a man of means', so Megan guessed that meant wealthy. Tom was certainly thriving since living with the Evanses.

'You seem really happy working on that stall, Megan,' Tom said, as they passed St Tydfil's Parish Church, its grey stone exterior and clock face nestled between the trees.

'I am, though I know it will be harder for me throughout the winter – Mrs Mathias has warned me of that.'

'It's good to see you looking so cheerful, though!'

For the first time in ages, Megan realised that Tom was absolutely right: she was.

Little did Megan realise that her short burst of happiness was soon to change with the arrival of the new Master and Matron at the workhouse.

Chapter Eight

Master and Matron Pomfrey arrived from the workhouse in Carmarthen a few days later. Originally from Yorkshire, Megan found their accents hard to tune into at first.

Workhouse rules were strictly enforced and now there was no dilly-dallying around, if ever there had been before, no freedoms of any sort for inmates. Megan feared the pair would prevent her from working on the cake stall, but so far hadn't done so. Now no inmate could afford to be late for a meal or try to miss out on prayers in the chapel, because if they did they were rounded up and made an example of in front of everyone. It was a humiliating experience which Megan hoped would never happen to her. She'd enough of that with Miss Hamilton. One morning, Eira was made to stand in front of all the inmates on a wooden podium during breakfast just because she'd accidentally fallen asleep on her bed in the dorm when she should have been in the laundry. Megan guessed it was either Miss Hamilton or one of the other girls who had reported her misdemeanour. The Pomfreys were granting special privileges to those inmates who ratted on others. An extra bowl of soup and a slice of bread, or lighter duties for a day went a long way with some at the workhouse.

'This is the kind of foolish article who deserves to go on show for her lazy ways!' Matron had said to all as they sat waiting for the signal to begin eating their daily bowl of gruel. 'The girl shall miss her breakfast and stand completely still in front of you all. If anyone spots her moving or fidgeting throughout breakfast you are to report to me or Master Pomfrey!' The Master stood beside her with a staff in his hand. He nodded, then banged his staff on the wooden floor three times, which was the signal they all waited for to tell them they could eat. No longer could they pick up their spoons after a short prayer of grace and gobble it down like there was no tomorrow; now they had to wait for a signal and woe betide anyone who picked up their spoon too early. And the final humiliation came for Eira when Matron hung a small slate suspended on a string over the girl's head which bore the words written in chalk: '*An idle man will suffer hunger*'.

Megan recognised it as a biblical quote from Proverbs.

Whereas once there was a clear divide between the staff and inmates, where the inmates all stuck together, now there was division amongst them and Megan didn't know quite who to trust any more.

Thank goodness Harry and Alfie were now happily ensconced at Mr and Mrs Evans's home and didn't have to suffer this way. They had to work for their keep, though. Harry was up at the crack of dawn helping Mrs Evans pack up the deliveries for Tom to take out, back and forth, to customers all day long. Alfie, who was stocky and stout, helped chop up sticks, heft coal from the coalhouse to keep the fires in the house going, and generally was a real asset, and a favourite of Mrs Evans, who treated him like a son. Tom had told Megan that although Mrs Evans seemed to favour the ruddy-faced child, Harry and himself didn't mind one bit, as Mr Evans was always championing them, singing their praises. Tom had discovered from Mr Evans that Alfie bore a strong resemblance to a young child of the Evanses who'd died at the age of four. Though that didn't appear to worry Tom, it did concern Megan somewhat. She didn't want a stranger taking over her brother and trying to be his mother.

One afternoon after returning to the workhouse, Megan noticed a young woman she knew to be called Tilly Thomas coming out of Master Pomfrey's room in floods of tears. Her head slumped and shoulders shook in devastation.

'What's the matter, Tilly?' she asked, laying her hand gently on the girl's shoulder, but Tilly shook off Megan's hand, adjusted her clothing, and ran back to her dorm, almost as if Megan were invisible to her. But Megan knew something had gone on in that room. Maybe Tilly had stolen something and had been ticked off, and that was why she felt too guilty to speak about it to her? That's what it must be, Megan decided.

She voiced her concerns later that day to Eira, who thankfully seemed none the worse for her ordeal at breakfast. Megan had managed to sneak her a crust of bread and butter from Cook to combat the girl's hunger, but the shame of the experience would be harder to shake off, Megan guessed. 'I've noticed Tilly getting very upset lately,' Eira said. 'She took to her bed one day and it was hard to get her out of it. She cried for hours and hours.'

Megan thought for a moment: if Tilly had stolen something, such as food from the kitchen, then it seemed unlikely she'd keep getting upset about it and taking to her bed. It had happened in the workhouse before. It wasn't unusual at all. If an inmate stole a morsel from the kitchen and was caught, they would be punished, but after they'd served their 'sentence', either undertaking extra work or going without supper, then the slate was usually wiped clean for them. 'Something's not right here,' Megan said. 'We need to keep an eye out to find out what's going on. Perhaps the Master is thrashing her. Try to get her to talk about it, Eira. She likes you.'

'Hmm, I'll do my best but she's not talking much to anyone at the moment. She's off her food, too. I hate the new Master and his wife. Say what you like but Matron and Master Langley were firm but fair with us. They wouldn't have made me stand with a slate around my neck during breakfast for all at the workhouse to see.'

Megan nodded, realising the truth behind her friend's words. It was definitely a case of better the devil you knew.

It was Saturday bath night at the workhouse, the one day of the week where all the girls were expected to strip off and wash themselves all over, instead of their usual wash-down in a bowl of water. At first, Megan had found it a little embarrassing having to strip off in front of everyone, especially as some of the girls were more developed than others, but gradually she'd got used to it, realising that everyone was more concerned about how their own bodies looked than noticing anyone else's. Usually Megan kept herself to herself during this time, but on this occasion, as she was in the old tin tub next to Tilly's, they were chattering away as all the other girls had departed. They'd been late arriving as they'd been mopping the corridor together, but Megan hadn't wanted to bring up the subject then in case it got to the ears of the supervisor.

'So, what do you think about the new Master and Matron then, Tilly?' Megan asked as she rubbed herself all over with the red carbolic soap the workhouse supervisor insisted they used to keep themselves clean. It killed all the germs, she reckoned, but Megan thought it had a very strong smell that she didn't much care for.

'I think Matron seems all right . . .' Tilly said.

Megan glanced at her. 'What about him though, the Master? I don't think they're as nice as our last Master and Matron.'

Tilly said nothing at all and Megan stared at her. It was then she noticed some purple bruising on the girl's upper arms and what looked like scratches on her chest.

'How'd that happen?' she asked, narrowing her eyes with suspicion.

Tilly was now becoming a young woman and Megan was surprised to discover how rounded and full the girl's breasts had become. She was a good few years older than Megan.

Tilly said nothing, just lowered her body further into the tin bath, resting her head on the back of it and closed her eyes as if blocking out the world around her.

'Look,' Megan whispered, 'I know something's going on. There's no one else around, please tell me what it is.'

Tilly remained silent, eyes still closed as a lone tear coursed down her cheek.

Something was wrong, Megan was sure of it. The very fact that Tilly had not replied spoke volumes. 'Speak to me, Tilly, please. I won't tell anyone, honest.'

Tilly's eyes flicked open and she turned to look at Megan, but there was nothing behind them. For the first time, Megan noticed they looked dead; the light had gone out from within. Tilly didn't look like that when the other Master and Matron were still here. Why did they have to leave?

'Please tell me, Tilly. You can trust me.'

Tilly took a deep breath and let it out again, then began to speak, but her words sounded strangulated. She did not sound like the Tilly who Megan had known all this time. 'It was a couple of days after they arrived: they needed someone in the Master's room to light the fire. I didn't mind too much because I've done it before. It was better than having to clean the privies anyhow, but now I wish I hadn't volunteered. I'd far rather work with filthy waste than what that man made me do, which was even dirtier . . .' She began to weep and put her hands to her mouth to stifle her sobs.

At that moment, another couple of girls entered the washroom, so Megan quickly reached for her towel to cover herself and whispered to Tilly, 'I'm sorry we can't talk right now, we can speak later if you like . . .' She had no intention of upsetting Tilly, but the time wasn't right for the girl to reveal all and she didn't want to draw attention to her in front of the others.

The following morning after breakfast, Megan remembered she still had the wicker basket stored in the kitchen. She'd need to return it to The Lady at the Temperance Hall; she didn't want her to get into trouble.

After she'd helped Alicia wash and dry all the breakfast dishes, she went to find Cook, who was having a rest in a small room just off the kitchen that the kitchen staff used. She had fallen asleep in the armchair with her legs up on a stool in front of a roaring fire. Megan giggled when she saw the woman had her mouth wide open and she was making the strangest snoring noise she'd ever heard in her life – it was like a long wheeze, followed by a grunt, then all went quiet for a few seconds for her to wheeze again, and so it went on. On Cook's lap was a small white plate that bore the evidence of several cake crumbs. Cook didn't have to worry about the likes of Miss Hamilton, though. She wouldn't get a telling-off for sleeping on the job as her services were badly needed. The workhouse staff and the guardians loved her meals – when she had good ingredients, that was. When it was gruel it wasn't so nice for the inmates, but that wasn't Cook's fault; she could only use what she was given to work with.

'Cook,' Megan whispered, as she watched her chest rise and fall beneath her pinafore. Her white starched cap had gone all skew-whiff on her head. Cook grunted in her sleep. 'Cook!' she bellowed in her ear as she tugged on the sleeve of her dress.

The noise caused the woman to sit up with such a startle that the plate fell off her lap and smashed on the hearth.

Cook sat bolt upright and stared wide-eyed at Megan. 'Where's the fire, child?' She glowered.

'Sorry, Cook, but I need that wicker basket to get it back to Miss O'Hara at the Temperance Hall. If you pretend to send me on an errand, I can slip away.'

'Very well, Megan.' She was smiling now and Megan realised she had frightened the living daylights out of the woman.

Megan began to pick up the china shards of the plate and dropped them in a metal dustbin in the corner of the room. She watched as Cook yawned, stretched her arms above her head and pulled herself onto her feet. 'Now where did I put that basket?' She drummed her chin with her fingers as she contemplated where. 'Oh, yes,' she said finally. 'I hid it in the cupboard in the pantry for safe keeping.'

Megan followed her to the pantry, which was much colder than other parts of the kitchen, and watched as she located it and handed it to her. 'Don't forget, I've sent you to the market to check on the price of a large goose for the Guardians' dinner next week.' She winked, and Megan winked back. Cook would do whatever she could to allow Megan to escape the place, if only for a short while.

Megan was about to leave the kitchen with the basket hooked over her arm when she almost collided with Miss Hamilton. She felt all the air being sucked out of her lungs and remained rooted to the spot with fear.

'And where do you think you're going, young lady?'

Before Megan had a chance to find her voice, Cook intervened. 'I was just sending the child to the marketplace to check the price on a nice big goose for next week's Guardians' meeting, Miss Hamilton. I thought she could pick up a few things for me, an' all, on her way back.'

But it was no use, Megan could see by the look in Miss Hamilton's beady eyes that she wasn't having any of it. 'Get over to the chapel mortuary at once. We've got a funeral service today. A pauper man has passed away and I want you over there to clean the place. We can't leave the coffin unattended, so I shall expect you to remain there until the service begins, after you've finished sweeping the floor and cleaning the windows, that is.'

Megan felt the fear descend on her at the thought of being in the place all alone with a dead person. It was not so long ago her mother had died and her coffin had lain in rest at that chapel itself.

'Here, I'll take that basket from you, Megan,' Cook said wisely, removing it from Megan's arm.

Megan realised she was taking it for safe keeping but there was nothing anyone could do; Miss Hamilton was doing this on purpose. It was Megan's morning off from the stall today; now she wished she was working. She'd have to find a way to sneak off later when she'd finished on the stall to see The Lady, by hook or by crook.

Megan was in for a shock when she arrived at the chapel, as the lid of the coffin had been removed and she shuddered as she noticed the pale, emaciated, elderly man's body inside lying at rest. A bandage was wrapped tightly around his jaw and the top of his head to keep his mouth closed. Penny coins were placed over either eye to keep them closed, too. 'W—why hasn't the coffin got a lid on?' she asked the supervisor as she took a step back.

Was it her imagination or was Miss Hamilton smirking at her? Surely not on such a sombre occasion?

'The undertaker said his eyes were still open so I thought it best to keep him here with the pennies over them. We can't leave any stiffs around this place too long, they'll stink to high heaven. The sooner we have the service and get him buried the better. It's a blessing to dispatch another elderly pauper to our good Lord above!'

Megan could hardly believe the coldness of the woman. She spoke about this man as if he were a nuisance to the workhouse and she was glad to offload him. Then she watched as the supervisor turned to walk away.

'Aren't you staying here with me, Miss Hamilton?'

The woman didn't even turn back to address Megan, just said as she walked away, 'No, certainly not, and I shall be locking you in until the work is done. And don't go having any ideas about thieving those pennies, either . . .'

'No!' Megan shouted after her. She was going to be left alone with a corpse. Megan went to run after her, but it was too late: the key clicked in the lock on the other side of the door and she heard it turn, and the footsteps outside as Miss Hamilton walked away. She'd done this on purpose to scare Megan half to death. Well, she wasn't going to get away with it.

The hairs on the back of her neck stood on end as she turned back towards the pulpit and stepped closer so she could see the man in his coffin more clearly now – his big hooked nose was most prominent in her field of vision. She drew up closer. The poor thing was still in his workhouse uniform. His hands appeared calloused and bruised, probably from all that bone crushing he was expected to do, whatever his age. And what was that all for? It seemed to Megan as though sometimes they worked the inmates literally to death for the fun of it.

'Never mind, sir,' she said, now realising someone like a dead person wouldn't harm her; it was the likes of the living, such as Miss Hamilton, she needed to watch out for. 'I'll sort you out.' She went to the back room, where the minister had a desk and kept all the bibles and hymn books, and there she found an old lace tablecloth in a cupboard, which she draped over the coffin.

She then worked briskly to sweep the chapel floor. That old witch wasn't going to get her down, she was determined about that. She hummed away as she swept up some dead leaves that had blown inside the chapel, then she made sure all the hymn books had been set out for the service. The flowers in the vases on the windowsills didn't look too good – all droopy with missing petals – so she removed all the dead ones and poured out the old stagnant water, refilling them with clean water from a jug kept inside the chapel.

By the time she'd finished cleaning the windows – by standing on the sills and rubbing away with a bucket of soapy water and shammy-leather Miss Hamilton had provided her with – she realised she'd done a good job. She jumped down and went to whip away the tablecloth that was covering the coffin just as the supervisor unlocked the chapel door to check up on her.

She glared at Megan as if she couldn't believe her eyes that the girl could work so well and not be at all frightened. She had been scared to begin with, of course, but had got used to it – but there was no need for Miss Hamilton to ever know that.

Megan stared her out, determined that the woman would not break her at any cost. 'All done, Miss Hamilton,' she said brightly. 'I need to get to the cake stall now to give Mrs Mathias a break!'

Megan realised that by saying that, Miss Hamilton could hardly refuse her request.

'Very well, Megan,' she said. There was no more she could say or do as Megan had worked well under the circumstances.

It was a battle Megan felt, for once, she'd won, as the woman stood open-mouthed, looking around the chapel trying to find some fault or other, but there was none to be found.

Megan waved to Mrs Lloyd, the flower seller, who had just sold her last bunch of chrysanthemums for the day. Customers had dwindled away from the cake stall, so she began to pack away, placing the unsold cakes and loaves of bread in wooden trays and covering them with muslin cloths. She hoped Mrs Mathias wouldn't mind her packing up a few minutes early but she was on a mission. She hurried to push the heavy cart back to Plymouth Street, then ran all the way back in the direction of the town. Mrs Mathias had been flabbergasted when Megan had turned up early out of the blue offering to take over on her half day off from the stall, but when she explained how hard she'd been worked by Miss Hamilton that day already, the woman was all for it. There wasn't that much left to do anyhow and it would give her a good excuse to see The Lady afterwards without rousing suspicion at the workhouse. When Megan arrived, breathless from running as fast as her legs would carry her to the Temperance Hall, Kathleen O'Hara was seated in her dressing room, wearing a blue satin dressing gown trimmed with white fur. She looked every inch a star.

'Hello, Megan,' she said, beaming at her broadly as if genuinely pleased to see her. 'And how are you? You look as though you've been rushing?'

'I'm all right, miss.' She didn't want to burden The Lady with what had happened earlier on. 'I'm sorry I haven't returned that wicker basket, but if I do, they'll know I lost the other one.' That was true, as questions might be asked, so maybe it wasn't wise to return it anyhow.

'That's absolutely fine, young lady. 'T'ain't needed anyhow. We have several of them here and if anyone asks I shall offer to pay for it myself. You look perished, child! Come and have a cup of tea with me.'

'That would be lovely, miss,' Megan said.

'Well, sit ye down, child. I'll ask the cleaner to make us a cuppa and I expect you could do with something to eat?'

Megan nodded eagerly. 'Yes please, miss.'

A few minutes later, they were seated beside a roaring fire in the kitchen, The Lady now having changed into one of her day dresses. Set out before them was a large pot of tea and a plate of ham sandwiches, followed by a slice of apple pie.

'My dresser makes a lovely apple pie . . .' Kathleen said, studying Megan's face. 'It's her mother's secret recipe. So what have you been up to lately?'

'I've got a job five days a week, miss,' she answered enthusiastically. 'Selling cakes and bread for Mrs Mathias, who owns the tea room in town.'

'Oh, that's good news then, a welcome respite from the workhouse, I've no doubt.'

'Yes, miss. That day I saw you, and you helped me out of a tricky situation, I'd run after a young lad who stole an armful of apples from a market stall. I'd dropped my basket to get a hold of him.'

Kathleen blinked. 'And did you catch up with him?'

'I did too!' she answered proudly. 'Fortunately, he managed to give an angry crowd the slip. He could have been transported to Australia if caught, like two of his friends are going to be. They're from the China area of the town. But he's my friend now, miss. Griff, his name is, lives with his uncle, who's an old drunk by the sound of it.'

'I know the sort. So some good came of it all then, Megan. He now has a friend in you.' Kathleen took a sip of her tea.

Megan admired Kathleen so. A real lady she was, and all, drinking tea out of a pretty china cup, not like the tin mugs they had at the workhouse. 'Yes, we're friends now, miss. I was wondering . . .'

'Yes, go on, child . . .'

'Whether you might have any work for him here at the theatre?'

Kathleen frowned and then shook her head. 'Oh, I wish we did. Not at the moment. I could have a word with the manager, though. You never know, he might consider Griff for future use.'

'Thanks, Miss O'Hara.' Megan beamed. 'How come you're wearing a wedding ring, if you're a Miss?'

Kathleen chuckled. 'Actually, I am married. O'Hara is my stage name.'

'Does your husband mind at all?'

'To be truthful, he doesn't really understand why I can't use my married name of "Jenkin" but my manager thinks "O'Hara" sounds better – more theatrical, if you like.'

Megan didn't really understand the reasoning behind it all but guessed it was something stage folk knew. 'My friend

Griff can sing and he can juggle several apples at the same time,' she announced proudly.

'Really?' Kathleen seemed surprised. 'There's a local talent show due to be held here next month. You should encourage him to enter!'

'Oh, I don't know about that, miss. He'd probably be too ashamed in the type of clothes he wears.'

'No problem there – I can select some from the wardrobe department for him. Will you ask him to come and see me here tomorrow afternoon?'

Megan nodded eagerly. It could be just the chance Griff needed.

'What's wrong, Megan?' Kathleen asked, her voice soft and low as she studied Megan's face for an answer.

'Nothing, miss.'

But there was no fooling The Lady. So she asked again. 'Megan, I can sense there is something not quite right with you today. Are you in trouble over that wicker basket?'

'No, miss. But there is something else. I don't know if I should tell you or not, but I have to tell someone.' She bit her bottom lip.

'Well, I always say a trouble shared is a trouble halved, so go ahead and tell me what it is that's bothering you . . .'

Megan hesitated. 'Believe me, miss, when you hear what I have to say you will think badly of what goes on in that workhouse.'

'Please go ahead, Megan,' Kathleen urged. 'You do need to tell someone . . .' She sat forward in her chair to listen.

Megan drew a breath. 'I'm worried about a young girl at the workhouse, miss. Well, I say "young girl", but she has now become a young woman, if you know what I mean. She's almost fifteen years old . . .'

'And?' Kathleen asked, arching her neatly trimmed eyebrows.

'I can't quite put my finger on it, miss, but the new workhouse Master keeps calling her into his room, and when she leaves she is most upset. I noticed she was covered in scratches and bruises when she bathed herself yesterday.'

'Did you ask her what was wrong?'

Megan nodded. 'Yes, miss. She refuses to answer and lies on her bed sobbing, burying her head in the pillow. She's hardly eating any food at all. She's wasting away before my very eyes.'

'Hmm . . . We have to tread carefully here before making any accusations, mind you. Keep an eye out what is going on, and if you have any evidence of foul play, come and see me. My husband is a policeman with the Glamorgan Constabulary in the town.'

'Gosh, miss, a policeman's wife! I never knew anyone who was married to a policeman before.'

Kathleen smiled. 'Have you finished your cup of tea?'

Megan nodded.

'Good, there's more in the pot. We'll have another brew

and my sister-in-law, Lily Davies, has given me some Welsh cakes. We'll have one of those each, too.'

Megan smiled broadly. She'd gone from eating a pittance at the workhouse to getting her belly full of cakes, buns and bread and she didn't mind one bit. At this rate, she was going to end up as fat as a workhouse rat.

The workhouse doctor had been summoned to examine Tilly. It had been almost as though she were in a world of her own. She sat with the rest of the girls but just stared into space, and when they asked her how she was, she ignored them as if they weren't there.

Wanting to make sure that her friend was all right, and knowing that she wouldn't open up herself, Megan thought it might be a good idea to find out first-hand what was going on, so she squeezed herself behind a cupboard in the corner of the dorm room when no one was looking and after all the other girls had been ushered to leave. She was small enough not to be seen, she reckoned, but she was going to have to be careful she didn't cough or make a noise to give the game away. Her heart was beating so loud she feared they'd hear it, but so far, all the attention was on Tilly's prognosis.

Megan peered out of the cupboard and, thankfully, Miss Hamilton's beady eyes were focused elsewhere so she couldn't see her. Tilly lay on one of the beds while the doctor appeared to be examining her, holding out a finger in front of her eyes, which he moved back and forth. Miss Hamilton watched on eagerly, standing beside them.

'The girl's in an absolute stupor, Dr Griffiths,' Miss Hamilton was explaining. 'Can't get any work out of her at all, lazy article. If I didn't know better, I'd swear she'd hit the gin bottle.'

By the frown on the supervisor's forehead, Megan thought she looked really worried. Usually her face was mask-like with hardly any expression at all.

'Well, I'll be the best judge of any diagnosis, Miss Hamilton,' the doctor said. He was now listening to her chest through a stethoscope.

To her horror, Megan hiccupped.

'Did you hear something then, Doctor?' The supervisor turned her head, her dark eyes scanning the room. And then, apparently satisfied no one else could hear, she looked at Dr Griffiths.

'No, I didn't hear anything, Miss Hamilton,' he said as he carried on with his examination, checking Tilly's ears, finger-nails and mouth.

Megan did her best to stifle another hiccup by placing her hand over her mouth, and hoped they wouldn't be staying too long in the dormitory as she knew that another hiccup would be emerging soon. She tried holding her breath to see if that might help.

'You won't find anything really wrong with her . . . A good

thrashing she could do with!' Miss Hamilton said harshly, causing the doctor to stop what he was doing.

'A thrashing? Is that what's gone on here?' The doctor raised his voice. 'I noticed some bruising on the girl's left shoulder and some surface scratches on her chest and back.'

'Oh, no, no, Doctor. It was just a figure of speech that's all,' Miss Hamilton said, rather quickly.

'In my opinion, the girl is badly dehydrated. Get some fluids down her. She looks malnourished too. Just for the once, give her some of the good food you supply the Board with, she could do with it. Gruel and thin soup indeed! These inmates require meat, vegetables and fruit – they need their nourishment, ma'am!'

Miss Hamilton huffed. Megan realised there was no way she'd give the girl a leg of chicken like every greedy member of the Board got, nor a piece of plum pudding.

'That's all very well, Dr Griffiths, but too much meat makes this lot vicious. Remember the riot that Christmas? That was on your advice and what thanks did the Master and Matron get? Men overturning tables and trying to smash windows, children screaming and shouting . . . Too much iron in the blood for them to cope with. No, we need to keep this lot subdued or else they'll turn on us all.'

'I think you'll find that was alcohol, ma'am,' the doctor said stiffly. 'Someone took it upon themselves to give the inmates a slug of gin, all the young and old. Nothing to do with the meat at all. And from my understanding, that idea was passed by the Board of Guardians, so blame them!'

'Still, the meat couldn't have helped.' She always had to have the last word. Megan almost sighed but stifled it just in time for fear of being overheard.

'I'll write up a prescription for a good tonic. Make sure she eats well and gets regular fresh air. No work for the time being.'

'Very well, Dr Griffiths,' she said sombrely, but Megan could see a glint in her eye that indicated she would do no such thing.

When the doctor had departed, Megan watched Miss Hamilton whisper something in Tilly's ear, then she prodded the girl as if she were a piece of meat. At that moment, there was a knock at the door – some of the girls had returned to the dormitory and wanted to know if they could come back in now – causing Miss Hamilton to quickly step away. She headed out of the dorm with her head held high like a woman on a mission. She was angered by the doctor's words, that much was for sure, and Megan wondered what she would report back to the Master.

Indeed, what was the Master doing to Tilly in the first place? This was all his fault, of that Megan was certain. Why did Master and Matron Langley have to leave for pastures new anyway? If they were still at the helm, she was certain Tilly would not be lying in that bed covered in scratches and bruises staring into space.

She let out a loud hiccup as she emerged from behind the cupboard, which initially surprised the other girls, before they laughed in amusement. Thankfully the supervisor had left and was now out of earshot. She'd got away with it, but she was still none the wiser to what was going on.

Megan ran out into the corridor to catch up with the doctor. She had a question entirely unrelated to Tilly and it was causing her so many sleepless nights. It was bad enough her mother had died, but what really gnawed at her was not knowing why.

When she'd asked, she could sense he didn't want to give her an answer. She could tell he was deliberating, looking both ways up and down the corridor, probably mulling over whether telling her could cause him trouble.

Megan held her breath and finally he said, 'You have a very inquisitive mind, young lady, and I can see you are not going to be satisfied until someone gives you an answer.' He paused. 'Your mother was haemorrhaging blood from her womb. I suspect it was some form of malignancy . . .'

Megan didn't understand what that meant and she frowned. 'Please, what does that mean, Doctor?'

'I suspect it was a form of cancer.' His kind blue eyes looked at her with a great deal of sympathy.

'B–but I don't understand. She became unwell very quickly and died before I even had a chance to visit her, nor my brothers and sisters. No one told us.'

The doctor leant down to whisper to her. 'In my opinion, you should have been told. Miss Hamilton has known how things were for the past few weeks and that your mother was not going to get any better. I suspect you thought your mother was fitter than she was. Maybe she, herself, did not wish you to know how ill she really was. I was called to see her several times.'

Megan's eyes began to fill with tears and she swallowed a lump in her throat that threatened to choke her. 'But did she suffer?'

The doctor stood up straight and ruffled her hair. 'Not as much as she might have done had she not been in the workhouse. I saw to it she had regular doses of laudanum – that's special medicine to help relieve the pain. Now, you must not tell anyone I've told you any of this, understood?'

She nodded, feeling a small sense of relief that at last someone had told her what had happened. She also realised the doctor's job could be in danger if she spoke out. Miss Hamilton would have his guts for garters if she knew.

'Me? Stand in front of a flipping audience?' Griff was about to walk away, but Megan grabbed him by the collar of his jacket and turned him around to face her.

'Yes, you. I've seen you messing around juggling all sorts and doing cartwheels. And you can sing too!'

'Well that may be but I've never performed in front of a

lot of people before.' He stopped to think. 'Except once at the Vulcan Inn.'

Megan blinked several times. 'What happened?'

'It was my uncle. He was quite merry, and told the men how I could sing and dance, so he made me get up on the bar to sing a funny little ditty. They threw coins at me. Maybe they felt sorry for me. I was much younger than I am now. I was about six years old, I expect.'

'But don't you see, Griff? You could have an act. Kathleen O'Hara, the lady who sings at the Temperance Hall, said for you to call to see her tomorrow afternoon and she can lend you some clothes too.'

'I'll fink about it.'

'The word is "think" not "fink". And what's to think about anyhow? This could be your big chance.'

'All right, I'll try, but I mightn't get the chance to go on stage in any case . . .'

'And get yourself cleaned up before you go to see her. She's a proper lady, using nice handkerchiefs and drinking tea from a china cup and saucer.'

'Oooh,' Griff said. 'Too good for the likes of us then!'

Megan rolled her eyes. 'How wrong you are, Griff. The Lady is nothing like that at all. Actually, I took tea with her at the theatre earlier and I drank out of one of those china cups and sat with her in front of the fire.' Megan was trying to use a refined tone of voice.

'Oh, very la-di-da!' Griff stuck his nose in the air.

Megan gave him a sharp dig in the ribs.

'I've got an idea!' he said suddenly with great excitement. 'Why don't you perform with me, Megan? You could be my stooge!'

'I beg your pardon!'

'A stooge is someone who becomes the butt of the comedian's jokes,' he explained.

'I shouldn't very much like that,' she said, feeling hurt.

'Aw, don't be silly, Megan – it would only be a bit of fun.'

'I'll think about it.' She glanced at the clock face of the parish church, suddenly realising the time. 'I have to dash! Or I'll be in big trouble.' Megan had almost forgotten herself, what with the excitement from visiting The Lady and telling Griff the news about the talent show. It was already dark, and with winter drawing in, it was hard to tell what time of day it was.

Without waiting to hear Griff's response, she lifted her skirts and ran back to the workhouse, huffing and puffing with the effort. If she didn't get back in time there'd be no evening meal for her – which she could manage without as she'd already eaten with The Lady, but questions would be asked, especially by Miss Hamilton.

She was out of breath by the time she returned to the confines of the workhouse walls, taking a moment to catch her breath. She didn't want anyone to realise she'd been rushing to get back. After composing herself and having returned to the dorm, she was ready to leave with the others as they lined up in single file to enter the dining room. She hoped Miss Hamilton wouldn't notice she'd missed prayers at the chapel either as there'd be hell to pay and some kind of punishment meted out for sure.

Her heart sank. Tilly was nowhere to be seen.

'Eira, have you seen Tilly?' she hissed.

Eira shrugged her shoulders. Megan gritted her teeth. 'I thought I made it clear to you that you were to keep an eye out for her while I was at work.'

'Well, I've been working too, on me hands and knees scrubbing all the corridors whilst some people have it made working on a cake stall!' Eira folded her arms crossly. It was becoming obvious that the girl was jealous that Megan now had a little freedom, despite the fact that she'd had to work hard for it.

'You could have done the same thing yourself if you'd used your nonce!' Megan said, tapping Eira on the head gently with her finger. 'Tell the Matron you want to work somewhere instead of staying in this dump. They should want you to as they'll get your wages for your board and lodging.'

Eira scowled. 'No, thanks!' she said, tossing her dark curls. 'I'll stay put. I don't fancy setting up no stall at an unearthly hour, going out in the dark, and returning in the dark too! No, thank you very much!'

'Well, shut your trap then!'

'I saw Tilly going in the Master's room about half an hour ago,' a girl called Franny interrupted.

'Do you know why?' Megan asked. The girl shook her head, and she began to fear the worst. Turning on her heel, Megan belted down the corridor.

'Don't, Megan!' Eira shouted from behind her. 'You'll get yourself into trouble!'

But Megan didn't care. Tilly's welfare was too important to her. She was determined to find out what exactly was going on.

She arrived outside the Master's room and slowly tried the brass doorknob, but it wouldn't budge. It was then she realised it must be locked from the inside. At that moment, Matron passed by, the folds of her long black dress rustling.

She paused and glared at Megan. 'You, girl, what are you doing here? You should be in the dining room by now.'

'Please, ma'am,' Megan began to explain, 'someone said the Master wanted to see me, but I got no answer when I knocked on his door and the knob won't budge.' It was a half-truth, but a necessary one.

Matron tried the doorknob and got the same response as she rattled it with all her might. 'My poor husband,' she said. 'It must be his heart. Quick, go and fetch the porter, girl!'

Megan ran off down the corridor more fearful about what was happening to Tilly than about the Master. Something was wrong, she just knew it. She'd learned from experience that her inner voice rarely failed her.

'Wassa matter, Megan?' The porter, Bill Harris, stared at Megan. He was sunk into an armchair in his porter's room near the entrance of the building. He appeared to be having some sort of break as a cup of steaming tea was on the small table next to him. He neatly folded the newspaper he'd been reading.

'There's something wrong in the Master's room ... I couldn't open the door, and Matron tried too. She wants to get in. She fears he's had a heart attack.'

Bill removed his peaked cap and scratched his bald pate. 'Wouldn't surprise me, he eats too much!'

Megan got the impression Bill didn't much care for the man, but she had to get into that room. 'Please, Bill, I don't really think it's his heart, I'm afraid. Tilly was last seen going into that room. He's been calling her in there a lot lately and when she returns to the dorm, she's very upset, crying and lying on her bed for hours on end and missing her meals.'

Bill frowned. 'I'm right on it,' he said, standing and picking up a bunch of keys from the table. 'You'd best go back to your quarters and not follow me inside, young Mcgan, in case something's amiss ...' He rushed off in the direction of the Master's room, but Megan did not return to the dorm as instructed. She followed close at his heels. She had to ensure Tilly was safe.

The porter's footsteps seemed to echo down the long dark corridor, which seemed to add to the sense of foreboding Megan had. Somewhere in the distance, she thought she heard someone cry out, but that wasn't unusual in the workhouse.

Matron was still waiting, her face ashen and her hands to her mouth. 'I think I hear his heavy breathing,' she explained when they approached.

Bill raised his eyebrows, then located a key on the ring of keys he'd brought with him. 'I think, ladies, you had better stand back in case it's bad news . . .'

Megan guessed he'd said that not to upset either of them.

He inserted the key in the lock, then tried turning it as it made several clicking noises. 'It won't budge, ma'am,' he said finally, addressing Matron. 'It's because there's a key in place on the other side of the lock, I reckon. I'll try pushing it with my shoulder.' He tried several times, heaving his shoulder against it, but the strong, heavy door wouldn't give an inch.

Bill shook his head. 'I've an idea. I'll go around and see if I can get in from the sash window on the other side. Now, you ladies remain here,' he said firmly, and even Matron obeyed his words.

It was a few minutes later before he returned with Tilly at his side, trembling and crying beside him, fearful.

Megan opened her arms and the girl fell into them. 'What's

happened?' she asked softly, soothing the girl as she stroked her hair.

'He . . . he . . .' She looked at Matron and then away again, but couldn't get the words out.

'What happened, Mr Harris? Is my husband all right?' Matron asked, more concerned about the Master than young Tilly.

Bill nodded. 'Oh, he's all right, ma'am. It's the young girl I'm concerned about . . .' He lowered his voice a notch. 'I'm afraid I caught him *in flagrante* with this young lady.'

Matron's face reddened from the neck up. 'I hope you're not telling a lie, Mr Harris, or I'll have your job for this!' A large, prominent vein on her neck appeared to be throbbing.

'I speak the truth, ma'am. I need to see you in private,' he said, looking at both girls. 'Megan, take young Tilly back to the dorm with you,' Bill said, his voice softening.

Megan nodded and with her arm draped around Tilly, led her away. Whatever had Bill witnessed in that room? And what did 'in fragrance' mean? It sounded like a foreign language to Megan. Was it some kind of perfume? And why was the Master using scent?

Once back at the dormitory, Megan put Tilly to bed. This time, the girl wasn't weeping. She just stared into space and tried to speak, but no words were forthcoming; her teeth were chattering and she shook all over.

Later, when all the other girls had eaten their supper and

returned to the room, Eira approached to ask what was wrong, speaking quietly over the din of chatter.

'Something odd has happened,' Megan explained in hushed tones. She didn't want the rest of the girls to overhear. 'I tried the door to the Master's room but it wouldn't budge. Matron tried too, and then she sent me to get Bill. He tried a key in the lock but it was locked from the inside. He even tried breaking the door down!'

'Never!' Eira said. 'What happened then?'

'Bill went around to the window and I'm assuming he got in that way and rescued Tilly. He told Matron that the Master had been caught "in fragrance", but I don't know what that means.'

'Me neither,' said Eira. 'But whatever's happened, it's upset poor Tilly,' she added, taking a look at the girl. 'I think she needs to see the doctor again.'

'Me too.' Megan knelt beside the girl and stroked her fevered brow. 'I suppose it's up to Matron. All I know is the Master has done something very bad to Tilly.' Megan had forgotten to keep her voice down and missed the footsteps of Miss Hamilton, who was now towering over them, casting a shadow across the bed.

'The Master has done what?' She glared.

'He's . . . he's done something to upset Tilly,' Megan said, her teeth chattering and her voice sounding strange and croaky to her own ears.

'Don't be so foolish, girl!' Miss Hamilton shouted. 'You

shall be severely punished for your lies.' She flexed a thin wooden cane in her hands that made Megan tremble. 'Bend over and lower your drawers, young lady. You are about to be taught a lesson!'

Megan gritted her teeth and balled her hands into fists. Then, taking a hard long stare at the woman, she shouted, 'It's true, every damn word of it!' Then she ran, with Miss Hamilton in pursuit, down a long flight of stone steps, Megan's heart thumping wildly in her chest the entire way.

Miss Hamilton's shouts echoed down the staircase but she was no match for Megan, who had filled out nicely, lately, from the extra food she'd been getting from her new employer.

Megan finally made it to Bill's room, where he stood staring at her as Miss Hamilton stumbled into the room, the cane still in her hand.

'Stop that girl!' she shouted at Bill. 'I need to punish her for telling tales about the Master.'

Bill stood firmly and pushed Megan behind himself. 'No, you don't, Miss Hamilton,' he said. 'The girl is telling the truth. It was me who caught him *in flagrante* with his trousers down, in the middle of messing with young Tilly.'

Miss Hamilton's top lip curved upwards into a sneer. Her eyes widened and she huffed out a loud breath. 'The Master is a good man, he would never do a thing like that. He's God-fearing and moral. A beacon of light to all in here.'

'Go and ask his wife then!' Bill shouted sharply, and

immediately her face changed as if she suddenly realised Bill might be telling the truth.

Stunned by Bill's declaration, Miss Hamilton turned on her heel and left the porter's lodge.

'What am I going to do now?' Megan asked. 'I'll be in trouble, that's for sure.'

'No, you won't, Megan. When Miss Hamilton speaks to Matron, she'll realise the truth of what I already told her.'

Megan drew in a ragged breath. 'But you don't understand, that woman has it in for me – any excuse to thrash me.' She began to whimper, her bottom lip quivering with fear.

Bill placed his arm around her young shoulders. 'Now, *bach*, don't you be worrying, no harm shall come to you while I work here, not now I'm aware of your situation with the old dragon.'

Megan began to chuckle at the thought of Miss Hamilton breathing fumes of fire. She found the image in her mind hysterical and she laughed until her sides ached. She would never look at Miss Hamilton in the same way again.

Bill looked on with great amusement and he began to laugh too. 'Any time that woman scares you, young Megan, you remember what I said.'

'I will, Bill. You have proper cheered me up.'

She left the porter's lodge with her head held high, but her laughter ceased as her mind went back to poor Tilly. What would happen to her now?

Chapter Nine

Griff was really excited. He'd been to see Kathleen at the Temperance Hall and she'd fitted him out with an outfit for the talent show.

'Cor, she gave me a proper little suit with a bow tie and bowler hat and a walking cane! You should have seen me, Megan. I looked a right toff!' He paused a moment to gauge her reaction. ''Ere, ain't you pleased for me? It was your idea in the first place.'

Megan turned to face him. They were sitting on a low wall at the bottom end of town near the parish church, Griff having turned up unexpectedly to help Megan push her handcart back to Plymouth Street. 'Of course I'm pleased for you, Griff,' she said, tucking a stray lock of hair that had fallen into her face behind her ear. 'It's just that something awful happened at the workhouse yesterday evening and I don't know what the outcome will be.'

Griff grimaced. 'My mam always said it was best to share

troubles, not keep 'em to yourself. You listen to me about my Uncle Berwyn, the trouble I get when he's drunk . . .'

'I know I do, but this doesn't really involve me, Griff. It's a young girl there, something has happened with the Master. He kept calling her to his room, and yesterday the door was locked. The poor girl keeps crying every time she's been there, as if something awful has happened to her but I don't know what.'

'Maybe he beats her?' Griff offered.

'Yes, it could be that, but I heard the porter say the Master was caught "in fragrance" or something like that. I don't understand what it means – do you?'

Griff shook his head.

Now she felt bad for taking the shine off his news.

'I tell you what,' he said, his eyes lighting up as if he had just had a good idea. 'We could ask Florrie from the Vulcan. She might know.'

'Good idea,' Megan said, feeling a lot happier. 'So . . . tell me more about your act. What are you going to do?'

'A few tricks, I think, as well as singing a song. I had a good idea – the landlord of the Vulcan owns a scruffy little dog called Scamp. He's always following me around after scraps and the like – knows me well as I'm in there often enough looking for my uncle. Anyhow, I fought it might be a good idea to use him in me act.'

Megan felt like correcting him and saying, 'It's "thought"

not "fought",' but as he was so happy, she kept it to herself. Instead she said, 'That sounds a great idea, Griff.'

'The Lady says the theatre can lend me some props, like a hoop and stick, and even a ball. I plan to teach Scamp to jump through the hoop and balance the ball on his nose. I ain't never had any of those things meself . . .' he said sadly.

Poor Griff! At least when her dad was alive they'd had some toys at her house, even if some were homemade. She turned to him. 'That sounds great, but how do you know you can train the dog?'

Griff immediately perked up. 'He's already turning tricks at the pub. The men love it when he dances on his hind legs or jumps up on a bar stool. I reckon it'll be easy.'

'Can I help you train him?' Megan asked eagerly.

'Yes, of course you can.'

'We used to have a lovely dog, but when we had to go in the workhouse we had to give him away . . .' Tears filled her eyes and although she had been upset at having to leave the dog behind, she realised deep down it was her mother she was crying for.

'There, there, Megan. You girls don't 'alf bring on the waterworks.' He said it in a jokey fashion but she knew that he, of all people, realised what it was like to be an orphan, and if it wasn't for his Uncle Berwyn, he'd probably be in the workhouse himself. Sometimes she wondered if he would be better off there than looking after a drunken old wastrel who went on alcoholic binges for days at a time. No wonder Griff had hooked up with the Rodneys. Though now, after the two of them had been transported, he seemed to have stopped thieving, but he did need to make some kind of living for himself all the same.

When she returned to the workhouse she went in search of Tilly, but the girl was nowhere to be found, despite Megan looking everywhere.

'Where's Tilly?' Megan asked Eira when she got back to the dorm.

'Something's wrong,' she replied in hushed tones. 'She didn't come with the rest of us for breakfast, just lay on her bed again staring at the ceiling, and by the time we returned here, she was missing and she hasn't been back to her bed since.'

Megan frowned. 'I wonder what's going on with the Master, too.'

Eira shrugged. 'After what happened yesterday, you mean?'

'Yes. Now people will realise what he's like, he'll surely lose his job here.'

'I don't think he will, to be honest. Matron was laughing and joking with him earlier in the corridor as if nothing has happened at all.'

Megan's hand flew to her face. 'Surely not?'

Eira nodded. 'Yes, indeed. I was so surprised.'

'This isn't right at all. He could do the same thing again – I'm not even sure what he did in the first place but it must have been bad for him to lock the door, and of course we've all seen the way poor Tilly has been acting lately.'

'So has Dr Griffiths,' said Eira thoughtfully.

'Yes, that's it! He needs to be told of this,' Megan said. 'I'll try to find him later and see if he knows what's happened to Tilly.'

Later, she found the doctor examining one of the girls in the dorm. 'You'll live,' he said to the girl in a kindly fashion. 'It's the damp environment in here, that's where the cough came from. I've listened to your chest and it sounds fairly clear. Try to get as much fresh air outside as you can,' he advised. 'It's hard, as you don't get enough good food in here. I'm always asking for more fruit and veg on the menu. Maybe your new Master and Matron will finally listen to me . . .' He returned his stethoscope to his leather Gladstone bag and was about to depart when he noticed Megan in the doorway. 'Anything I can help you with, young lady? I thought I answered your questions the other day? Or didn't you understand?'

'Yes, I did thank you, Doctor. Could I speak to you alone please? About . . . another matter?' she asked, glancing at the other girl, who quickly got the message and left the dorm, leaving the doctor and Megan quite alone.

'What is it?'

'Well, sir . . .' She paused, unsure of how he might react.

'I'm worried about a young woman you recently examined. Tilly, her name is.'

'Child, I don't think I can discuss this wi—'

'But, sir! We don't know where she is. Something occurred with the Master the other day. I've been noticing he's been calling her to his room and afterwards she's been very upset.'

The doctor's eyebrows shot up.

'Then yesterday, Matron couldn't get into his room,' she continued. 'It was locked. Bill, the porter, couldn't open the door either so he looked through the window and said he found the Master "in fragrance" with Tilly. Matron looked shocked.'

The doctor's face drained of all colour. 'You're sure about this, Megan?'

'Yes, sir.'

'The correct phrase is "in flagrante", by the way, which is what I assume you mean. Is that what you heard Bill saying?'

'Yes, sir. You can ask him yourself.'

The doctor muttered something under his breath which Megan couldn't catch, then said in a normal tone, 'I shall go and have a word with Bill myself right now. Thank you for telling me, young lady.'

Oh dear – had she now opened up a can of worms? But she felt it needed to be said and she still didn't know what had happened to poor Tilly.

Tilly did not return to the dorm that evening either. Megan stared at the empty bed in the corner of the room. They all knew better than to comment on it for fear Miss Hamilton or Matron should overhear, and by the following evening there was a new girl called Annie Higgins in that bed, which worried Megan greatly, for it meant Tilly would not be returning to the workhouse.

After breakfast the following morning, she went in search of Bill before she was needed at Sunday morning prayers in the chapel, but there was a new man at the lodge.

'Do you know where Mr Harris is?'

The man was sitting on a stool munching on a meat pie. He licked the gravy off his chubby fingers. It looked as if Cook was taking good care of him. Megan's mouth began to water after her meagre breakfast of a thin, grey gruel.

The man shook his head. 'Don't know no one by that name. I started here this morning at short notice. I guess he's done something wrong and been made to leave. I was told some man had been given the elbow.'

Megan's stomach lurched, all thought of food suddenly gone. This was a travesty. Bill had been made to leave, and so had Tilly, it appeared. They knew too much. And all the while the Master and Matron were carrying on like nothing had happened at all.

The following day, Griff met Megan at her stall. She was quite busy, so he hung around watching her at work. Scamp stood at his feet, tethered by a piece of cord used as a make-shift lead. She had to wait until she'd served her customer and the people browsing the cakes had drifted away before she could speak to him, but he seemed content enough to wait, playing with the little mutt and scratching behind his ears affectionately.

'So this is Scamp.' She smiled and bent down to stroke the small, scruffy, wire-haired dog. He was ginger and white, and so cute. 'Hello, boy!'

Scamp sidled up to her and laid his head on her lap, his deep brown eyes looking up at her as his tail wagged vigorously.

'He likes you,' Griff said, with obvious pleasure.

'So what are you up to?' She patted Scamp's head and stood.

'I was thinking once you've returned your handcart we could go to the Temperance Hall so I could get some practice in with Scamp. The Lady, Kathleen, said it would be all right.'

Megan beamed. It might be just the tonic she needed to keep her mind off poor Tilly right now.

Griff hung around to help her with the stall. Every so often he'd shout out to passers-by, 'Roll up, roll up, get your delicious cakes and buns 'ere, be a nice treat for your hus-band's tea, madam!' Or if it was a man, he'd shout, 'Come on, sir, wouldn't you like to please your lady with a nice sticky bun or an apple pie! The best in town from Mrs Mathias's tea room down the road, freshly baked every day!'

'You're a natural at this. A proper little showman!' she laughed, which caused Griff to blush beet red. It made him even more handsome than he already was, which in turn made her blush a little. She knew she was always a lot happier when she was in Griff's company: her heartbeat quickened and she felt a warm glow all over her body. Was this what the romantic love poets spoke about? She thought maybe it was.

She had a couple of leftover rock cakes, which she gave to Griff.

'Cor, thanks, Megan. Won't your boss lady mind, though?'

'No, she told me I can have a couple as those will be hard as iron by tomorrow. She won't be able to sell them to anyone. They really will be like rocks.' She giggled.

He grinned as he tasted one. 'Right nice they are, and all,' he said, chomping away.

She was always taught not to speak with her mouth full but he was enjoying the cake so much that she hadn't the heart to tell him. She watched as he fed Scamp with a few titbits. Although he had nothing in life, he always made sure to share what he had. He was kindness itself. That's what she liked about him.

'I'll keep the other cake for my uncle.' He stuffed it into his jacket pocket.

Megan fretted a lot about Griff's relationship with his uncle – the fact that he overlooked how badly Uncle Berwyn treated him and still cared about him baffled her. She'd noticed the tell-tale bumps and bruises and the sad look in his eyes sometimes, yet he always seemed to make an excuse: he'd walked into a door or lamp post, he'd say. He always covered for his uncle and never admitted that the bruises came from the end of his fist. And she should know, after everything she had been through with Miss Hamilton. The supervisor was sneaky: she ensured the marks she left on Megan were hidden beneath her clothing so neither the other inmates nor staff suspected a thing. Of course, Cook and Mrs Crossley knew what was going on, but even they had never witnessed the woman beating her. Miss Hamilton was too clever for that.

'Look, Megan!' Griff shouted when they had packed the last sticky bun away. There wasn't much left on the stall today. It had been a good day of trading; most items had sold out.

She turned from the handcart to see Scamp dancing around on his hind legs as Griff shouted, 'This way, boy!' Scamp would go in one direction and then the other, all the while still balancing on his hind legs, following Griff's gentle encouragement.

Megan clasped her hands together in delight. 'That's so clever. Did you teach him to do that, Griff?'

He nodded eagerly. A crowd of onlookers had gathered to watch. 'Look at this too, Megan!' He curled himself into a little ball on the ground and commanded, 'Jump, boy, jump!' Scamp immediately got down from his hind legs and leapt over Griff's body. Then, when Griff stood up, Scamp jumped into his arms.

A ripple of appreciative applause came from the onlookers and Griff bowed to the crowd. 'I thank you!' he said with a flourish of his hand. He clearly had them rapt, and Megan could imagine just how well his act at the talent show would go down. She was so pleased for him.

She ran over and planted a kiss on his cheek, causing him to step back in surprise, but there was a huge smile on his face.

He put Scamp on the ground and began to push the handcart for Megan. The daily walk with the cart to Plymouth Street didn't seem half so gruelling in Griff's cheery company, and there was something else she was happy about, too: they were going to see The Lady afterwards.

Kathleen looked overjoyed to see the both of them and made a huge fuss over Scamp, too. They ran through a rehearsal where Scamp practised jumping through the hoop and attempted some funny stunts where he balanced on an old barrel and jumped on Griff's shoulder. It made Megan's sides ache from laughter. Then Kathleen arranged for them all to have tea and sandwiches in her dressing room. It was the best day she had had in a long while. Megan wished life could always be like this.

Whilst they were sat drinking tea, Griff messed around, crooking out his little finger as he held the delicate cup whilst reciting, 'I'm a toff now, don't you know!' Kathleen turned to Megan and asked her about Tilly.

Megan explained all that had happened.

'Oh, that doesn't sound right to me at all,' Kathleen said, her mouth gaping open, shocked by Megan's words. 'Something awful must have happened in that room and it's being covered up.'

'Well, I told the workhouse doctor, miss, so let's hope something will come of that,' Megan said. But deep down she worried now in case she'd get into trouble because of it.

'Always remember this,' Kathleen said wisely. 'You have done what your conscience has told you to do. 'Tis the godly thing to do. You have nothing to reproach yourself for.'

Griff, who had been feeding some leftover crusts to Scamp on the floor, whipped his head around and looked at the pair. 'I forgot to ask the barmaid about that funny word, Megan,' he said. 'To be honest, I forgot how to say it.'

'That's all right, Griff,' Megan said. 'I find it hard to say too.'

'What word might that be?' Kathleen drew her eyebrows together in puzzlement.

'"In-flag-granty", miss. At first, I thought it was "in fragrance" till I was put right by Dr Griffiths, but he didn't tell me what it meant.'

'In which way was it said?' Kathleen asked.

'Well, when Bill the porter looked through the window of the Master's room he said the Master was caught in-flag-granty with Tilly.'

Kathleen went silent. She knew what it meant, Megan

could tell. She thought that Kathleen was trying to think of a way to explain it to Megan and Griff. It must be a very complicated matter, she thought to herself.

'It's usually used to describe someone who has been caught in the act of some sort of criminal behaviour,' Kathleen eventually said.

Perhaps fearing Kathleen was going to say something about him pinching apples from the market, Griff's cheeks began to redden and he made an excuse to leave the room. Scamp followed at his heels.

Kathleen continued, 'It might be that the Master was caught being intimate with Tilly, from all you've told me, Megan. You know what I mean by that? Do you know how babies are made?'

Megan nodded. One of the older girls in the dorm had told her last year. Another girl had turned up at the workhouse with a swollen stomach and had been made to wear a different uniform to the rest of the girls. The dress was red in colour and singled her out from the others – she stood out like a sore thumb. She was treated in such a humiliating fashion for her misdeed and Megan had felt sorry for her. It hadn't been her fault; a married man she'd worked for 'had taken advantage of her', as Eira had put it. She gave birth to an infant who sadly died days later, and then the girl was made to go back to her employer to work. It sounded awful and Megan often wondered what had happened to her after, whether it had happened to the poor girl once again.

'It could be the Master was trying to have his way with young Tilly or maybe he already had.' Kathleen looked concerned. 'This is very worrying. All you young girls are at risk. If I were you, I'd go and check again with the doctor that it's been reported.'

'Yes, miss,' Megan said seriously. 'At the moment Matron is acting like nothing at all has happened, even though she heard Bill the porter telling her what he saw. I suspect Miss Hamilton, the supervisor, got Bill dismissed after he told her what he'd seen.'

'A conspiracy of silence . . .' Kathleen said thoughtfully. 'If nothing is done then I shall be telling my husband to send the police there. This is not right at all.'

Griff returned at that moment, holding his jacket, evidently ready to leave. 'Thank you for the tea and sandwiches, Miss O'Hara,' he said. 'When shall I call again to rehearse?'

'Tomorrow afternoon should be fine, Griff,' she said kindly. She glanced at the wall-mounted clock in the dressing room. 'Megan, you'd best get back to the workhouse too before you're missed. You don't want to be getting into trouble.'

Megan looked at the clock, her heart missing a beat. It was later than she thought. She'd done it again. 'I'd better run,' she said to the others and, before they had a chance to reply, she was on her way out of the building.

*

She just managed to join the queue for supper before Miss Hamilton appeared and could know that anything was wrong. Her beady eyes glared at her.

'Miss Hopkins,' she said. 'I need to see you in my office later.'

Oh no! Had she indeed noticed she was late returning to the workhouse?

All through supper, Megan could hardly eat a mouthful for worrying about the situation. The hard potatoes, overcooked cabbage and fatty piece of mutton were hard to swallow – and tasteless, too. She glanced across at the table where Matron, the Master and Miss Hamilton sat. They had a big roast chicken, which the Master divided up between them using a large fork and carving knife. Several silver salvers were on that table too, no doubt full of rich pickings beneath. The smell wafted over to her. It was so unfair; they always got the best of everything.

After supper, when the girls were lined up ready to leave the dining room, Miss Hamilton appeared beside her and, taking Megan roughly by the elbow, she steered her off to the office. Pushing open the door, she was told to remain standing, whilst Miss Hamilton sat on a large leather chair behind a sweeping walnut desk.

'It's come to my attention, Miss Hopkins,' she said, peering over her gold-rimmed spectacles, that you were witness to some sort of incident in the Master's room the other evening.'

Megan gulped then nodded. 'Yes, ma'am.'

'So, what exactly did you see?'

'I . . . I didn't see anything . . .' Megan began to tremble but didn't want to show the old crone she was scared. She rested her leg against the large desk to support herself. 'There was no answer when I knocked on the Master's door and I tried to turn the doorknob, but it just wouldn't budge. It was then I called Matron and she couldn't open it either, so we got the porter who tried his key, but he said there was a key on the other side keeping it locked. And then he went outside to look in through the window and said he had seen the Master *in flagrante* with Tilly.'

'Do you know what that phrase means, Miss Hopkins?'

Of course, Kathleen had explained it to her just that very afternoon, but something told Megan that it was best to keep her mouth shut.

'No, Miss Hamilton.'

'Very well then.' Miss Hamilton wrinkled her nose as if in disgust. 'Whatever you've been told, it's all lies, I'm telling you. Mr Harris has been dismissed. You are not to report a word of this to anyone. Understood?'

Megan shivered from top to toe as Miss Hamilton stood and produced a leather bullwhip from her desk drawer. 'Now this is what really bad children get in the workhouse. You wouldn't want me to use this on you, would you, Megan?'

'N—no, ma'am.'

So that was the price she had to pay: silence, or be whipped to within an inch of her life. What could she do?

Griff returned Scamp to the landlord of the Vulcan Inn. He was a large, well-built fellow called Fred Harper, who sported mutton-chop whiskers and had bulging biceps bursting out of the sleeves of his shirt. Uncle Berwyn had once told him he was built like that as he loved a bit of mountain bare-knuckle boxing and kept himself fit. Yet, although he was scary to look at and handled his customers well, Griff had come to realise that inside he was a gentle giant of a man, after getting to know him the past couple of weeks. He had pangs of guilt for stealing that coal from his yard. After all, the man was allowing him to use his dog and he allowed Griff to take him for walks or visit whenever he wished. But somehow he couldn't find it in his heart to tell the man what he'd done. And all the thanks he'd had for stealing that coal, too! He thought back to that cold night when his uncle hadn't even come home to the fire he'd carefully banked up for him, and which had gone out by the morning.

He patted Scamp on his head and the dog looked up at him with his big, soulful brown eyes. Then he waved at Fred and went home.

When he got into the house, there was an unusual odour. It wasn't nasty or anything like that; in fact it was quite pleasant. It was some sort of perfume women wore and it reminded him of roses. Oh, what a lovely smell it was, an' all.

He called out, 'Uncle?' but there was no reply. So he went over to the fireplace and noticed that, for once, the fire had been kept in, and not only that – the old table in the corner was set for tea. There were two mismatched cups and saucers and two plates, one holding a currant bun and the other a custard tart. Blinking, he couldn't believe his eyes. What had brought about this change in his uncle? Maybe his sister had persuaded him to give up the booze once and for all?

There was a teapot on the table and the kettle was boiling on the fire so, taking some initiative, he brewed up the tea. His uncle couldn't be too far away, he guessed, and would be pleased he'd got it ready for him. He was taking a nibble on the currant bun when he noticed something on the floor. Bending down, he picked up the white scrap of material. It was a white lace handkerchief, just like his mother used to use. He inhaled deeply; this smelled of roses too. A lady had been here, but where was she now?

Suddenly, overhead, he heard movement: a bumping around and then heavy footsteps on the stairs. His uncle appeared in the doorway, his eyes bulging, face red. 'What the bleedin' hell are you doing home at this time of the day, you little rascal?' He was only partially dressed, wearing his trousers and braces over his long combinations. His hair was messed up as if he'd been in bed. Maybe Griff had woken him up.

'S—sorry, Uncle. I just took Scamp back to Fred at the pub and there was nowhere else for me to go as it's perishing outside.'

'I've told you before, whenever you go out, you're to bring something back home for me, understood?'

Griff stood there trembling. 'Yes.'

His uncle's eyes wandered to the table where he noticed something was amiss. 'What have you done to that table? Have you been eating my food?' he thundered.

'No, sir. I mean, yes, but I thought one of the cakes was for me as there were two.'

Spittle began to form on his uncle's lips as he stepped nearer and raised his hand as if about to wallop him across the head, but the sound of something falling from above, caused his uncle to freeze.

'Who's upstairs?' Griff asked.

His uncle's expression had changed from one of anger to shock as his mouth gaped open. It was obvious he didn't want Griff to know someone else was in the house. And then it clicked: that's why he'd been angry that Griff had eaten part of the bun.

Griff took this as his cue to get away and he ran as fast as his legs could carry him back in the direction of the Vulcan Inn. His uncle was no match for him when it came to a race and he soon arrived at the alleyway and scaled the wall of the pub and into the backyard. Scamp was sitting there, almost as if he'd been waiting for him to return, and bounded over to where Griff was stood, pleased as anything to see him. He licked away at Griff's face as if he were a tasty bone.

'Ssh, boy,' he warned. 'Seems like I'll be sleeping out here with you for the night.'

There was an old tarpaulin in the corner, which he dragged over the pair of them, and on Scamp's rag bed they both lay, curled up together, gazing up at the stars.

Chapter Ten

Megan set up the market stall the following morning with a heavy heart. Work was brisk and Mrs Mathias called by near the end of the day to collect the majority of the day's takings. She often did this as she feared Megan could be targeted and accosted on the way back to Plymouth Street. There were many pickpockets and plain bad people in the area who stole to fill their empty stomachs. Most folk seemed law abiding, but Mrs Mathias said she could spot a wrong 'un at forty paces.

Usually, though, Griff made it his business to accompany Megan back to Plymouth Street with her cart after her working day was done. It was a time she relished, him turning up with Scamp at his heels, the short walk back to the bakery. They would chatter away together, then call in to see The Lady at the Temperance Hall, where they were both welcomed like old friends. It was the nearest both had to a mother figure.

Griff was getting on in fine style with his act. Scamp had learned how to jump through the hoop, balance on the barrel and respond to commands to leap onto Griff's shoulder. Kathleen had taught Griff a music-hall-style song to perform called 'A City Gent Am I'. It was quite funny, though designed to be sad in places. It was a song about a poor young lad who had fallen on hard times and yearned for the high life. He'd decided to call his act 'Tramp and the Little Scamp'.

I'm just a homeless little tramp, a starving lad am I,
I take my dog, my little Scamp, to beg at passers-by.
But when I'm rich and there's no ditch, you will hear me say,
I am a City Gent, am I, in every single way . . .

I'm just a homeless little tramp, a starving lad am I,
I take my dog, my little Scamp, to beg at passers-by.
But when I'm rich you'll look at me and everyone will say,
You're a City Gent, you are, in every single way . . .

Megan loved the song and began clapping as soon as Griff had finished his rendition.

'Oh, Griff, you're so talented!' she exclaimed. 'It's really clever how you got Scamp to jump on your shoulder as you sang!'

Griff blushed. 'Thank you, Megan. I'm working on making him howl at the end of the act, too!'

'That will really bring the house down!' Kathleen enthused.

Griff and Megan exchanged glances, having no idea what The Lady meant, but Megan realised it must be something good.

Afterwards, Kathleen asked Megan if Tilly had returned to the workhouse.

'No, miss.' Megan shook her head. 'Miss Hamilton called me into her office and told me I wasn't to breathe a word of what had gone on to anyone and that Mr Harris was a liar and that's why he was dismissed. Then she threatened me with a leather whip she keeps locked away in her desk drawer. But Mr Harris was telling the truth, miss. He's not a liar.'

'But that's preposterous!' Kathleen said, her nostrils flaring. 'That woman is a big bully! I've a good mind to go around there and have a word and give her a jolly good whipping! T'ain't right them picking on young children, and I bet that workhouse Master has done that kind of thing before. Do you know where he worked last?'

'Somewhere in Carmarthen, miss,' Megan said.

'And what's his surname?'

'Pomfrey, miss.' Megan's knees began to knock together with fear, but she didn't want to show The Lady just how scared she really was.

'Now listen to me, Megan. You will not get into trouble as I shan't say how I obtained the information, but I will ask my husband to check up on workhouses in the Carmarthen area. It might take a while as letters will need to be written to make a background check. But if we discover that this kind of thing has happened previously, there'll be a good chance it is true. Meanwhile, I'll ask my husband to visit Bill. Would you know where he lives?'

'Yes, miss. It was the street opposite ours in Troedyrhiw. I forget the street name now as I've been away from there for some time.'

'Well, if you can just let me know roughly where it is, I'm sure my husband would be able to find it.'

Megan explained the best way she could how to get to his house. Luckily she remembered her old house street and number so it wouldn't be too hard for them to find it. Kathleen sat at her dressing table and jotted it all down on a piece of paper using a fountain pen. Megan glanced over the woman's shoulder to admire the neat and elaborate handwriting.

Kathleen set down her pen and turned to face the pair of them. 'Very good. Now, how about we run through that routine again, Griff?'

Griff nodded eagerly as Scamp woofed with delight. It was so nice being here that Megan wished she could stay forever, instead of returning to that cold dark place up the hill.

It was several weeks before Kathleen got news to Megan that the Master had left the workhouse in Carmarthen under a cloud, just as the previous workhouse Master had indicated.

Documentation had been located showing that he had been accused of 'interfering' with a young woman at the establishment. An inquiry had been held but the main witnesses had withdrawn their evidence at the last moment. Cook had told her that it was probably because those at the Carmarthen workhouse feared losing their jobs, and she quite understood why, because something similar had happened at another workhouse she'd worked at as a young lass. She herself had been called to court over the Master getting fresh with a young kitchen maid, though she hadn't realised what had been going on at the time, and he had also approached her himself, but she'd been relieved in the final instance when the case was called off. It was only her instinct that told her something had gone on, but the Master didn't lose his job in the end at all. Cook still had to work for him, and at least it kept a roof over her head at the time.

'You mustn't judge people for trying to survive as best they can,' she'd told Megan, but nevertheless Megan still felt an injustice had been done.

At the cake stall in the marketplace the following day, Kathleen had come to visit Megan.

'A case needs to be made,' she said firmly. 'The police are going to enter the workhouse and ask to speak to the doctor who examined Tilly and try to find out where she is. Bill Harris has agreed to give a statement, and I'm afraid you, too, will probably be called to give evidence, Megan.'

Megan began to whimper. 'I don't want to, miss. I'm too scared. I'll be whipped by Miss Hamilton. Everyone will turn against me.' She remembered Cook's words about how her Master had remained at the workhouse.

'No, they will not. I shall see to that, and whilst the case is ongoing, I'm going to make provision for you to stay with my brother and sister-in-law in Abercanaid. Evan Davies is a minister at the chapel and his wife, Lily, runs the school there. You'll be quite safe with them for a while.'

That cheered Megan up – to get out of the workhouse for a while – but then her thoughts changed. 'But what about my sisters? They're still there . . . The staff might take it out on them.'

'I admit, I hadn't thought of that. It would be a good idea if we got them out of there too whilst this case is ongoing. It could hit the newspapers big time. "Workhouse Master Interferes with Inmates – One Disappears" . . .' she said, imagining the front-page headline. 'I don't know if anyone will believe us, though, but I'm going to do my level best by those children, you have my word on that. I might need to speak to the Board of Guardians and explain how it will be in their best interests to send both your sisters to live with respectable members of the community.'

'But who could take them in?' Megan asked.

'Maybe Lily and Evan could take the three of you for the time being. I'm sure Mrs Morgan would help out too.'

'Who's she?'

Kathleen's face broke out into a huge smile. 'She's a lovely elderly lady who runs a little shop in Abercanaid. She took a young girl in herself called Betty and has been bringing her up as her own child. Don't worry, my family and friends shall help you three until all of this blows over. Or maybe Mrs Mathias could take you in, Megan, and both your sisters could lodge with Lily.' She stopped. 'In fact, that sounds the best idea all round.'

Megan shook her head. 'Oh, I don't know about that. She knows I'm a good worker but I don't know if she'd have me to live with her.'

'Would you like me to ask her for you?' Kathleen said kindly.

Megan breathed out a breath of relief. 'Would you, please?'

Kathleen nodded, 'Yes, of course. We'll get that sorted for the three of you, then we can concentrate on Griff's final rehearsals with Scamp. The talent show is only next week.'

And so it was arranged that both sisters, Lizzie and May, were to live with Lily and Evan at Abercanaid and, to Megan's surprise, Mrs Mathias received her into her home near the bakery. It was nice for her to sleep in a warm, comfortable feather bed at long last, but Megan ensured she paid for her keep by helping Mrs Mathias around the house, as well as working at the stall. She was a widow whose children were all grown-up and off her hands, apart from a twenty-two-year-old son who remained at home, but worked in the bakery. His grandfather had started the bakery business but now Eli worked there along with an elder brother called Jed and another called Morris, both of whom were married.

If Megan thought she had to get up at the crack of dawn to work on the stall, then Eli had to get up even earlier to help bake the bread. He seemed to have a wracking cough that his mother put down to the flour dust. She badly wanted to get her younger son out of the business but said it might be even worse for his health if he went underground or to the ironworks.

Eli was a nice lad, but he looked quite pale and wan. Megan wondered if it was because he worked through most of the night and slept during the day. She thought he needed more daylight and definitely more fresh air. In contrast, her brother Tom, who was only a few years younger, was as fit as a butcher's dog from all the walking and lifting he did, and all the good nourishing food Mrs Evans gave him. She was good to all three of her brothers and she'd even invited Megan and her sisters to Sunday tea that weekend.

The girls were settling in nicely with Lily and Evan, and although Megan knew it couldn't be a permanent arrangement, it was a welcome respite from the workhouse.

At Sunday teatime, all six children were eating under the same roof and made such a fuss of one another. Mrs Evans had baked a whole ham for the occasion and prepared a nice salad to go with it. Then, for dessert, there was tinned peaches and fresh cream.

'It's so good to see you children all together,' Mrs Evans enthused when all had been fed. Mr Evans snoozed quietly in his armchair by the fireside, much to the amusement of Lizzie and May, who were tweaking his moustache. Every so often he'd wrinkle his nose, and they'd back off, then he'd go back to sleep. Mrs Evans and the boys found it hilarious. Megan, though, had other things on her mind: the upcoming inquiry at the workhouse and the fact she'd be called to give evidence.

'Come on now, Megan,' Mrs Evans said thoughtfully. 'We'll leave the young ones playing, and you and Tom can come and speak to me in the scullery.'

They sat at the small table and Mrs Evans poured the three of them a nice hot cup of tea. 'I've seen that worried look in your eyes,' she said gently. 'Now, what is it? You've no need to worry about your brothers, they're all happy here.'

Tom nodded in agreement. 'We're having a great time. It's not all hard work. Mr Evans has been taking us fishing and for mountain walks, and Mrs Evans is like a mother to us all.'

Megan shook her head. 'Oh, if only it were that simple . . .' She ended up telling them both about what had been going on at the workhouse.

'He ought to be horsewhipped, by rights!' Mrs Evans said, banging her hand down on the kitchen table.

'I wish I could thump him and get away with it!' Tom said fiercely. 'I don't want any of my sisters going back in there with someone like him around. Why is there no protection for these young women? And as you rightly said, Megan, where has Tilly gone to? I vaguely remember her at the workhouse. She's a very pretty young lady.'

'That might have been the problem,' Mrs Evans said thoughtfully. 'She was womanly-looking, but she's still no more than a child. It makes my heart bleed for all the Tillys out there.'

Megan stared at Kathleen, blinking profusely. She just could not believe her ears. 'You're leaving for London today, miss?' They were in Kathleen's dressing room at the Temperance Hall.

Kathleen bit her bottom lip before replying. 'I'm afraid so, Megan. You see, last week I was talent-spotted by a London agent. He loves my voice and feels he could find work for me on the London stage!'

Megan realised this opportunity meant a lot to The Lady. *Her* lady. The lady who had helped both her and Griff at a time of need.

'Don't look so downhearted, Megan. I've waited for this moment all of my life, and we shall keep in touch, but you and Griff must promise not to breathe a word of this to anyone as I have to just go. My husband doesn't understand my need to sing on stage there. He believes the Temperance Hall and Merthyr Tydfil are all I should need in life, and of course, being a good wife and future mother. But I long for so much more . . .' Her eyes looked sad and Megan's heart went out to her.

'So, when are you going, miss?' Megan asked. She had a huge lump in her throat that refused to go away.

'Tomorrow. But don't worry. Griff has been trained up well for his chance on stage, and I shall expect you to tell me how he's got on. I'm sure he and Scamp will go down a storm with the audience . . .'

Megan nodded as tears filled her eyes. Kathleen hugged her warmly and she didn't seem to mind one bit that Megan's tears were soaking the sleeve of her fancy satin stage dress. Kathleen dipped her hand into her pocket and handed Megan a clean white lace handkerchief.

'Now dry your eyes, Megan, or else you shall have me crying too, and that just won't do.'

'Sorry, miss,' Megan said, breaking away. 'I don't mean to upset you, but Griff and I shall miss you so.'

Kathleen turned away to pick up her reticule from her dressing table. She opened it and took something from it to hand to Megan. It was a small white card with embossed fancy lettering on it. 'This is my agent's card. You can write to me there, and before I leave, I shall take Mrs Mathias's address from you, so I can send you a postcard or a letter. Some day I will return to Merthyr, I promise you that much, Megan.'

Megan smiled. It was a bittersweet moment between the pair of them, but at least there was hope they would be reunited some day.

The Lady's departure was a huge knock for both Megan and Griff, but before long it was time for Griff's performance, and they needed to put all of their focus on that.

Waiting in the wings at the Temperance Hall, ready to be called out onto the stage, Griff looked the picture of splendour in the outfit Kathleen had so kindly lent him. Megan was proudly at his side, and Scamp circled around his heels excitedly.

'Go on, break a leg, Griff!' Megan said brightly.

'Er, what do you mean?' He glanced at her sideways, obviously nervous at the thought of his impending performance.

'The Lady told me it's what performers say to one another for good luck!'

'Oh, thank you, Megan.' He beamed, and then kissed her on her cheek. 'You're all the good luck I need.'

She felt her cheeks flame, but a warm feeling transcended all over her, and it felt so good.

The compère's voice suddenly filled the auditorium, pulling them away from their little moment of affection. 'And now we have a rather special act. Introducing "Tramp and the Little Scamp". Give them a big round of applause, folks!'

The red velvet curtain drew back slowly, and Griff went to move forward onto the stage, but it looked like he was frozen to the spot. He glanced at Megan for help. Maybe it was the limelight flares that floored him, or maybe hearing the thrum from all those people in the audience. Whatever it was, Griff obviously had stage fright. Kathleen had told her all about that. How she wished The Lady was still here with them!

What would she do right now?

'Go on, Griff, you can do it!' Megan said, and gave him a little push, but he remained frozen. People in the audience started to boo and hiss, to which Scamp barked back, whether from anger or excitement Megan didn't know. But if this carried on he was liable to run off somewhere, and she didn't want that to happen. So, calm as she could be, she walked onto the stage.

The audience silenced.

Megan looked at them all, not caring what they thought of her. 'You lot should be ashamed of yourselves!' she scolded. 'My friend Griff, here, has worked for weeks to prepare for this act for you all, and he's scared to come on stage, even more so now you're all booing at him. Please give him a chance. It's nerves, that's what it is.'

'Gerroff and take that scruffy mutt with you!' a man shouted from the crowd. Megan looked back to see that Scamp had followed her out onto the stage. Then someone threw some rotting fruit, narrowly missing Megan's face. She felt like she wanted to cry.

Then, as if wakening from a stupor, Griff sprang to life, and she felt his comforting arm around her shoulders. He was no doubt upset that anyone could hurt his Megan. He led them back to the wings where he spoke firmly to the stage manager. 'I shall go on to perform my act, but please take Megan away and see she is safe.'

The man nodded, and led her away. She smiled at Griff as he grinned back at her. The compère returned to the stage and announced, 'And so I give you . . . "Tramp and the Little Scamp", folks!' This time, people cheered and there was no more booing or hissing, just a curious silence, waiting to see whether he would go through with it second time round.

Megan watched him from the back of the stalls and was so proud of his performance. Following a tricky start, his act went down a storm. Scamp performed all the tricks Griff had painstakingly taught him: he jumped through hoops and balanced on the beer barrel on his hind legs, but he also surprised everyone in the audience by jumping into the arms of the compère when Griff pretended to scold him – this part was a new addition the compère had been keen to take part in. People were rocking with laughter and, later, almost crying as Griff performed his ballad. At the end of the act, they were on their feet, clapping, whistling and stomping as they yelled out for more. But there was no more, as another act was due on next.

Griff, who had tears of joy in his eyes, called for Megan to come on stage with him and they both took a bow. 'I couldn't have done this without this little lady nor without the help of Miss Kathleen O'Hara!' Griff said proudly.

Griff's act eventually won the talent show and he was awarded a shiny sovereign for his efforts. They were also approached by the organisers who were keen he come back, to his utter delight. As Kathleen had left the theatre in such a hurry, there weren't any arrangements for her replacement. So they decided that one of the regular performers, a female singer, would step up to take Kathleen's slot, which meant that Griff could take hers. He now had a job, and not only that: one that brought him, as well as the audience, a great deal of joy. He was over the moon.

'It's all thanks to you, Megan,' he said, hugging her and giving her a big smack of a kiss on her cheek as he walked her back to Plymouth Street. Scamp was back on the lead and he'd been given a big bone for his efforts.

'I'm so proud of you, Griff,' she said shyly.

As they reached Mrs Mathias's house they stood under the lamplight and he said, 'One day I'm going to marry you, Megan Hopkins. You'll see if I don't.'

Then he turned and left her on the doorstep touching her cheek where he'd just kissed her.

Chapter Eleven

The following day, word was sent to Megan via Cook that she would soon be asked to give evidence in the inquiry against Master Pomfrey. Megan's stomach lurched at the very thought of it. Cook had come to see her at the cake stall and tried to break the news gently, as she knew she would be distressed.

'Look, Meg, I know it ain't what you want to do, but the rest of us in the kitchen are on your side. I might be called, too, as I saw him once taking Tilly into his room. I thought nothing of it at the time, but now in light of recent goings-on . . .' She lowered her voice and crossed one hand over the other as she said, 'He must have been having carnal knowledge of the girl.'

What did 'carnal knowledge' mean? Megan had no idea, but guessed it must be the same thing as '*in flagrante*'.

It was strange to see Cook away from the workhouse kitchen. She was wearing a brown-and-cream-checked shawl over a floral dress, which looked as though it could be her

Sunday best, and under her arm she held the very same wicker basket Kathleen had given to Megan. Perhaps Cook had noticed Megan's appraisal of her, as she then said, behind the palm of her hand, 'I had to pretend I needed to go shopping in the town to get away. I'm wearing my best shawl so I don't stand out as one of the workers.' She gestured in the general direction of the workhouse. 'Anyhow, I thought you ought to know.'

Megan gulped as she tried not to tremble at the thought of being called to the inquiry. 'I'm really scared, Mrs Woodley.'

'There now, girl, don't let on so. If you don't give evidence, that brute might get away with it. I've heard the good doctor will be saying his piece, an' all, so I dare say you won't be the only one.'

Megan let out a breath of relief to hear that. Dr Griffiths was a good man. He would tell the truth, she was sure of that. 'That's good to know,' she replied, feeling somewhat reassured.

'I'd best buy a few fancies for the Board of Guardians meeting later this afternoon. Greedy bunch of pigs, they are, with all those inmates 'alf starving to death whilst they dine like nobs. I've been busy baking all morning but 'ad instructions from Matron to make an extra nice feast today. I reckon the old bird is trying to soften them up before the inquiry takes place.'

Megan guessed Cook was probably right. 'How many would you like?'

'Hmm . . . I'd say ten sticky iced buns and ten custard tarts, to be on the safe side. Oh, and pop in a few fondant fancies. Mine ain't good enough for them, that's for sure. I'll be glad to see the back of those pompous Pomfreys!'

Megan wished in her heart that would be the case, but she wasn't holding her breath.

Stallholders were beginning to pack up, costermongers piling leftover fruit and vegetables into wooden crates, which they loaded onto the backs of horses and carts. The lady from the faggot-and-peas stall had served her final customer for the day, and Mrs Gibbons, who sold second-hand clothes, had bundled them all onto the back of a handcart. People were beginning to drift away from the marketplace. Another working day was over.

Megan glanced around to see if she could spot Griff anywhere. *That was odd. He was usually here by now to walk her to Plymouth Street.* Oh well, she couldn't hang around. She'd just have to push the cart herself. It was becoming more and more difficult as the days were getting colder, and now it was becoming icy underfoot.

She managed to push the cart as far as the parish church, when a gang of young scruffy urchins rammed into her, causing the cart to begin rolling out of her hands down a slight incline.

'Stop that at once!' she heard Griff's voice call out, and the young gang raced off in the direction of Caedraw, as if fearful of the older lad.

'Are you all right, Megan?' he asked, drawing close to her.

'I'm all right, Griff. They startled me, was all.' She turned to see that the cart had crashed into a low wall running alongside the church.

Griff approached it and knelt down beside it, and upon close inspection said, 'I'm afraid one of the wheels has worked a bit loose.'

'Oh no.' Megan knelt beside him on the frosted ground and sobbed, not caring how cold the pavement was. This was all too much.

'What's the matter?' He asked gently as he looked into her eyes.

She told him what Cook had said about the inquiry. 'So now I have to give evidence soon. I knew all about it and didn't worry too much before because Miss O'Hara was still here. But now she's gone to London, I feel I have to cope with this alone.'

'No, you don't have to,' Griff said tenderly. 'I'll always be around for you, Megs. Look, I'll wheel this back to the bakery for you and I'll borrow some tools from Eli and get it mended. It'll be right as rain in no time, you'll see. Check your takings, as I don't trust that gang. They bump into people to flummox them and then the poor folk find they've been robbed blind.'

They both stood, then she checked the small drawstring purse she had secured on a string around her neck. Thankfully it was still full to bursting with coins. It was the very day

Peggy Mathias couldn't show up to collect the takings as she was too busy. Megan would have hated to have lost all that money. She let out a long breath of relief. 'No, it's all here, thank goodness.' She paused for a moment. 'Is that what you used to do with the Rodneys, Griff?' She narrowed her eyes. 'You seem to know a lot about their little ploys.'

'Oh, no, no!' He held up his hands in defence. 'I admit, I did sometimes nick things from the market stalls, but that was because I was starving. No, as soon as I saw them doing that sort of thing, I stopped going around with them, particularly when those two boys were taken to court. They'll be halfway to Australia by now.'

Megan smiled. 'I should have known better,' she said. 'I know deep down I can trust you, Griff.'

He cocked a smile at her. 'Well, very glad to hear that, my lady,' he joked, and Megan could see the steam from his breath exhale on the frosty air. It was a deathly cold day; the pavements and roofs glittered white like icing on a Christmas cake.

Griff was as good as his word, and he pushed the wobbling handcart back to Plymouth Street. He hadn't even mentioned his winning audition at the Temperance Hall last night, but she could tell he was overjoyed. When they arrived back at the bakery, he got the tools from Eli, who was up out of bed after a day's sleep, and then Griff set about fixing the wheel for Megan before it got dark. Mrs Mathias, who lived in the house a few doors away, insisted Griff stay for supper. She warmed up a steak-and-onion pie that had already been cooked in the bakery with some potatoes, peas and carrots, and thick gravy.

'Cor, thank you, missus,' Griff said gratefully. 'I haven't had a meal like this in years.'

'Go and wash your hands, young man,' Mrs Mathias scolded good-naturedly. 'Can't have you seated around my table with hands like a navvy.'

Megan's stomach growled with hunger. It had been a long day working at the stall. Finally, she, Griff, Eli and Mrs Mathias were all seated around the table. Griff was just about to make a lunge to begin eating his food when Mrs Mathias held him with a beady brown-eyed glare. 'This is not how we do things under this roof, Griff,' she said, with some consternation. 'I shall say grace first, then you are allowed to eat up. When my late husband was still alive –' she looked heavenward and then back at Griff, who was watching her open-mouthed – 'myself and the boys would have to wait for him to pick up his knife and fork before we could begin eating ourselves, and this was always after my husband had said grace.'

'Please, missus' – Griff's eyes widened with curiosity – 'who is Grace?'

Megan and Eli tittered.

'Grace, young man, is a form of prayer before partaking of any food. It is to show that we are grateful for the food He provides us with . . .' She turned to face her son. 'Eli, tonight you can say grace.'

Eli nodded sombrely. 'We thank Thee, Heavenly Father, for the food You have provided us with this very evening. Amen.'

'Amen,' said one and all, followed by Griff, who had now picked up his knife and fork, ready to eat. Megan noticed he'd held his knife and fork in the wrong hands and so corrected him. He ate clumsily throughout the meal but at least he was trying his best. He was obviously not used to sitting around a table eating food like this. Her heart went out to him.

'Megan tells me you did well at the Temperance Hall last night at the talent show,' Mrs Mathias said brightly, trying to put Griff at ease after her earlier scolding.

'Yes, missus. I won the show but it wasn't all me. Scamp the dog helped me win it and Megan helped me, too.'

Mrs Mathias beamed at Megan. 'Oh yes, our Megan here is a very good girl . . . I shall be sorry to see her go back to that workhouse. Speaking of which, I have something to tell you later, dear . . .' she said, her expression transforming to a serious one.

Oh dear. What had she done? She hated the thought of being stuck in that place all day. It was her only escape, working on the stall for Mrs Mathias. It took her out of herself, being able to chat to folk. They weren't at all like the people at the workhouse – there she had to mind her P's and Q's, and if she said something out of turn, then she'd get a backhander. The folks that visited the stall were quite pleasant, and she had got to know most of the regular customers. Yes, working for the Mathias family made her feel wanted and appreciated. She could be herself. It would break her heart to have to leave them all.

Megan's heart sank at the very thought of it. Griff, sensing this, gave her a reassuring smile. 'You'll be all right, Megan,' he said.

'Have you been worrying about it, Megan?' Mrs Mathias tilted her head as if in sympathy with Megan's plight.

'Yes, ma'am, they're not very nice in that place. Well, some of the staff are, like Cook, but Miss Hamilton, the supervisor, has it in for me. She once made me work for hours in the laundry room.'

'And you weren't allowed any food during that time, were you, Megan?' Griff chipped in.

'No, but luckily the lady who runs the laundry room gave me something to eat and drink on the quiet without Miss Hamilton seeing.'

'That's terrible,' Mrs Mathias said. 'I know these places are necessary, but you'd think they'd employ good staff, not awful ones like that Miss Hamilton and that Master you told me of.'

The rest of the meal was spent in silence, as if Mrs Mathias were mulling things over in her mind. Megan glanced at her from time to time, hoping the woman's expression would somehow herald a clue to her thoughts. She didn't want to be rude and ask outright. Still, whatever happened next, Mrs Mathias had been kindness itself, and if it wasn't to last, then at least she had some good memories to look back on.

Finally out came dessert, a creamed rice pudding with the delicious aroma of nutmeg. Mrs Mathias really was an excellent cook. After they'd eaten, she said, 'Well, Megan, you've done so well on my stall. You've won everyone over. I'd like to give you a job in my tea room. One of the waitresses is about to have a baby and I could do with someone I can trust to help out. What do you say?'

Megan couldn't believe her luck. 'Oh, thank you, thank you!' She beamed, dropping her spoon into her empty bowl with such a clatter it made Griff jump. She ran around the table to peck her employer on the cheek.

'Why, Megan, I didn't expect you to get so excited! I'm only offering you a job. You'll be on your feet all day and it's hard work, mind you!'

'Oh, Mrs Mathias, you don't know how much this means to me. I thought for a moment earlier on . . .'

'Thought what, child?' Mrs Mathias studied Megan's face.

'I thought you were sending me back to the workhouse for good.'

Mrs Mathias swallowed hard, and she looked away to dab her eyes with the edge of her pinafore. 'Aw, Megan, you've got me crying now, *cariad*. I'd never do that to you, you're already like a daughter to me. The daughter I never had.'

Eli yawned. She might not have a daughter, but she did have a son, Megan realised. She hoped Eli wasn't too put out by the outpouring of affection his mother was lavishing on her.

Megan's eyes filled up hearing Mrs Mathias say those words, but they were tears of joy. It felt so good to be part of a family at last. It reminded her of the days when all her family were together, not divided by the workhouse.

Griff beamed. 'Yer'll make a great little waitress, Megan!' he enthused.

Megan glanced across at Eli who was nodding off into his uneaten bowl of rice pudding. She wondered about him sometimes, as he often seemed to fall asleep unexpectedly.

'Come on, soft lad.' Mrs Mathias roused her son. 'Go back to bed for a couple of hours. You've got a long night ahead of you.'

When Griff had gone home and they were washing the dishes together, she turned to Mrs Mathias. 'Should Eli be falling asleep like that so often, Mrs Mathias? It doesn't seem right to me.'

'Don't fret about it, *cariad*. It's the long hours he does at the bakery. He's not as strong as his brothers. He's got a weak constitution.'

But Megan didn't think it was that at all. She'd once disturbed him and found him hiding something underneath his bed. He didn't seem weak to her at all, but he was certainly hiding something from his mother. Deciding to say no more about the matter for now, she carried on drying and stacking the plates. It could wait. She'd check under his bed when he was in work later on.

Later, as both women relaxed in front of the fire, content with a cup of cocoa each under the dim light of an oil lamp, Eli popped his head into the living room.

'I'm off to the bakery now!' he said, making for the door.

'Here, son. Come here. Could you take these with you?' Mrs Mathias said, reaching down for a pile of newly washed white cotton jackets and trousers she had brought home earlier in the week. But Eli barely acknowledged her, though he had clearly heard her. The expression on his face almost looked as if he were trying to stay away from them. Megan wondered why.

As soon as he'd slammed the door behind him, Megan set down her cup. 'I'm just going to fetch my book from the bedroom,' she said. Peggy, who had resumed her busy click-clacking with her knitting needles, nodded.

Up in Eli's bedroom, all appeared neat and tidy, but it wasn't until she dropped to her knees and lifted the bed-covers that she found what she was looking for. She felt underneath the bed until her hand hit a hard object, which she drew out and held up to the light. It was a half-drunk bottle of whisky. No wonder Eli had been dropping off to sleep earlier and not getting too close to any of them, for fear they should smell it on his breath.

She deliberated whether she should tell Peggy about her son's drinking, but decided for the time being not to. For now she would keep it to herself. There was no use causing any alarm until she discovered the truth behind it.

And so Megan began work at Mrs Mathias's tea room in the town. It was a stone's throw away from the parish church, and Megan loved to hear the chime of the bells in the distance. It made her think of her mother, for a very strange reason. She had always used to say that the chime of church bells indicated 'hatches, matches or dispatches', a saying that had always baffled her. When she asked what she meant by that, her mother would smile and say she'd find out some day. So the first day she began working at the shop, she'd asked Mrs Mathias, who told her it meant 'births, marriages and deaths'.

The tea room was quite quaint. There were ten tables in all, six of which could seat four people at a time, and the other four tables were smaller and seated two. The tables were dressed with clean white linen tablecloths every single day – Mrs Mathias was quite particular about that. In the centre of each table was a pristine white lace doily, on top of which was a thin stemmed glass vase holding one or two flowers. It gave the tables a nice touch.

Her favourite table was the one just in front of the bay window made of leaded glass. It was a table for two which

Megan thought quite romantic. She'd yet to see any sign of lovers seated in that spot – more often than not it was occupied by elderly ladies who gossiped about everyone; that seemed to be the sort the tea room attracted in general – but she held out hope that one day she might see love blossom there.

Husbands and wives would often enter the tea room, and Megan could usually tell the state of the relationship immediately, just by how they reacted towards one another. If it were good, the husband would be very attentive, drawing out his wife's chair and settling her to sit down, then asking her what she'd like to eat and drink. If it were a fractious or boring relationship, quite often the husband would pay little heed to his wife and at the first opportunity open a newspaper.

There was one couple who, in particular, she found strange. They always appeared very furtive with one another, speaking in hushed tones. 'Married, the pair of them!' Mrs Mathias had informed Megan.

Megan had frowned. 'But if they're married to one another, why the secrecy?' It didn't make sense at all to her. Megan had been quite bemused by it.

'Not to one another!' Mrs Mathias had chuckled.

Megan thought she understood, but why on earth a couple would not have a cup of tea and a fancy with their own husband and wife was beyond her thinking.

Griff made an excuse to call in every day. He was doing

well at the Temperance Hall – his act was going down a storm.

'The way you're going, Griff, you'll be joining Miss O'Hara on the London stage!' Megan enthused.

'Not on your bleedin' Nellie!' Griff said.

''Ere, less of your language,' Mrs Mathias mimicked, giving him a good-natured cuff around the earhole.

'Sorry, missus,' Griff said, a cheeky grin on his face. 'But Megan should know I won't leave her to go on any London stage.'

'That's nice to know.' Megan beamed and felt her face grow hot. Griff had that kind of effect on her. She put her hand in her pocket. 'That reminds me! I forgot to tell you I got a letter from The Lady yesterday.'

Griff's eyes shone in expectation.

'Go on, the pair of you!' Mrs Mathias said. 'Megan, you're due a short break. Go into the kitchen and read Griff that letter.'

'Oh, thank you, Mrs Mathias,' Megan said, grateful that the woman understood how important The Lady had been to both herself and Griff.

Griff could barely read. Megan had been teaching him herself, and he was coming along nicely, but she thought he'd have trouble reading joined up writing.

She unfolded the letter on the scrubbed pine table in the centre of the kitchen.

Dear Megan,

I am so pleased to hear that Griff and Scamp won the talent show and what wonderful news that he has regular billing at the Temperance Hall! Please pass on my best to him.

I am doing well here and making new friends. I am boarding with a landlady at her pub. But you will never believe this — finally, my husband has relented and is coming to join me here for a short while. He has booked some very fine lodgings for us to stay in.

I am due to appear on stage soon so I will make this letter short. I will be performing for a figure of world renown, but I am sworn to secrecy. I shall tell you after the performance who that person was. It is oh, so exciting.

I hope things are going well for you and that your stay with Mrs Mathias is a long one. Lily tells me your sisters are doing well at Abercanaid, and that there is a couple in the village hoping to adopt both girls. I am so pleased for them both.

I will write again as soon as I am able and shall tell you my exciting news!

Kathleen O'Hara.

It was signed with kisses.

After she finished reading, Megan stared at the letter. Rereading the words made her miss The Lady all the more.

'What's the matter, Megs?' Griff asked.

Megan sniffed. 'It's just . . . I'll be the only one left of my family now who has to remain at the workhouse. After the Master's trial I'll have to return. I don't know how I'll cope going back in that place, especially with Miss Hamilton taking such a strong dislike to me.'

'How that woman could dislike someone so lovely and sweet as you, I'll never know,' Griff said kindly. 'Any more news about you giving evidence in his trial?'

'Not a blooming sausage! I haven't heard a thing.'

Mrs Mathias entered the kitchen and looked at the pair. 'Come on, Megan, give the lad a cup of tea.' She picked up a tray of cakes which were covered with a clean tray cloth, then looking at the pair said, 'Suppose it wouldn't hurt for me to give you two a Welsh cake . . .' She lifted the cloth and placed the tray on the table so they could both take one. 'I notice your hands are a lot cleaner these days, Griff,' Mrs Mathias remarked.

'Yes, missus. Thank you.' He munched away as if he'd never eaten one before in his life, dropping crumbs all over Mrs Mathias's floor.

'I notice you still need to brush up on your table manners, mind.' She winked at Griff. Then, sniffing loudly, she covered the cakes with the cloth, and carried them out to the tea room.

The kettle had boiled, so Megan made them a cup of tea.

'Lovely cuppa, Megs,' Griff enthused. 'Good colour. When my Uncle Berwyn makes tea, he keeps using the same tea leaves and it's the colour of gnats' pi—' As if remembering his manners, he carried on: 'Well, never you mind. It's very weak, is all I'm saying.'

'It'll be Christmas soon, Griff,' Megan said softly. Holding her tea, she hoped she looked just as ladylike as Miss Kathleen O'Hara.

'Yes, I know. Won't be much fun with my uncle, though. He'll be out for the count, but at least this year I've got some earnings of my own, so we won't starve.'

Megan had to admire Griff's fortitude. 'I'll be having Christmas dinner with Mrs Mathias and her family. I'm sure if I ask her, she'll invite you too.'

Griff's face fell and he shook his head. 'I'd love to come, of course I would, but I can't leave my uncle – even though he'll be spark out for most of it. I'm all he has, now my auntie and his baby are gone. He lost touch with this sister a long time ago.'

Megan understood. She nodded. 'Maybe you can come for tea on Boxing Day then. I doubt if Mrs Mathias would want to invite your uncle – she hates to see someone so out of control on drink.'

'I know,' Griff said quietly. 'But look on the bright side. At least you won't be at the workhouse this Christmas.'

Megan knew all too well that Christmas Day would be the one day of the year when the inmates would be fed properly. The Board of Guardians ensured they had a beef dinner followed by plum pudding. The inmates always looked forward to it, but under the present circumstances she'd rather eat scraps intended for Scamp than enter that place again. But she still had the niggling feeling that Mrs Mathias might send her back there soon . . .

Chapter Twelve

Megan wandered up and down Merthyr High Street. The shops were full of Christmas spirit. If it wasn't the holly-decorated windows, then it was the large geese strung up by their legs at the front of the poulterer's, ready to be plucked, roasted and eaten by families around a Christmas table, or the little painted wooden soldiers that stood proud in Mr Adler's toy shop, ready to be taken home and eagerly opened by the well-to-do kids on Christmas morning. There was a hustle and bustle of festive activity all around the town in general, and she loved this time of year so much. And best of all, this Christmas, she wouldn't be in the workhouse.

Mrs Mathias had sent her on an errand to pick up some red poinsettias to go on the tables at the tea room. She also had instructions to look out for some holly and mistletoe to decorate the place, too. On the way to the little flower shop on the High Street, Megan almost collided with a man carrying a large brown-paper parcel under his arm. She was about to apologise when she noticed it was Bill, the porter, who had been working at the hospital.

'Well, hello there, young Megan,' he said, with a big smile on his face. He juggled the parcel with one hand, while he attempted to tip his bowler hat with the other.

'Hello, Mr Harris. You're looking very cheerful.'

'Yes, I'm back at the workhouse now, since all that business with the Master has been sorted out.'

Megan felt her heart thump in her chest at the mere mention of the Master. 'But how can that be? There has been no trial yet.'

Bill's face clouded over with confusion. 'The Master was acquitted of any wrongdoing and he's been moved to another workhouse. Didn't anyone tell you?'

She shook her head before finding her voice. 'But you knew he was guilty!' She stamped her foot on the ground. 'I was supposed to be called to give evidence. And what about Tilly?'

'Tilly is back at the workhouse.'

Was it her imagination or did Bill look shamefaced? 'But where did they send her to in the meantime, Bill?'

'I think it was the workhouse in Cardiff, I'm not too sure now. In any case, it was thought that Tilly was too feeble-minded to present her case. Her evidence was too fragile to stand up in court, apparently.' He began to look around, as if afraid of being seen talking to her. 'I'm afraid I have to go. Mrs Harris is waiting for me at the post office. I have to send this package off to our daughter before Christmas, you see. She lives in Hereford. I'd better go—'

'But hang on a moment, Bill. Didn't they believe the doctor's evidence? *He's* not feeble-minded. What happened there?'

He shrugged his shoulders. 'I've no idea. Anyhow, Merry Christmas to you, young Megan!' He lifted his hat to her and replaced it on his head. Before Megan had a chance to protest any further, he turned his back on her and strode away. It was obvious he was delighted to have his job back and didn't want to risk it any further. Megan sighed. It was true what Kathleen had said about a 'conspiracy of silence'. She knew that calling Tilly as a witness wasn't very persuasive, but the doctor's word would make a strong case. Whatever had happened to stop the trial from going forward?

A few days later, Megan decided to return to the workhouse to ask Eira about the situation. She found her tidying up the girls' schoolroom when she arrived.

'Megan!' she said, her big eyes shining brightly. 'Are you coming back here?'

Megan dropped her wicker basket and hugged her friend tightly, then drew away, her expression sombre. 'I don't know. I suppose now I hear the trial is over, I should return, but I don't want to leave Mrs Mathias's house. She hasn't told me to go yet, but now the Master and his wife have gone away . . .'

Eira beamed. 'Yes, I'm so glad that pair has left here.'

'I only just found out.'

'We've got a new Master and Matron now, Mr and Mrs Baker from Swansea,' Eira said, smiling. 'They treat us well.'

'And Miss Hamilton?'

'She's still here, unfortunately, but she seems kinder these days.'

Megan wondered whether it was because the Bakers had reprimanded the woman or simply that she no longer had Megan around to terrorise. After all, the woman was particularly nasty to her alone, not so much to others. 'What about Dr Griffiths? Do you know if he gave evidence? Or why I wasn't called to do so? I'm really frustrated by it.'

A cloud appeared over Eira and then she bit her bottom lip. 'I wouldn't really know much. No one tells me anything here. Now, tell me, what's been happening for you, Megan?'

Although the girl tried to sound bright and breezy, her tone of voice didn't match. Something told Megan that something was amiss here.

'Please, Eira,' she said, touching her forearm. 'I do need to know. If you think it will upset me, you're wrong, because it will upset me even more if I never discover the truth. I saw Bill, the porter, earlier, and he didn't want to tell me much either. Someone must know something, they simply must.' Megan looked deep into Eira's eyes. She had such a kind nature, she knew she could rely on her.

Eira nodded. 'All right then, Megan, but it's going to upset you. You wouldn't know, but the real reason the Master got off is because . . . Well . . . Tilly was due to give evidence, but then she was found drowned in the bathroom. Miss Hamilton discovered her body – she said it wasn't a pretty sight. There was an empty bottle of gin beside her . . .' Eira turned away, as if the memory were too painful to even speak of, her shoulders wracked with grief.

Megan put her head in her hands and wept. It was too awful to even think of, poor girl. It was all that man's fault. She dreaded to think of everything the poor girl had been through in her young life.

There, but for the grace of God, go I.

She wiped away her tears with the back of her hand.

Eira turned to face her and touched Megan's shoulder gently. 'Go and see Mrs Woodley in the kitchen before you leave. She'll tell you more. She's been asking after you.'

Megan hugged Eira once again, then retrieved her basket and went in search of Cook.

The kitchen was noisy with the clattering of tin pans, plates and cutlery being tossed into the sinks to be washed. It was just after dinner and the women were talking nineteen to the dozen as they worked. It was a sound she loved to hear, so familiar to her, now a distant memory. In that moment, she realised that, out of everywhere in this workhouse, this was where she'd felt most at home.

'Hark at Madam here!' Annie, one of Cook's assistants, shouted to the other women in a good-natured way. 'She's come up in the world: just look at that pretty floral dress and white pinafore! In pristine condition, too! You're looking lovely, girlie. How's life treating you?'

'Oh, ever so good,' Megan answered truthfully. 'I love working at the tea room.'

'Oh, you're there now then, Megan, are you?' Cook arrived on the scene. 'What happened to the cake stall?'

'Bessie, a new girl, has taken it over and now I work in the tea room.'

'Come here,' Cook said, drawing Megan towards her. 'Give us a hug! I've missed you that much, I have. Enid!' She shouted at a young girl in the corner. 'Make us a cup of tea. Bring a couple of those currant buns I squirrelled away from that last Guardians' meeting!'

Megan smiled. It was good to be back – in the kitchen, at least. Cook sat her down at the scrubbed pine table and they chatted for a while. 'You haven't just called to see me, though, Megan, have you?' she asked. Her bright cornflower-blue eyes crinkled at the edges, and Megan could see her salt-and-pepper hair, peeking out from beneath her mop cap.

'No, Mrs Woodley. I want to find out what happened in

the Master's trial. I was supposed to give evidence but wasn't called in the end.'

'Ssh!' Cook said, putting her index finger to her own lips. 'Walls have ears!' She lowered her voice. 'All I know is that poor girl then did away with herself and he was let off with the offence and sent elsewhere.'

'Eira told me about that. I was sad to hear it. It's all his fault, the Master's.'

'Happen you're right about that, Megan, but it's all over with now, any road.'

'But what if he does it at another workhouse?' Megan said. 'The lady from the Temperance Hall's husband, the police officer, said that Mr Pomfrey left the last workhouse under a cloud. What if this isn't even the first time?'

'Aye, that may be so, but there's not much we can do about it now. The trial's been cancelled.'

Megan held back her tears and swallowed hard. 'But what about the doctor? Did he give evidence?'

'I don't believe so, Megan. There was an injustice done that day. You know it, I know it, and so does the Board of Guardians, but no one is willing to hold their heads above the parapet and say so for fear of getting shot at.'

It made Megan very sad to think the Master had got away with it. 'Eira said Tilly drowned herself in the bath and she had a bottle of gin by her side. She wasn't a drunk, that I knew of.'

'Oh dear, Megan. You are still too young to understand these things. She didn't drown herself. Poor Tilly was trying to get rid of an unwanted pregnancy.' Tears brimmed over from Cook's eyes and she dabbed them with a cotton handkerchief. 'It was well known here that's why she was sent away – so Matron wouldn't have to walk past the girl seeing her pregnant with the Master's baby. She only returned here from the Cardiff workhouse for the trial. They even made her wear one of those red dresses to single her out as an unwed mother-to-be, it was total humiliation for the girl. But in the end, well, you know what happened.'

Megan felt the blood in her veins turn to ice. 'I can't believe it, I never knew,' she said soberly. 'She was only fourteen.'

'Apparently by the time of the trial she was fifteen years old, which was deemed old enough to know what she was doing. The Master's defence barrister tried to make out that the girl seduced him and that he was only a man of "flesh and blood", whatever that is supposed to mean. They called her a "Jezebel".' Cook laughed in disbelief. 'As if that poor little thing would try to come between the Master and his wife! That's as much as I know, any road.'

'But that wasn't true, Tilly was an innocent young girl.'

'Aw Megan, I know that . . .' Cook leant forward in her chair and softly stroked Megan's face. She tucked a stray piece of hair that had fallen from her mop cap behind her ear. 'But of course the members of the jury wouldn't know Tilly's character. And the Master would have put on a good show of being a God-fearing, good husband, I'm sure.'

'And of course, Tilly isn't here to tell the tale . . .' Megan said sadly.

'Try not to be downhearted, gal,' Cook said. 'At least some good has come out of it. We have the Bakers here now, and they're quite nice and have shaken things up. They appear to be keeping an eye on old Hamilton, too, and Bill the porter has been taken back on, so that has to be good.'

Megan forced a smile, but deep down she knew in her heart an injustice had been done. At the end of the day, more than one soul had died: there was the Master's unborn child to think of, too.

Megan returned to the tea room with her shopping. She had been gone a long while, but it was as if Mrs Mathias could sense something was up, as she ordered her to remove her shawl and sit in the back room while she finished dealing with the customers. The shop was quite busy and that made Megan feel guilty, but she needed time to compose herself.

When trade had died down, Mrs Mathias joined her for a chat. After Megan told her about what she had learned that day, she was outraged.

'Why, I never! That brute has only gone and got away with it . . . and that poor young girl, pregnant with his child. Megan,

I have this to say to you: I don't want you ever to return to that place again. I'm going to have a word with the new workhouse Master about keeping you with me a while longer yet.'

Megan was up on her feet in an instant, wrapping her arms around the woman's neck. She inhaled the soft rose-petal perfume Mrs Mathias always wore, and it comforted her so, as it reminded her of her mother. 'Oh, I am more than pleased, Mrs Mathias. I am overjoyed.' Tears were streaming down her face but she was smiling at the same time. She felt Mrs Mathias's soft powdery cheek against her own and at that moment she realised just how much she really cared about her welfare.

'Hang on now, *cariad*,' she said, breaking away from the embrace to speak plainly with Megan. She obviously didn't want to raise her hopes too much. 'I'll need to get it from the horse's mouth first. They'll probably have to put it to the Guardians.'

Megan understood that, though she couldn't help her excitement from showing. Apart from going to visit her friends, she never wanted to go back into that place, not ever.

This was going to be the best Christmas ever. She just knew it.

Mrs Mathias tapped the side of her own nose with her index finger. 'Just leave it all to me, Megan. I'll have a word with Mr Baker for you. He sounds a lot nicer than old Pomfrey. I'll do my very best for you, child. You can count on that.'

Chapter Thirteen

It was lovely not having to push the cart up and down the town and not having to stand around for hours at a time serving customers in the ice-cold conditions. Poor Bessie now had that particular task, but to be fair to Mrs Mathias, she had knitted the girl warm gloves, a scarf and a beret to protect her from the weather. She also made sure Bessie could call into the tea room for a hot cuppa and something to eat twice a day, while someone else manned the stall.

Mrs Mathias had begun to treat Megan very much like a daughter now. She'd only ever had sons and poor Eli was looking frailer by the day. Megan feared for his health, though she didn't think Mrs Mathias noticed her own son's condition.

They were still waiting to hear back from the Board of Guardians about Megan's adoption – it seemed that they wouldn't know anything now until after the New Year. Every night, Megan prayed that the Board would allow the adoption to go ahead.

One morning, Megan awoke and went downstairs to discover that Eli was not at the breakfast table as he usually would be, following his night shift at the bakery. Mrs Mathias was at the stove, stirring a big pan of porridge.

'Run along to the bakery, Megan, and check what soft lad is doing,' she had instructed, a hint of irritation in her voice. They both needed to get to the tea room and didn't really have time to be worrying about Eli.

Megan walked outside into the street and an ice-cold blast of air hit her face. She almost slipped on the pavement, it was that icy.

The bakery, which was located at the end of the street, was a low, red brick building with high windows. It appeared to be closed, but on further inspection, she managed to push on the metal latch which unlocked the door. That was odd. Eli always went straight home for his breakfast. Why would he still be here? She pushed open the heavy door and looked around the dark, deserted building.

'Eli!' she called, her voice echoing into the dark. 'Eli! Are you still here?' The echoing was quite eerie and she shivered from top to toe.

There was no answer. Looking around the place, she could see that all the wooden pallets that were normally loaded with bread had gone, so she knew they were out for delivery. But why would Eli leave the place unlocked?

She was about to turn away to leave when she tripped over

something on the floor. Falling forward, she caught herself on a counter and gazed downwards. She felt bitter bile rise up to her throat as she realised it was Eli. He was lying on the floor, an empty whisky bottle beside him. She knelt down and felt his cold body. He was still breathing but it was very shallow and his skin was a pale grey.

'Eli,' she said, tapping his face with her fingertips. There was no response, so she threw her shawl over him and flew back up the street to Mrs Mathias's house.

'Come quick!' she shouted. 'It's Eli. He's lying on the floor at the bakery and he's barely breathing!'

By the time they had got back to the bakery, Eli was sitting up on his haunches, gazing around. 'Where am I?' he asked.

'You're all right now, soft lad,' Mrs Mathias said, and knelt down so she could hold his head to her bosom, rocking him back and forth as if he were a young infant. When they thought he could handle it, they helped Eli onto his feet, who was now trembling from head to toe. It took them some time to get him back to the house. He was unsteady on his feet so they had to stop and allow him to sit on windowsills and low stone walls. Megan thought too late to run back to the bakery and fetch her handcart to push him in, but they were almost home.

Once inside the house, they sat Eli down on a kitchen chair. 'We'll have to leave the shop shut today,' Peggy told Megan between breaths. It had taken it out of her helping Eli, who'd been a dead weight as he'd clung on to both of them the short distance from the bakery. 'Go and see if you can find Dr Richards – he lives opposite the parish church – and send him here. Tell him I'll pay him well for his time.' She handed Megan a few coins.

Before leaving, Megan called Peggy to one side. 'I found a bottle of whisky beside him at the bakery. I think you should know . . .'

Peggy blinked several times. 'What are you suggesting, Megan?'

'It's not the first time. I noticed him hiding something under the bed once and I later went to check what it was. I'd become suspicious as he's so often falling asleep.'

'But that doesn't mean to say he's a drunk, Megan. You know how tiring his job is.'

'It was a bottle of whisky I found then too, Mrs Mathias, hidden under his bed.'

Mrs Mathias shook her head sadly as Megan's words began to sink in. It was all starting to make sense now. Poor Eli couldn't cope with the strains of life.

Megan retrieved her thickest shawl from behind the kitchen door. 'If I find the doctor and send him here, would you like me to open the tea room on my own? I know what to do,' she said.

'There's a good girl, you are. Yes, please. You rush and send the doctor here, Megan, right away. I know Eli's colour is coming back but he's coughing and wheezing a bit.'

Peggy was right. Eli was looking more himself and was even asking for his breakfast, but he needed to be checked out.

'Don't worry, Mrs Mathias. I'll go right away.'

Peggy made her son a cup of tea whilst they waited for Megan to send the doctor there.

Megan ran as fast as her legs could carry her to the doctor's house, which was a large double-fronted house at the lower end of the town. His housekeeper took her to the doctor, whose surgery hadn't even begun for the day, so he said he'd go to the house right away.

Megan gave the doctor the address, then made her way to the tea room, unlocking the door with the thick brass key and locking herself inside before anyone arrived – just as she'd seen Peggy do on many an occasion.

A delivery had been made earlier at the back of the shop so she brought it in, carrying it from the lightweight wooden pallets, and laid it out in the kitchen. Then she checked all the tables were properly laid out, throwing away any dead flowers and replacing them with the red poinsettia plants, which made a nice festive change. Finally, she put on a couple of kettles to boil before the first customers arrived – some just called to purchase an assortment of cakes to take away with them, whereas others stopped to take tea, and she needed to make sure there was a brew on for the first customers.

As expected, there was already a handful of people waiting outside as she opened the tea-room door. There were a pair of sisters who usually liked to come to the tea room as a treat before they began their shopping in the town. They were elderly and unmarried – Clara and Isabella – and Peggy said they were very set in their ways. Why they'd never married puzzled Megan, but after questioning Mrs Mathias she'd discovered that they'd had to look after their ailing mother and that had always come first. Megan could see that in their day they would have been beautiful young women: both had high cheekbones and eyes of the brightest blue, though their hair, which they wore piled up on their heads beneath their bonnets, was silver grey. Proper ladies they were, and all, just like Miss O'Hara.

As the day passed, the shop filled up with customers and it became harder to cope taking orders as well as serving everyone. Usually she and Peggy worked well together as a team, but it was a lot of work for one person, particularly as there were cups and saucers that needed washing too.

Luckily Griff turned up with a big smile on his face. 'Where's the missus?' he asked, as he found Megan carrying a plate of fancies over to a table in the corner.

'She's had to stay at home to look after Eli, so I'm on my own today.'

'I can help you if you like. I'll clear those tables away for you.'

'Thanks,' Megan said, relieved. 'I know you can't read and write much at the moment, but you've got a good memory.

Could you remember what people want to eat when they order?' She gazed at him in expectation.

'Course I can. I'll take orders for you and clear tables,' he said brightly.

'I can't pay you but I'll give you a glass of lemonade and some cakes to take home for you and your uncle.'

'He'd like that.' Griff rubbed his nose.

'Well, before you start, go and wash your hands with soap and water in the bosh in the kitchen.'

'But my hands are clean!' Griff protested.

Megan placed her hands on her hips. 'Mrs Mathias says even if hands look clean, sometimes they're not. So before we serve food we always wash our hands. It's the rule of the tea room. We don't want to give people bad stomachs, do we now?'

Sheepishly he nodded, and within a few moments she heard the splashing of water in the bosh. She smiled to herself. Griff was a good lad but sometimes she forgot that he had been brought up differently to her and she had to teach him certain manners.

And so Griff took orders and cleared tables while Megan made cups of tea and dished up cakes. At the end of the shift, after the last customers had left and she'd locked up, they sat in the back room drinking glasses of lemonade.

'What's the matter with Eli?' Griff said, before taking a sip of the cool liquid that Peggy kept in the pantry. It had been so busy they hadn't been able to talk at all during the day.

'I found him collapsed in the bakery this morning. He looked awful, to tell you the truth. It looks like he's drinking whisky – a lot of it. There was an empty bottle beside him when I found him. I had to get the doctor before I came here. I have no idea what's wrong with him, whether it's the whisky or something else. We should know by the time I get back.'

Griff shook his head. 'Well, I hope he doesn't go the same way as my uncle—'

'Did I tell you Mrs Mathias has applied to adopt me?' Megan said, trying to change the subject. Griff always got so sad when he spoke of his uncle.

Griff nodded. 'Yes, you did. Has she heard any more?'

'Nope. There will be a Board of Guardians meeting about it in January. I hope they'll allow it. All my other siblings have already left the workhouse. If my mam knew, she'd be so happy to know we'd all made better lives. I do miss her ever so much.'

'One day, Megan, you and I shall have a tea room like this,' Griff said, taking her hand. 'We'll own several of them in the town and people will come from near and far, ain't that the truth!' He cocked a cheeky grin.

Though he was looking a lot cleaner since he'd started working at the Temperance Hall, she still worried about that uncle of his leaving him alone a lot of the time.

Griff walked Megan back to Plymouth Street and waited outside Mrs Mathias's house, hands dug deep in his pockets, while Megan went to check on Eli's condition. She returned a few moments later.

'Mrs Mathias says you're to come inside, Griff. Eli seems all right at the moment. The doctor thinks it's working with the dust from the flour that's causing him lung problems.'

There'd been no mention about the whisky bottle, and Megan guessed the woman hadn't told the doctor, for the shame of it all.

As Christmas approached, Megan wondered what she should get for Griff as a suitable present. She wanted to get him something special with the money she'd earned working at the tea room. It wasn't a great deal of money but for once in her life she was earning. She'd spied a penny whistle in a shop window in the town and thought it might be an idea for him to learn how to play it – it might come in useful for his act.

She purchased a pretty pearl brooch for Mrs Mathias. They weren't real pearls – she'd need to own her own tea room before she could afford those – but it was a lovely piece of costume jewellery, something she'd loved to have bought for her own mother. Thinking about her mother reminded her it was the first ever Christmas without her, which gave her an empty feeling inside the pit of her stomach. Last year, on Christmas Day, the whole family had been allowed to be together at the workhouse for a quick visit. It was a joyful day and the Board of

Guardians had supplied the inmates with a special feast. For once they ate as well as the Master, Matron and everyone else.

Megan wondered what she could buy for her brothers and sisters. Peggy had suggested she sewed the girls a rag doll each. She had plenty of leftover material in her work basket — cottons and even a little silk — to make the dolls a pretty dress each. She purchased a whip and top for Alfie, a wooden sailing boat for Harry, and for Tom she knitted a warm scarf to wear on his delivery round. The only other person to buy for was Eli, and she hadn't a clue what to get for him. He was still on bed rest. Peggy had employed someone else to take over his duties for the time being. She did worry about him, though. And despite keeping away from the bakery as the doctor had recommended, he still coughed and wheezed on a daily basis, his complexion still pale and sickly-looking. Peggy said that by January she had no doubts he'd be fit and robust again. Eli had never looked robust to Megan, not even before his sickness.

But despite her sadness for her mother and her worry for Eli, it really thrilled her to see people coming into the tea room carrying gaily wrapped presents, their cheeks pinched and flushed from the frosty air. She'd hear them chatter about their plans for the festive season and loved their stories.

'Yes, Peggy, we'll be spending Christmas with Alf's folk in the country. They came to us last year, so it's our turn to go there this year. It won't be such hard work for me . . .'

'Ooh, Peggy, I've bought my little Winifred this beautiful china doll. When I saw it in Edmonds' Bazaar I knew she just had to have it. Won't her face be a picture on the big day itself?'

'Could we order a couple extra of your miniature Christmas cakes to have with our tea, Peggy? They look ever so nice and I'd love to take a few home to my Harry. He has such a sweet tooth . . .'

As Megan went about her business at the tea room, she noticed Peggy had a strange gleam in her eye and kept humming to herself. That was odd. She seemed so pleased with herself, but that was nice as she had worried so much about Eli of late. At the end of the working day, when it had grown dark and the last customers departed, wishing them both a Merry Christmas as they left, Peggy locked the door and sat at one of the tables.

'Megan, please sit down, I have something to tell you.'

Megan drew out a chair and sat opposite her. She wasn't usually allowed to sit at one of the customer tables with its pretty white tablecloth and vase with flowers, so this was a first for her.

Peggy had donned her gold-rimmed specs. Megan watched as the woman smiled broadly. Then she dipped her hand into her pinafore pocket and extracted a letter, which she opened out onto the table. She smoothed it with the palm of her hand. It was written in elegant copperplate handwriting.

'Do you know what this is?' Peggy asked.

Megan shrugged. 'A letter from The Lady in London?'

'No, Megan. It's a letter from the Board of Guardians at the workhouse . . . Shall I read it to you?'

Megan nodded. She had a lump in her throat and she felt like the air had been squeezed out of her lungs. Peggy began:

Dear Mrs Mathias,

In response to your request to become the sole guardian of one Megan Hopkins, formerly of St Tydfil's Union Workhouse, we would like to inform you that a meeting was held on Wednesday last in regards to the matter. The request was put before the Board of Guardians, who decided it would be in the child's best welfare that you become the sole guardian. An application for adoption of the child can now proceed—

Mrs Mathias did not need to read on any further: Megan had all the information she needed. She sat there and opened her mouth to speak but no words came out.

'Don't you see, Megan? You shall not have to return to the workhouse ever again! Now you can live me with permanently!'

As Megan digested the information, a tear trickled down her cheek. 'Oh, Mrs Mathias, I am just so happy. I realised you'd made an application to adopt me but I didn't think it would ever go ahead! I thought somehow it might never happen for me.' She wiped her cheek with the side of her apron. 'It's such a wonderful surprise, thank you, thank you! I've never been so happy in all my life. I can't believe you want to adopt me!'

'Now, now, Megan,' Mrs Mathias said, her warm brown eyes twinkling with kindness. 'Haven't I always said you are like a daughter to me, and now you shall be so. It's all official! I can call you my daughter at last.'

Peggy was on her feet and then cuddled Megan as they both wept tears of joy. This was going to be the best Christmas ever, even better than the year Father Christmas had brought her a wooden cradle for her favourite doll.

Chapter Fourteen

Megan was so excited to tell Griff of her good fortune. She was dying to tell him the good news about the adoption. It had been a good few days since she'd last seen him, and with it being so busy at the tea room she hadn't had the time to seek him out. She'd been concerned about his absence, though. He'd been practising hard at the Temperance Hall for a special show during Christmas week, so of course he must be very busy, but he hadn't called into the shop or to Mrs Mathias's house for days, which was most unlike him.

She'd vowed to herself that if he did not call by today, she would seek him out herself – even though she hated setting foot in the China district. Young ladies had set foot in that place never to return home again; Peggy had told her so on many occasions. She said there were bad people there who ran gangs of pickpockets and prostitutes. Megan still wasn't sure what a prostitute was, mind you, though she had a fair idea that maybe the man who had accosted her that time had something to do with it.

Florrie at the Vulcan said she hadn't seen Griff or his uncle for days either. Megan had had to seriously plead with her before she relented and asked Fred the landlord if she could nip out for a few minutes to take Megan to Griff's house. The landlord had shook his head at first, but eventually, reluctantly agreed. Florrie seemed to have a knack for getting around the man. But when they approached the house, all was in darkness and there was no answer, despite Florrie knocking several times, even on the window.

Megan felt tears prick the back of her eyes.

Florrie peered through the dust-covered window. 'Sorry, beaut, can't see a thing in there. It's darker than down a coal pit.' Then, on seeing Megan's tears: 'Aw, don't dwell on it, *cariad*. Go and see if Griff's rehearsing at the Temperance Hall.'

That seemed a good idea, so after brightening a little, Megan thanked the girl and made off for the theatre. But when she arrived she was in for a shock.

'Griff, the boy?' The cleaner said, scowling at Megan as she flicked her grey duster. She tossed it on a counter, then wiped her hands on her already grubby pinafore. 'He ain't 'ere any more. The gossip has it that uncle of his has taken him orf to London to get him on the stage there. He's seen rich pickings in his nephew. Griff's a good lad, mind you. I feel sorry for him if he's been forced.'

Megan tried to speak but was mute, then she forced out the words, 'Do you know which London theatre they might have gone to?'

The cleaner shook her head. 'No, first the stage manager knew of it was when the lad failed to show up for rehearsal the day before yesterday. One of the other cleaners mentioned that Griff had told her he feared his uncle would take him away. She noticed he was full of bruises as if the boy had been beaten or something. The dog, that Scamp, he seemed to be more nervous than usual. Did his business on the stage. Ruby – the other cleaner – weren't happy about that. She was the one who had to clean up the mess. But I told her the dog didn't usually do that kind of thing. He must have been really scared about something. Griff, bless his heart, was so careful to make sure the dog was walked before he went on stage to avoid that sort of thing. Something must have gone wrong for the lad.'

Megan lowered her head, fearing she might cry in front of the woman. 'I wish I could find him . . .' She sniffed.

''Ere now, don't be letting on or you'll 'ave me at it an' all. Let's hope that uncle of his sees the error of his ways and brings him back soon,' the woman said softly. Megan guessed that Ruby must have been the cleaner she'd seen that first day she'd met Griff, the one who had been so rude to her.

She thanked the woman and left the Temperance Hall downhearted. What if she were never to see Griff again? She simply could not bear that.

Griff trailed behind his uncle along the streets of London.

'C'mon, boy, hurry up. There are a few more theatres and music halls I want to try before tonight!' His uncle's voice was gruff and rasping. He felt so sad being made to go to London; he was quite happy in Merthyr Tydfil. But his uncle thought the streets of London were paved with gold and, given Griff's recent success on the stage, he saw what he could make out of him.

It wasn't just that Griff missed Merthyr. He hadn't had the time to even explain to Megan or say goodbye. Scamp had also been returned to the landlord at the Vulcan Inn. They couldn't take him with them, and his uncle had said they'd easily buy a new dog in London. He went as far as to say that there were so many strays around the place, it would cost them nothing at all. That was his uncle all over, always thinking of the pennies.

But Griff didn't want another dog. He wanted Scamp. It broke his heart to be parted from him. Uncle Berwyn promised that some day, after they'd made their fortune, they'd return to Merthyr Tydfil. He'd even tidied himself up and had been off the drink for a few days, which was most unusual for him. Griff wondered what had caused his sudden change once again, but didn't dare ask. It couldn't be a woman again, could it?

At heart he liked to think his uncle was a good man, but when Griff had refused to go to London, his uncle had beat him black and blue. He still had the bruises to show for it, though they had now turned a yellowy green. It still hurt when he tried to sit down, but at least he hadn't been forced to go into the workhouse and he was thankful for that.

Berwyn had suffered a blow to the head a month ago when he was set upon by two men in the town. His behaviour seemed to have got worse since. He'd said they'd robbed him blind, but Florrie had told Griff it was his uncle who had owed them money. He wondered if that was another reason why they had come to London – to escape the moneylenders.

The lump on his uncle's head from the beating had lasted for a couple of weeks as had the two black eyes. He'd refused to leave the house, but the good thing about it was that he'd sobered up as he was keeping away from the taverns in the town.

In London they were turned away from every music hall and theatre his uncle tried. It seemed no one was interested in a 'kid and a dog' show, and where was the dog anyhow?

That night, his uncle paid for them to lodge at a rundown hovel near some of the theatres. The house itself was four storeys high and stank to high heaven of gin and sweat. Men in tattered clothing who looked like they hadn't had a wash in days came and went; women in brightly coloured dresses and smelling of strong scent seemed to come and go, too. At night, it was hard to sleep as he heard the sound of shouts and yells, arguments, and people singing. He even heard of it being referred to as a 'dosshouse' by one man.

The people around him spoke with funny accents, too. It was hard to understand what they said and they couldn't seem to understand him either. Some people even thought he was speaking in Welsh.

The following day, after a communal breakfast of dry bread and dripping, and tin mugs of weak tea, Uncle Berwyn and Griff made their way around the theatres and music halls once again.

'What can the boy do?' one stage manager at the Palace asked his uncle, after he had blagged his way into the man's office.

'He can sing and dance – he had a sell-out show in Merthyr Tydfil with his dog.'

The man raised his eyebrows, then twiddled his moustache. 'We might have something for him here, if you have the dog?'

'Sorry, we don't,' Uncle Berwyn said soberly. 'The dog died under the wheels of a horse and cart just last week . . .' Then on cue, as his uncle had instructed, Griff began to sob. He was so sad anyhow it wasn't hard to do.

'Now, lad,' the stage manager said. He had a different

accent to other people in the area Griff had come across. 'No need to cry. Perhaps you can perform your act for me without the dog? Singing and dancing?'

Griff wiped away a tear on the sleeve of his jacket, then was led on stage. A pianist played some sheet music his uncle had brought along. It was a sad song that Griff had rehearsed over and over again, called 'I'm Only a Boy'.

The stage manager, whose name was Mr Gittings, beamed once he heard Griff's melodic voice. No one else had given him a chance so far. 'Wonderful,' he enthused. 'I can see something like this going down a storm here. He's just what we need. Our last child star had to leave . . .' He whispered something unintelligible to his uncle, and Uncle Berwyn nodded soberly.

'Tragic,' he muttered.

After it was decided that Griff be taken on a trial basis, his uncle took him for a slap-up lunch at a little chophouse down the road. Griff was just finishing off his meat pie and potatoes, followed by apple tart and custard, when his uncle's voice took on a serious tone. 'There's someone I'd like you to meet a bit later,' he said. 'Her name is Bronwen and she's also from Merthyr Tydfil. Bronwen and I are going to marry here in London. You might have noticed, I've smartened myself up lately and kept off the drink?'

Griff nodded, then put down his spoon, even though he badly wanted to eat his apple tart. 'Yes . . .' This was the lady who'd left her handkerchief at his uncle's house, he presumed.

The one he'd heard that time upstairs when he'd eaten that currant bun that had been meant for her. She must be something special to make such a big impact on his uncle. And the reason he'd kept off the drink all this time too.

'Well, that woman has been the making of me. I met her a few weeks ago in the Vulcan Inn. She's a cleaner there, just lost her husband, and she's good for me.' He smiled and winked at Griff, then threw him a silver sixpence. 'Keep that, you've worked hard today and you've got a lot more work in front of you later. You remember where the digs are?'

Griff nodded. 'Yes, I do.'

'Well, I'm meeting Bronwen from the train and we'll be spending the rest of the day together. That should buy you some more food, I'll see you tonight. I'll settle the bill on the way out. Stay where you are for now.'

And with that, his uncle stood and headed for the door, leaving Griff speechless, realising he was all alone in London for the next few hours.

When Megan returned home, she told Peggy what she'd been informed earlier that day: that Griff had been taken to London by his uncle.

'Oh, that's terrible, Megan!' she said, bringing her hands to her face in horror.

If Megan had to, she'd travel to London to find him

herself, she thought. Couldn't be that hard, could it? She had her savings from working at the tea room.

As if reading her thoughts, Peggy patted Megan's hand. 'Now don't you be having any strange thoughts about running off to London to find Griff – it's a big place and there are some bad people there, just like there are in China, *cariad*.'

Megan shivered. 'I won't,' she said.

'There's a good girl. But what can we do?'

Megan seated herself at the kitchen table. 'The only thing I can think of is to send a letter to Miss O'Hara. She's in London.'

'Yes, and she's moving in those circles too,' Peggy said thoughtfully.

Megan had no idea what Peggy meant about 'moving in those circles' but Peggy sounded hopeful, so it must be good. As if noticing Megan's confusion, Peggy said, 'It means Kathleen is living in that sort of world, working on stage. She might have contacts or actually bump into Griff himself.'

Megan smiled. So there was hope after all.

'Come on,' Peggy said. 'I've got some nice beef stew and dumplings for our supper. I'll pour you a glass of milk and bring you pen and paper so you can write to Miss O'Hara. I'm sure you owe her a letter, don't you?'

Megan realised that Peggy was right, she'd been so busy she hadn't replied to Kathleen's last correspondence. She'd sent Megan a postcard of herself at the music hall – very pretty she looked, too – where finally she'd been able to reveal the special person she'd performed in front of. It was Queen Victoria herself, no less! Imagine that, Megan thought. The Queen of Great Britain. How amazing.

And Megan also had good news to share with Kathleen. She'd been so busy she hadn't found the chance to tell her how the Board of Guardians had agreed to make Mrs Mathias her guardian.

Days took a similar path for Griff: in the morning they would eat in the chophouse, and then his uncle would give him a sixpence or a few pennies to fend for himself for the rest of the day. But at least he had his rehearsals at the music hall to keep him busy. His uncle was besotted by 'the lovely Bronwen', as he called her, but Griff had yet to meet the woman. They kept to themselves, and Griff was glad of it.

So it was with some surprise that Griff found his uncle stood with the woman outside the music hall one day. She had dirty-blonde-coloured hair – his uncle had described it as honey blonde, but to Griff it wasn't a nice colour at all – and she had a brassy look about her: she wore thick dark red lipstick and rouge, and she smelled strongly of rose-petal perfume. Her dress was cut a little too low for what would be considered decent back home in Merthyr.

'Hello, Griff, we've come to take you to your new home!' Uncle Berwyn said proudly. 'This is my Bronwen!'

Griff forced a smile. He'd taken an instant dislike to the woman and he didn't know why.

'What a cute little boy!' she squealed, removing Griff's flat cap and then ruffling his hair. She pinched his cheeks so hard it hurt.

He fisted his hands at his side, disliking her even more. 'New home?' Griff asked, once she'd stepped out of the way, giving him some breathing space.

'I'm renting rooms for us. We can't live in that fleapit in Windsor Road now, not after you being a performer on stage. It's not good enough, lad.'

'Yes, and I'm coming to live with you, Griff.' Bronwen linked her arm with Berwyn's and snuggled into him. His uncle gazed at her with such longing in his eyes that Griff felt like a gooseberry.

'But you're not even married to one another!' Griff said in astonishment, surprised at how, after months of grief, his uncle had so conveniently forgotten his deceased wife and child.

His uncle's face reddened. 'Now, there'll be no need for that, Griff. In London, it doesn't matter if we're married or not as yet. No one knows us here like they do in Merthyr Tydfil. If anyone asks you are to say I'm your father and Bronwen here is your mother. Understood?'

'I can't tell a lie!' Griff said, blinking in astonishment.

'Well you'd better do or you'll feel the back of my hand!'

his uncle growled, causing Griff to shiver with fear. His uncle held his hand inches away from Griff's head.

'Berry Bear, there's no need for that. Griff will behave himself, won't you?' Bronwen said in a sickly sweet tone. His uncle dropped his hand to his side as if he thought better of what he'd been about to do to Griff.

Berry Bear indeed!

Griff couldn't understand why his uncle was acting so smarmy around this woman, who looked like a common tart to him – she wouldn't have looked out of place on the streets of China back home.

He just nodded.

'Good lad, you know it makes sense.' His uncle softened his tone. 'Now we're off home, so I can show you our new lodging rooms. Then we'll dine out!'

Griff shuffled along behind the pair of them, who each seemed amused in the other's company. In the past, although his uncle hadn't been around that much – when he was sober, at least – Griff had commanded his attention, but now with Bronwen on the scene, he didn't get as much as a look-in.

They arrived outside the tall, imposing building. It was on a tree-lined street and was a step up from the dosshouse on Windsor Road, though still a little shabby on the outside.

Inside, though, it did not smell of stale sweat, urine, tobacco or gin, like the other had, and Griff was immediately relieved.

His uncle showed him around the new lodgings proudly;

there was a bedroom with a double bed, dressing table and wardrobe, a small kitchen and larger living room.

Griff removed his cap and scratched his head. 'But where do I sleep?' he asked.

'There's a little cubbyhole used for storage in that alcove by there,' his uncle explained. 'It's in the kitchen near the stove, so it will be nice and warm for you. Bronwen has put a nice soft pallet, pillow and blanket for you there.'

Griff opened his mouth and closed it again. It looked to him like somewhere a servant would sleep – or a dog.

'Don't worry, Griff,' Bronwen explained. 'It will be comfortable for you and I've bought some curtains cheap at the market which I'll hang up to give you some privacy.'

Griff glowered at her, realising she was trying to be nice to him. But if she hadn't come along, at least he'd have had a bed for the night.

'I've changed my mind about taking you out for supper,' his uncle said quite suddenly. 'Bronwen made some stew earlier. You can have some of that with a crust of bread while me and her go out for the evening, you ungrateful little scallywag!'

Griff didn't know if he was imagining it or not but he thought he detected a look of pity in the woman's eyes.

It was well past midnight before the duo returned, sounding very merry, clinking glasses as if they'd brought their drinks home with them and sounding very lovey-dovey with one another. With some relief, Griff heard their bedroom door close shut.

It wasn't as bad in the alcove as he first thought. It was quite comfortable and he could read using a candle, as long as he didn't hold it too near the curtains and ensured it was safely snuffed out for the night. He tried to reassure himself that he needed to count his blessings, just like Mrs Mathias had told him the last time he visited.

But the thought of Mrs Mathias just turned his thoughts to Megan. How he missed her . . .

Chapter Fifteen

On Christmas Eve, Megan received a beautiful festive postcard from Kathleen saying she would indeed keep a lookout
for Griff, but as yet had not encountered him. She wished
Megan and her family a Merry Christmas and a Happy New
Year and said she was thrilled to hear Megan's good news. On
the front of the postcard was a picture of a large Christmas
tree that was nicely decorated and beside a roaring fire, with a
little black cat curled up by the fireplace. Megan smiled as she
placed the postcard on the mantelpiece. She had earlier helped
Peggy to decorate the living room. There was a holly wreath
on the wall and a small fir tree in the corner, with a silver star
atop and real white miniature candles in their holders adorn-
ing it. Mrs Mathias had told her, though, to be careful and not
leave the tree unattended if lit, and definitely not to leave the
house without snuffing out all the candles first.

Although she was looking forward to Christmas, there was
a distinct heaviness in Megan's heart. She missed Griff like

mad and not knowing exactly where he was or how he was doing hurt her, casting a cloud over the celebrations.

Peggy's tea room was closed for the next two days, so she should have felt good about having time off from work, but she liked the busyness of work as it allowed her not to think.

She'd been invited to the Evanses' home for Boxing Day tea and all her brothers and sisters would be there too, so at least that was something to look forward to. Mrs Mathias and Eli were invited too, but Eli was still a little weak and frail, and Peggy said he needed looking after, so they declined the invitation.

If only she were with Griff right now, she knew all would be well.

Griff awoke to the sounds of grunts and groans coming from the bedroom next door. His heart beat nineteen to the dozen. For a moment, he could not get his bearings; it was dark and – what was that in front of him? He pushed some heavy material out of the way, only to remember he'd been asleep in the small alcove and the material was the curtains Bronwen had made for him. Maybe the woman wasn't so bad after all, but who was that making the grunting noise? Was his uncle ill or something? He heard the sound of mattress springs squeaking steadily. Thinking he'd better check it out, he scrambled out from the alcove and stood on his feet. The scullery kitchen was dark and he could barely make out the shapes of the counters.

'Uncle!' he shouted. Then there was a deadly silence and the sound of something heavy falling to the floor. In the darkness, he made his way to the door, stumbling over a chair and the edge of the pine table as he went. He'd made it to the landing, where a thin sliver of moonlight shone in through a high window, allowing him to see more clearly. He was about to touch the doorknob to his uncle's room when he felt a hand clamp down heavily on his shoulder.

'What have we here then?' a man's gruff voice said, with a strong cockney accent. In his hand he held a lantern which shone in Griff's face, causing him to blink profusely.

'Please, sir,' Griff said. 'I heard some funny noises, so I was going to my uncle's room to check all was well.'

The man grabbed Griff in an armlock around his neck, which gave him difficulty breathing. 'A likely story, I can tell. You were trying to rob the people in these lodging rooms.'

'N–n–no. You've got it wrong, sir. My uncle lives in the rooms on this floor. Knock the door and ask him.'

The man pushed Griff so roughly that he fell to the floor, then he hammered on his uncle's door.

'What's all the palaver?' his uncle shouted as he opened the door. Bronwen stood behind him in a flimsy nightgown.

The man held the lantern near Berwyn's face, making flickering shadows dance upon his skin which made him look quite spooky, like a ghoul Griff had once seen in a story book. His hair was messed up, his eyes widened with puzzlement – he was clearly wondering who could be knocking on his bedroom door at this ungodly hour.

'This young lad was wandering about on the landing. He says he's with you. You know you're only paying rent for two. If you're hiding him here you shall have to pay extra.'

Berwyn shook his head slowly. 'I've never seen that lad before in my life, Mr Connor.'

'I thought as much. Ain't no room for waifs and strays in my building. I'll whip his backside and then toss him out onto the street. He's lucky I haven't decided to call the rozzers on him!'

Griff could not believe his ears. His own uncle was denying his very existence. Surely Bronwen would vouch for him? But she stood there shaking her head, her ample bosom spilling out from beneath her low-cut night gown.

'But I'm not a thief,' Griff said, as he scrambled to his feet. 'You can ask the stage manager at the theatre where I work.'

'A likely story!' The man growled. 'A liar as well as a thief!' Then he proceeded to kick Griff down the stairs. 'I'm going to take my belt off to you, lad. You ought to be in a reform school!'

Fearing worse punishment, Griff made for the door and turned the latch. Thankfully, it opened first try and he slipped out on the freezing cold street. What a situation he should find himself in, he thought! Christmas morning, running for his life.

He had no idea where he was running to, but eventually found himself back at the theatre. He hid at the back door where there was storage room for crates, props and all sorts. He bundled himself in there beneath some old hessian sacks to try to keep himself covered up. At least they provided some warmth against the biting cold air.

He had just drifted off to sleep when suddenly he felt something scamper over him. Opening his eyes, the beady black eyes of a small rat stared back at him. He screamed and the rat ran off as if frightened too, disappearing behind one of the crates. Even in the confines of this store cupboard he felt unsafe. There would be no one at the theatre until tomorrow for the next performance – Christmas Day was the one day of the year it closed.

Tomorrow, he would speak to the stage manager before his uncle got the chance to turn up and demand payment for Griff's work. Until then, he just needed to figure out where to sleep and how to keep warm. He was only thankful he'd gone to bed fully clothed last night when he'd fallen asleep or else he'd be homeless, unclothed and bare foot.

Griff managed to find a stale crust of bread that someone had thrown out for the birds in the alleyway. It was filthy dirty, but he took his chances and ate it, he was so starving. Noticing a church open nearby for Christmas services, he yearned to go inside but felt he might be tossed out of there due to his shaggy appearance, so he stood near the doorway, removing his cap as people passed him on the step to enter the church. A gentleman in a top hat and long black coat threw a few pennies into Griff's cap, which took him by surprise. He'd never begged before, but if people were willing to salve their consciences at Christmas, so be it. Within a few minutes, he had quite a few coppers in his cap as well as a shiny silver sixpence.

He made his way across the street and found a pie shop that was open, despite it being Christmas Day. The woman who ran it introduced herself as Kitty Hollings and said she'd opened today to sell some old pies at cost price for the needy and destitute. Well, he was that, all right. He was blooming starving. With the money collected, he bought two meat and potato pies, deciding to keep one for later. He might not find anywhere else to eat and he doubted the shop would be open long, as Kitty herself would be having her own Christmas dinner. She was a portly woman with a kindly face that, going by her wrinkles and salt-and-pepper hair, meant she could tell a tale or two in life.

'What yer doing in these parts, darlin'?' she asked as she placed a jug of gravy down in front of him to go with the pie.

'I'm from a place called Merthyr Tydfil in Wales, missus . . .' Griff was starving and longed to get stuck into the pie, but didn't want to appear rude.

'So how come you ended up 'ere in the East End of London?'

'My uncle made me come here. I had an act at the music hall in Merthyr but he brought me here to perform on stage.'

'And my guess is you want to go back home?' She narrowed her eyes suspiciously. ''Ere, you're not telling tales, are you?'

'No, missus. It's the truth. My uncle got me a place on stage in London and he's got a girlfriend see, so got us lodgings in the area ... but last night I got kicked out by the landlord as my uncle hadn't paid for me to be there.'

'You poor thing, and your uncle didn't stand by you?'

Griff shook his head as his eyes began to fill with tears. 'No, missus. I spent the night sleeping in an old storeroom at the back of the theatre, getting trampled on by a filthy rat.'

'How comes you got money then?' She placed one hand on her hip.

'I stood outside the church down the road with me cap off and people started tossing me coins, so I came here to buy a couple of pies, one to eat right now and one for later.'

'You can keep yer money, lad. It's Christmas Day. Eat up both pies and I'll fetch you some plum pudding and custard for afters. I live over the shop and you can stay 'ere with me for the time being. You can work for your keep!'

Griff nodded eagerly. He immediately liked Kitty Hollings, she seemed a good sort.

*

Griff couldn't believe how he'd landed on his feet. He didn't mind working for Kitty at all. In fact, he quite enjoyed it. His first task was to get over to Baxter's, the butcher's shop, the following morning to ask for some scrag-ends of beef and chopped kidney for Mrs Hollings's pies. Kitty had entrusted him with a few silver florins to purchase the ingredients. He wouldn't have been so trusting of someone he didn't know, but that's the sort she was, so he wasn't about to let her down.

As he stood staring in disbelief at the silver coins in his hand, she ruffled his hair. 'Now get along with you, lad. No shirking around. I need those ingredients so I can get started on me baking. An' watch out for that uncle of yours.' He looked at her and could see the genuine concern in her eyes.

He nodded. 'Cor, thanks, missus.' For once, he felt free as a bird and it was all thanks to Kitty.

She reminded him of Mrs Mathias back in Merthyr. His thoughts turned to Megan and what she was doing for Christmas. He hoped she wasn't missing him too much. One day he'd get back to see her, he would. He had thought about writing her a letter but then thought she might worry too much, so maybe that could wait until he was back on his feet.

As he walked along the street he hummed the song he'd performed at the Temperance Hall. How he missed Scamp, too. He hadn't even got the chance to say goodbye to him before being dragged off to London. Well, at least Scamp had a permanent home at the pub and regular food in his belly. His owner had been nice enough to take him back, rather than just unleashing him out onto the street, as Griff suspected he might.

He booted a stone into the gutter and dug his hands deep into his pockets. He enjoyed the simple pleasure of touching the coins jangling there, even though he only had them for a short while. Now where was the butcher shop Kitty had mentioned?

He turned the corner to find himself on a cobbled street full of colourful shops. Some were closed as it was the Christmas season, but there were a few shoppers around with nicely wrapped packages in their arms. Last-minute purchases, he thought. There were well-dressed women in smart dresses and matching hats, fur-lined capes and hands kept warm in matching muffs; men in tailcoats and top hats walking arm-in-arm with loved ones. He passed one couple who had two small children ambling beside them. The little girl was so pretty, with ringlets in her blonde hair and pink chubby cheeks; she clutched her dolly for dear life and Griff guessed it was a special Christmas present. The boy, who was about his age, held a wooden sailboat in both hands. Their eyes shone with the magic of the season. What a lovely-looking family. He watched as the mother placed both hands on her children's shoulders and guided them inside a cake shop. How he yearned to belong to a family just like that one. There was an emptiness inside him that had yet to be filled.

He noticed a shop ahead where there were row upon row

of turkeys, chicken and geese strung up outside from the eaves, and on the long wooden table set before the window were several rabbits and pheasants. The smell was quite overpowering and he realised he'd reached the butcher's shop Kitty had spoken of. Now what was it she wanted? Some scrag-ends of beef and some kidneys for the pie fillings. She'd written it down on a piece of paper for him, so he'd show the butcher that. He looked up at the sign which was painted on a black board in white fancy lettering. His reading had vastly improved now since Megan had taught him so well and he hoped he wouldn't lose his newfound skills now she wasn't around.

'Alfred Baxter, purveyor of poultry and fine meats', the sign read. He didn't understand what the word 'purveyor' meant but nevertheless he stepped inside the shop, its black-and-white tiled floor scattered with sawdust.

There was a small queue gathered at the counter, so he waited his turn as he watched the large man serve the customers in front of him. The man had ruddy cheeks and slicked-back dark hair, and set about weighing various pieces of meat and poultry on his set of silver scales. He wrapped them up in sheets of brown paper and a covering of old newspaper, before tying up the packages carefully with string and placing them into the customers' baskets or under their arms.

When Griff finally reached the counter, the man said, 'Well, lad, I ain't seen you around these parts before.'

The way he'd been chatting so easily to the other people in

the queue, it appeared that he knew them all well and all their business.

'My name is Griff, sir. I'm staying with Kitty who owns the pie shop up the road. She wanted me to buy these ingredients.' Nervously he handed the note to the butcher.

The butcher peered at it and stroked his chin with his chubby hands. 'Ah, her usual order then. I'll tell you what I'll do, I'll sell her the same stuff for the same price but as it's Christmas and I'm in a good mood today, I'll throw in a couple of pig's trotters for the both of you, how does that sound?'

Griff nodded eagerly. He hadn't tasted trotters in ages. As he waited while Mr Baxter weighed the meat and wrapped it, he thought how kind the man was, and perhaps the reason he'd given him those trotters for free was because he'd taken pity on him as he looked so thin.

Griff handed the man all the money as he hadn't a clue how much it would be and he couldn't count all that well. The butcher gave him change as well as returning some of the original coins. He didn't know if he'd paid the correct price, but the man seemed kind and he guessed that Kitty trusted the man anyhow.

Mr Baxter handed him the well-wrapped package and he went on his way, calling behind himself, 'Thank you, Mr Baxter. We'll enjoy those trotters.'

'Get away with you, lad.' The butcher chuckled. 'Anyone

would think I was giving you the Crown bleedin' Jewels!' He stood in the doorway, arms folded, as he watched Griff walk along the street, now with a bit of a swagger as he was feeling quite at home in London, now he was away from his uncle.

The young lady who served him at the grocer's shop wasn't half as friendly as Mr Baxter. She seemed stuck-up, with her nose crinkling as if there were a bad smell under it. She thought she was a cut above him, but he didn't care. At least she didn't question him or act as if he were about to thieve something, and for that he was grateful. He ordered a sack of plain flour, packets of lard, suet and butter to be delivered within the hour to Kitty's pie shop. He watched as she dealt with his order and noted the address down with impeccable handwriting in a red ledger.

Except for Megan and Scamp back in Merthyr, his worries were over. He had a new job and a roof over his head with a very nice lady indeed and he couldn't wait to tell her about the gift from the butcher.

When he returned, Kitty gave him a good breakfast of porridge and toast, and even half of her kipper and a cup of tea. It was the best breakfast he'd ever had in his young life.

'Now, I think you'd better lie low around that theatre for a while in case your uncle or that harlot he's shacked up with show up and try to take you back with them,' she advised. 'They see you as a money-making machine, that's for sure. In fact, I'll go over there meself and see if I can get the stage manager to call here to see you.'

Griff blinked. He couldn't believe that a total stranger could be so kind to him, but then again, that's what Megan had once been, a total stranger, and look how she'd helped him.

Megan enjoyed her Boxing Day visit to the Evanses' household. It was good to see her brothers and sisters once again. They chatted and laughed and played parlour games that Mr Evans organised whilst Mrs Evans put the finishing touches to a trifle she'd made for the occasion.

Whilst everyone was busy chatting, Tom took his sister to one side. 'What's up, Megs?' he asked, with a concerned look in his eyes. 'Aren't you happy staying with Peggy?'

'Oh, yes, I really am,' she enthused. 'It's just that there's still no word from Griff and I'm worried sick about him.'

Tom's eyes clouded over and in hushed tones, so his younger siblings could not hear, he said, 'Trouble is, London is a big place and I think you'll have to accept the fact that you might never see him again . . .'

Tears welled up in her eyes, it was a thought she'd been unwilling to accept but now it felt like when her parents had died. The thought of the loss tore at her heart; it was a low-down pain that came from deep down in her stomach, a sort of emptiness that could never be truly filled.

'Come on, you lot!' Mrs Evans said heartily. 'Dinner is waiting to be served, get yourselves to the table for the dinner and if you eat it all up, I'll give you some of that trifle!' They didn't need asking twice. All of the children, including Megan herself, looked upon Mrs Evans as a surrogate aunt.

During the dinner Megan was preoccupied with thoughts of Griff. *I must find him again. Maybe somehow I can save up enough money to go to London? Or if not, maybe Mrs Mathias can give me some wages in advance. There has to be a way to find out where he is. He'd really love to be here with us right now, I know he would.*

Tom nudged her elbow as she moved a piece of meat around on the plate with her fork. She'd hardly been listening to all the merriment going on around her. 'A penny for them, Megan?'

She turned to face him with tears in her eyes. 'I'm just thinking about someone, that's all.'

He touched her hand. 'We'll have a talk about it on the way home.' Then, turning to Mrs Evans he said, 'I can't wait to try that trifle, Mrs Evans. It looks lovely.'

Mrs Evans beamed. It was obvious she loved feeding everyone up, especially her new surrogate family.

When they'd finished and Megan had helped with a pile of dirty dishes to be washed up, she put on her cloak, and then Tom walked her home to Plymouth Street.

'Now tell me,' Tom said as he walked down Twyn Hill, 'what was so upsetting earlier, Megan? I'm guessing it was something about Griff?' He'd stopped dead in his tracks causing her to pause too.

She huffed out a long breath. 'It's just I can't bear to think of what's happened to poor Griff. I really must find him again.'

Tom, who was often the voice of reason said, 'But London is a big place, Megan. How can you possibly find him? There are so many people living there, it will be like looking for a needle in a haystack.'

Megan realised her elder brother was speaking sense, but she couldn't let the feeling go. 'I know, I just feel so sorry for him and I know he would never have gone without saying goodbye to us all. He must have gone against his will. His uncle is a real nasty piece of work.'

'That's very likely, Megan. From what you've told me about Griff's uncle, he's a man without scruples. An immoral sort. I think the best you can hope for is that one day Griff will return to Merthyr of his own accord and come looking for you . . .'

Megan nodded and they both fell into step once more, walking the rest of the way in silence.

He left her at the door with a kiss to her cheek. 'Now don't you fret, Megan. You still have us, your brothers and sisters, and the Mathias family too . . .'

She hugged Tom and then waved goodbye to him from the doorstep, but as she entered the house, it was in uproar as Jed, one of Mrs Mathias's sons, pushed past her. She realised he wasn't being rude, as he wasn't usually like that – something was very wrong. All thoughts of Griff flew from her head. Had something happened to Mrs Mathias? Please, God, no!

She took the stairs two at a time, and upon reaching the top, she found the rest of the family in Eli's room. Morris was one side of Eli's bed on bended knee, almost as if in prayer, whilst Mrs Mathias sat on the other side, stroking her son's brow. She looked up when she saw Megan. 'Jed's gone to fetch the doctor,' she said solemnly, but without panic. 'Eli's been coughing up blood . . .'

Chapter Sixteen

Megan stood staring at the trio. This was too unimaginable for words. Eli's face was a deathly shade of puce and he was struggling to breathe.

'Sit him up!' Megan said. 'My father used to suffer with his lungs from the coal pit and my mother used to put lots of pillows behind him.'

Peggy nodded and went in search of more pillows.

'It will help him to breathe more easily,' she explained to Morris.

Morris studied her for a moment. 'For someone so young, you seem to know so much, Megan,' he said.

'Being in the workhouse I saw all sorts of ailments,' she explained.

'And some deaths too, I expect,' Morris said lifting his brow.

'Yes.' She was just about to tell him about her mother's death when Peggy returned with the pillows.

'Help me sit Eli up,' she said to Morris.

'I'll help, Mrs Mathias. You sit on the chair,' she offered, drawing nearer to the bed.

Peggy looked all but worn out. 'There's good in you, love,' she said, as she sank down in the winged armchair in the corner. 'I need to put some more coal on the fire.'

'Don't trouble yourself, Mam,' Morris said. 'I'll stoke up the fire and add fresh coal.'

'And I'll make you a nice cup of tea,' Megan said, patting Peggy's hand, realising what a strain the woman was under.

Megan helped Morris to lift up Eli and she plumped up the new pillows to put behind him. He gave her a grateful look, before emitting another bout of painful sounding coughs.

A few minutes later, after Peggy had finished her cup of tea and with the fire attended to, Jed showed up with the doctor. The boys left the room so he could examine Eli, leaving his mother for support and Megan sitting quietly in the corner.

After listening to Eli's lungs with a stethoscope he asked about the bleeding. As Mrs Mathias told him everything she could, the doctor proceeded to examine Eli's poor emaciated body.

'It's tuberculosis, I fear. Otherwise known as "consumption".'

Megan felt like all the air had been drawn out of her lungs. She heard Peggy sob. Eli let his head drop into his hands, and she heard a weak 'No' come from him.

'I'm afraid you'll have to give up your work at the bakery.

You're contagious. Also, keep all bed linen clean and either boil your handkerchiefs or preferably burn them. Keep all visitors away from the house . . .' the doctor instructed.

'*Oh fy ddaioni*,' Mrs Mathias muttered in Welsh, which meant 'Oh my goodness'.

The doctor opened his Gladstone bag and handed her a brown bottle of medicine. What it contained, Megan had no idea. Peggy dipped her hand into her pinafore pocket and handed the doctor some coinage, then thanked him for his time.

When he had left the house, Peggy's hands flew to her face, 'Oh, *cariad*,' she addressed Megan in the hallway, 'what shall I do about the bakery and the cake business?'

Morris and Jed, hearing their mother's distress, drew beside her. 'We'll keep the bakery going, Mam,' Jed said, 'and we'll keep well away from the house during that time. How about Megan keeping the tea room going?'

'Yes, that's all very well, but she'll have to move out of here now, for her own sake,' Peggy said soberly.

'She can stay at our house,' Morris said, 'until Eli is better. She'll be a help with the new baby when he or she decides to put in an appearance, too!'

'Sounds a good idea to me,' Jed added. 'As long as you don't mind, Megan?'

Megan nodded. So she was going to have to take over the tea room herself. Could she do it? she wondered. She would give it a go – she had managed one day in charge by herself, and she'd do anything for Mrs Mathias.

And so a couple of days later, Megan began working as boss of the tea room, with another young girl called Elsie working there under Megan's supervision. At first, Elsie was good to work with; she took orders well, but when she'd found her feet after a week or so, she began to boss Megan around. She was older and several inches taller, which made Megan begin to feel intimidated by the girl.

It isn't fair. I've come so far. I worked hard to get out of the work-house and now that cheeky madam is trying to tell me what to do. I had enough of that with Miss Hamilton. Elsie hasn't had to work out on the stall in the freezing cold for hours on end until her teeth chattered and her fingers and toes turned numb and blue with cold, or had to push the heavy handcart back and forth from Plymouth Street every day. She's just come here and had it easy, with me showing her the ropes, and now she wants to take over and tell me what I should be doing all day.

If the adoption doesn't go through then I might end up back in that horrible place, and not only will I have lost Griff, I'll lose my job and being with a family, too. I just couldn't bear that to happen.

Megan began to ponder the situation with Elsie. What could she do, though? If she told Mrs Mathias, it could upset her. She had enough to contend with trying to nurse Eli back to health. Megan realised there was no way now she was going to allow her to leave for London to seek out Griff when she was needed at the tea room, and even if she did allow it, she might not have a job to go back to as Elsie would have stepped into her shoes.

And why hadn't Griff been in touch anyhow? She'd taken the trouble to teach him how to read and write properly, yet he couldn't even be bothered to write her a letter – he could send one to the tea room if he didn't remember Mrs Mathias's address. Maybe the truth of it was, all the time she'd been pining for him, he'd forgotten all about her, and that made her so sad.

The main thing for now, though, was to sort out the situation with Elsie, who was becoming increasingly bossy by the day. If it wasn't 'Megan, set that table' or 'Clear up those dishes, hurry up now, will you?' then it was 'Go and make the teas!' or 'Make sure you wash those dishes clean now!' You'd have sworn Elsie was the one who had been working at the tea room the longest, not Megan. It began to eat away at her until she could stand it no longer.

One day, after Megan opened the shop, with Elsie looming over her and following her around barking out orders all the time, she turned suddenly and with arms folded and chin jutting forward, she drew herself up to her full height and said, 'If you don't stop telling me what to do, then I will have nothing else to do other than report you to Mrs Mathias. She can find another young girl quite easily, there are enough of them around.'

Elsie stepped back, her bottom lip quivering. Megan's forthright approach had knocked the girl off guard. Then, as if trying to lord it up, she towered over Megan. 'And if you do that, me and my friends will wait for you when you lock up every night and pull away at your pigtails. My mother told me you're a good-for-nothing workhouse girl. And I think you deserve a hard slap!' Elsie raised her right hand and stepped forward. If Elsie landed a blow, Megan decided she would kick her in the shins, but there was no need as, at that moment, someone stepped into the tea room. She recognised the fragrance so well.

Distracted, Megan turned to face The Lady, and quickly felt a hard slap across her face. She fell backwards and hit her head on one of the tables.

Elsie looked down at her with a look of horror on her face. Her hands flew to her face. 'Oh, Megan, I'm so sorry I didn't mean to hit you so hard . . .'

Megan's head was spinning. The Lady bent down and cradled her head. 'But you did mean to hit her. I saw you,' Kathleen's Irish voice said firmly. 'Now go and get a cold compress – a wet tray cloth or napkin will do.'

Elsie fled, almost toppling over a chair in her haste. She returned within a couple of minutes with a cold, wet napkin, which Kathleen held to Megan's head. 'I'm afraid you're going to have a big bruise there and maybe a little lump too, Megan,' she said soothingly, then she stared hard at Elsie. 'Go and fetch Megan a glass of water at once!' Now Elsie was all demure and obedient. 'How come you young girls are running this tea room on your own?' Kathleen whispered.

Megan groaned, her head felt muzzy and was beginning to throb. 'Mrs Mathias has to look after Eli – he has consumption, miss. I'm staying at her other son's home, Morris his name is, and he has a lovely wife called Violet and she's due to have a baby soon.'

'I see,' said Kathleen, with grave concern. 'Now, Elsie, don't just stand there gawping. Help Megan back onto her feet, seeing as how you were the one that knocked her on the floor to begin with.'

Elsie looked up sheepishly through thick lashes and, taking one of Megan's arms whilst Kathleen took the other, she helped to steady her on her feet.

Kathleen made her sit in a chair. 'Now get your sea legs, girlie,' she said. 'Take your time. Elsie can see to this place for an hour or so, and she can bring me and you a pot of coffee for two and some fancies, can't you, Elsie?'

Megan thought it very grown-up to be offered a coffee. She'd only tasted it once before when Peggy had first introduced it to the shop after serious competition from the coffee taverns in the town. She gave Elsie a haughty look. After what she just did, she wouldn't be offering her a cup.

Elsie smiled and nodded, now compliant and willing to please the both of them. Kathleen sat opposite Megan at the table and whispered behind her gloved hand, 'I don't think ye'll be getting any more bother from the likes of her,' which caused Megan to burst into fits of giggles. It was so good to have The Lady back home.

Megan couldn't wait to go and visit Cook and Eira at the workhouse the following day to tell them all about what had happened. She could well imagine their laughter at the thought of Megan and Elsie grappling on the tea-room floor when The Lady walked in on them. Oh, how they'd have a good giggle at that over a nice cup of tea and a selection of sticky buns Megan would bring along. At least she still enjoyed visiting that awful place whilst there were people there she cared for.

The next day Megan was making her way to the kitchen to see Cook when she was accosted by Miss Hamilton in the corridor.

'And what do we have here then?' the supervisor sneered. 'The little bitch who caused so much trouble that she got the previous workhouse Matron and Master moved on elsewhere!'

Megan trembled. She could sense how angry the woman was by the tone of her voice.

'You just wait until you have to come back here some day, Megan Hopkins. I'll thrash the living daylights out of you for telling such filthy lies about the Master and that filthy little whore called Tilly.' Her eyes flashed with fury.

Tears welled up in Megan's eyes. 'You evil witch!' she shouted. 'The girl is dead and all because your precious Master got her in the family way. She went through hell and you were responsible – you knew the truth of how that girl suffered!' Megan surprised herself at the depth of her anger. All the years of frustration at her bad treatment at the hands of the supervisor came to the fore.

Miss Hamilton raised her hand and slapped Megan, a stinging blow across her cheek, which caused her to rebound and stumble backwards and fall to the floor. The basket she was carrying fell from her grasp and some of the treats she had brought spilled out onto the stone floor. But still the woman carried on with her punishment, this time kicking Megan with the toe of her boot right in the direction of her stomach. 'You and your filthy family have made my life hell!' she shouted.

If she stayed on the floor much longer, Megan realised, she wouldn't be getting back up again. It was as if the woman were possessed by a raging demon. What had got her so angry?

There was only one thing for it. Megan reached out as the woman went to boot her once more and caught her foot. Miss Hamilton too stumbled backwards and fell on the floor herself, hitting her head as she landed.

Quick as a flash, although slightly winded, Megan rose to her feet, clutching her stomach. 'What has my family ever done to you, that you have treated me like this?'

Miss Hamilton fought to push Megan away, but anger had

made Megan more powerful and she'd grown a couple of inches this past year. She was getting taller and stronger week by week and she now loomed over the woman's body.

'Answer me, you evil witch!' she shouted, and took a hold of her neck.

A gurgling sound emitted from the woman's throat as her eyes appeared to bulge out of her head. For a moment, she feared she had killed her and quickly removed her hands. She saw Cook rush out of the kitchen and come to kneel at her side.

'Megan, what have you done to Miss Hamilton?' She stared solemnly at Megan.

'I think I've killed her, Mrs Woodley.' Now she'd be in trouble for sure. 'She started on me first, though,' she explained.

'I don't doubt that for a moment, pet,' she said sympathetically.

Then there was a long groan and, to her surprise, Miss Hamilton pulled herself up into a sitting position rubbing at her sore neck as Megan looked down on her.

'Well, you old cow,' Cook said, 'you deserved that for laying into our Megan. What have you to say for yourself? The girl deserves an answer.'

Miss Hamilton didn't say a word, and glared at the cook with venom in her eyes.

'Tell her,' she insisted between gritted teeth.

Whatever was Cook talking about? Megan wondered. She

didn't realise that the two women might regularly speak together, apart from when Cook defended her from Miss Hamilton's savage attacks.

Miss Hamilton hesitated before speaking, and Megan gasped at what she had to say. It was the last thing she expected to come out of her mouth. 'Once upon a time I was your father's beau . . .' she began, her voice sounding croaky. 'We were due to get married but then he met that mother of yours and that was the end of that. He broke off our engagement. Just think how much that hurt me. He chose your whore mother. Why would he do tha—'

Not wanting to hear any bad words about her parents, Megan launched herself at Miss Hamilton, but Cook held her back, hushing her softly. 'Listen, pet.'

'I cried for months afterwards. I didn't want to go out anywhere. I was living in Abercanaid at the time and it felt like the whole village knew about it. It was total humiliation. He rejected me.'

'You're a liar!' Megan shouted at the woman.

The supervisor shook her head. 'It's true. Why do you think I always have it in for you? It's because you look just like her, you filfthy waif. You're a constant reminder of the woman who stole my true love. She had the grace to die, but you're still here. Everywhere I look. Even when you leave, you're still always here. I can't stand the sight of you.'

It was all beginning to make sense now, even though Megan

didn't want to believe it. She did look like her mother, far more than her sisters did.

'Finally, you admit it,' said Cook with hands on her hips. 'That's no excuse, if you ask me. Megan has done you no harm whatsoever.'

'Maybe not,' said the supervisor. 'But someone has had to suffer for what *she* did.' She spat out the word 'she'. 'Seeing you both at the workhouse was sheer torture.'

Megan thought back to the cruel way Miss Hamilton had kept her away from her dying mother, and the way she'd sent her into the room when her mother was already dead to give her the biggest shock of her life.

Miss Hamilton reached out for the railings of the wooden banister to pull herself into a standing position, breathless as she did so, shaky on her feet.

'If the new Master and his wife find out about this you'll get dismissed from here!' Cook shouted.

'No,' Megan said, shaking her head. 'I don't want her to be fired. It's only me she's that nasty with around here. It won't solve anything at all.' It pained Megan to think her father had ever been involved with such a person, and thank goodness he'd met her mother and fallen in love with her instead, else she and her brothers and sisters wouldn't be here right now. 'I think the woman's to be pitied . . .' she whispered under her breath as she caught the supervisor's eye. 'Poor soul doesn't understand the meaning of love or forgiveness.'

Cook nodded. 'Well, if it were me, I'd have her burned at the stake, Megan. You're a better person than I am, that's for sure. Come on into the kitchen and leave that old witch to her own devices . . .' She wrapped an arm around Megan and led her into the kitchen. Behind her, Miss Hamilton brushed down her skirts and slunk away with her head bowed low, the wind finally taken out of her sails.

Once inside the kitchen, Cook couldn't wait to tell all the staff how Megan had finally got the better of the supervisor. They all gathered around and laughed and patted her on the back, telling her what a brave young lady she was. She didn't feel brave. She was reeling from the news that her father had ever been involved with that horrid woman.

But, in an attempt at celebration, Cook and Eira shared a cup of tea and plate of sticky buns with Megan, and she couldn't help but be relieved that it was all over.

'I don't think Miss Hamilton will bother you ever again, Megan,' Cook said, taking a sip of her tea.

Megan smiled back. No, she didn't think she would, either.

Under Mrs Hollings's supervision, Griff made his way to the theatre. 'Where have you been, boy?' Mr Gittings, the stage manager, glared.

Mrs Hollings had her umbrella in hand, ready to wallop him if he started on Griff, but after Griff had explained the circumstances, the man relaxed and stroked his chin. 'That makes sense, I suppose. That uncle of yours and his, er, lady friend, turned up here yesterday demanding recompense for your performances. I withheld payment as I felt they were up to something, but to be honest, I thought they were going to take the money and run with you before you'd worked the full week out, so I refused. But I did arrange for them to call tomorrow providing they brought you along.'

Griff's heart hammered in his chest and his breaths became short and shallow. 'Please, sir, I never want to see my uncle again.'

'Yes, he's been beating the lad,' Mrs Hollings chipped in.

Mr Gittings looked on sympathetically. He twirled his moustache as he usually did when deep in thought. 'I think I have a solution,' he said. 'Look, you need to get away from these parts, to somewhere they won't find you. I'll send you to one of our music halls across town – only on a temporary basis, mind, but we can swap acts to work out your contract. Then I'd lie low if I were you. Either with Mrs Hollings – but you risk being caught in the East End – or . . . I have an idea. I have a cousin and his wife who live in Oxford. They're childless, they might take you on.'

Griff looked at Mrs Hollings, who nodded her head. 'You're welcome to stop with me, of course you are, lad, but think of the opportunity you might be getting.'

Griff didn't know quite what to think, but he needed to

get away from this area in case his uncle found him again and whipped his hide black and blue. He drew a long breath before answering. 'Yes, sir. That sounds a good idea,' he said. 'Thank you. If you can please ask them for me. I'll be no trouble to them, honest!'

And so Griff waited to hear back from Mr Gittings's cousin and his wife. In the meantime, he vowed to work hard for the man at the alternative theatre, and Kitty Hollings, too, until the day came when he could leave London once and for all.

Working on the stage again was like a welcome respite for Griff. He soon slipped back into his old routine and Mr Gittings even got a little black terrier called Molly to accompany him on stage. Molly wasn't as easy to train as Scamp had been, but with persistence and using a lot of leftovers from Mrs Hollings's pie crusts, he soon had her jumping though hoops and balancing on an old beer barrel just as Scamp had done in Merthyr.

Of course, Griff didn't have top billing; he was way down the line-up. But he didn't mind one bit as he had made friends with the other performers: there was 'Franco the Fire-Eater' and 'Sinbad the Sword Swallower' – he had no idea how they did what they did, but people seemed to love their death-defying performances. And there was 'Good Time Gal Gilly from Gateshead'. Now, she wasn't a patch on Kathleen, who was very ladylike indeed. She was a coarse sort of performer who liked to play up to the men in the audience by lifting her skirts and showing her ankles. Griff had even seen her bloomers once in rehearsal, causing him to blush from head to toe. Yet, she was maybe more respectable than some of the women who walked the streets of China, and she was ever so friendly when she wasn't playing up to the crowds.

One night, after a performance, Griff was heading off back to the pie shop when he heard footsteps behind him. Every time he turned around to see who was following him, the footsteps ceased and he could see no one there. He was nearing the Devil's Acre area that was as notorious as China itself with its slums and vagabonds – he often shivered as he passed by that way – so he decided to cross over the road to get away from whoever it was who appeared to be following him. That was when a young lad rushed past him, almost knocking him over as he ran off down the street. Griff was just about to complain loudly when he felt a heavy hand clamp down on his shoulder in a bone-crushing grip. Fearing it was his uncle, he was about to yell for help when he heard an unfamiliar voice.

'Hello, hello, hello!' a voice boomed out. He tried to turn about, but the man now had him gripped firmly by the collar, so that his feet were a couple of inches off the ground. 'Got you at last, you little tyke!'

The man dropped him from his grasp and Griff could see

under the yellow rays of the street gaslight that it was a policeman. Why was he calling him a little tyke?

'I'm sorry, sir. I don't know what you mean. I've just been performing on stage at that theatre back there and am on my way home now!'

The constable studied him under the gaslight. 'A very likely story, lad. A young lad fitting your description has been rumbled after being involved in a distraction burglary. He was taken to a large house by a man and pushed in through a small window – only small enough for someone like yourself to have got through. The pair got away with a sack of silver and precious jewellery. Come on, laddie, you're coming with me!'

The constable tightened his grip on Griff's jacket, dragging him over to the next street where a horse drawn Black Maria awaited.

'But you've got it wrong,' Griff protested. 'It wasn't me. I was on stage this evening, you can check with the stage manager, Mr Gittings, if you don't believe me.'

'You be quiet, lad,' the constable warned as he bundled him inside the Black Maria, next to a burly man and two other young lads.

Griff felt a lump in his throat and tears in his eyes, but he didn't want to show any of them he was about to cry. He couldn't believe this was happening to him. And poor Kitty would worry herself all night about why he hadn't returned home.

As the cab trundled along in the semi-darkness, Griff felt

the man's eyes on him, whilst the other two boys just sat there staring out of the barred windows.

'Whatcha been caught for, son?' asked the man, who smelled strongly of gin.

'I haven't done anything,' Griff said. 'I was just walking along minding my own business when that policeman brought me here. He reckoned I'd been involved in a burglary with a man in a big house.'

The man laughed. 'That were me. And I know you weren't with me but that lot won't believe it. The lad with me ran off. They probably reckon you're him.' He leant forward and studied Griff. 'Say, if you're interested in joining the gang, I can give you work. You're just the right size to get in through small windows. Whatcha say?'

Griff was just about to protest and say he had a job at the theatre and lived with Mrs Hollings at the pie shop, when he thought better of it. If the man found out where he lived and worked he could come looking for him in the future. So he decided to play along as he might end up sharing a cell with those three.

'Sounds a good idea, count me in!' he said in as bright a voice as he could possibly muster, and he hoped the copper sitting at the front with the driver couldn't hear.

At the police station, he was bundled into a cell with the other two lads and the man was carted off to another cell, flanked by two policemen, much to Griff's relief.

As Griff sat shivering in the corner of the cell he thought about being back in Kitty's comfortable rooms above the pie shop with that wonderful smell of stewed beef and onions in the kitchen below. He'd had a bed there all to himself. It had been so good while it had lasted.

He tucked his knees up under his chin and hugged himself, trying to think of all sorts of things not to make himself sad. An image of Megan with her dark curly ringlets and her bright smile came to mind, but as quickly as it came, it disappeared. As the lights were dimmed in the corridor outside he heard one of the other lads whimper in another corner of the cell. The older-looking lad came to sit beside him and asked, 'Is it yer first time in the slammer, mate?'

'Yes and I shouldn't be here now. I ain't done anything wrong.'

'They all say that,' said the lad. 'My name's Jimmy, what's yer's?'

'Griff.'

'Griff, yer got a funny speaking voice, if yer don't mind me saying so. Yer not from round these parts, are yer?'

'No, I come from a town a long way away.' He didn't much feel like explaining himself so he changed the subject. 'What are you here for, Jimmy?'

'Me and my brother, Sam there, we were sent on the rob by our father. We been caught before, so don't think we'll gerrof this time, that's why Sam is so upset. We'll be up before the beak in the morning.'

'Beak?' Griff imagined some giant bird. What did Jimmy mean by that?

'The judge. There's a courthouse next door to this police station. We'll all of us 'ave to give an account of ourselves in the morning. But I can't believe you ain't done nothing, Griff.'

'It's true, I'm telling you. I was walking home and this boy runs past, nearly knocked me over, then a policeman collars me. I must look like a wrong 'un, I suppose. I fink the boy must have been the one the copper was chasing, but he got me instead. The most I've ever stolen is a bunch of apples and some coal, and I feel bad about both of those things already.'

Griff found himself telling Jimmy all about his uncle and what life had been like for him before, and in turn Jimmy told them about his life on the streets with his family. It sounded like they'd both been dealt a bad hand, but the fact still remained that Jimmy had commited the crime he was in here for, whereas Griff hadn't. By the time they'd finished talking, dawn was beginning to break. He let out a long groan.

He heard a key in the lock and the burly policeman from the previous night said to the three of them. 'Right, let's be having you, lads.'

'But we ain't 'ad nuffink to eat or drink yet,' Jimmy protested.

'Well, you can have all the bread and water you like when the judge puts you all behind bars and throws away the key!'

'Rozzers, eh?' Jimmy looked at Griff and rolled his eyes.

Griff sniffed, trying to hold back tears. Kitty might never know what happened to him and maybe if the judge sent him to Australia, he'd never see Megan's smiling face again either. He wiped his runny nose on the sleeve of his jacket and he remembered that day in the churchyard when Megan had told him to use a handkerchief. He'd come a long way since then, but some of his habits had remained.

Griff watched as Jimmy and Sam were led away to the courthouse by the policeman. Griff was led by another policeman into a different room, where there were two elderly men waiting to speak to him. They were seated behind a large walnut desk and opposite them was a single chair. On the oak-panelled walls were various paintings of distinguished-looking policemen.

Cripes, I must be in big trouble being brought to a room such as this. I ain't ever seen anything so grand in all me life.

He hovered near the chair, yearning to take a seat. He was so tired from a night on that ice-cold cell floor, his legs would hardly hold him up.

'Remain standing, boy,' the younger of the two, who had a small twirled moustache, commanded. Griff straightened himself and hoped his legs would not buckle in front of them.

The elder of the two men, who had white hair and whiskers, peered at him over the top of his spectacles. 'Right,' he said, with a ledger open in front of him and a fountain pen in his hand. 'Name?'

'Griff Rhys Morgan, sir.' Griff stood with his hands behind his back, determined to make a good impression.

'Age?'

'Twelve years old, sir.'

'Hmm, not very big for your age, are you, lad?' He sniffed. 'Now then, any previous convictions?'

'Like for what, sir?'

'Theft and the like,' the younger man chipped in.

Griff was about to say no, but felt he couldn't bring himself to lie. 'No convictions, but I have stolen goods a couple of times when I was back in Merthyr, but didn't get caught and I'm very sorry for that. Sorry for stealing the goods, not about not getting caught, that is . . .'

The younger man whispered something in the elder man's ear and both nodded to one another.

'And what did you steal?' the one with the ledger asked.

'An armful of apples, sir, but it was only cos I was hungry, you see. I was living with my uncle and we'd go days with no food. His wife, me auntie, died in childbirth, then he lost his job at the ironworks and then took to the drink, so money was scarce. Then another time I stole some lumps of coal. But my uncle told me to do it and if I hadn't, he would have beaten me.'

'And why were you living with your uncle in the first place, Griff?'

'My parents are dead, sir. If my uncle hadn't taken me in, then I would have ended up in the workhouse.'

The man nodded. 'I see. And why were you brought here last night then, young man?'

Griff shrugged. 'Sir, it was all a mistake. I was walking home after I performed on stage at the theatre. I've been staying with Mrs Kitty Hollings who owns the pie shop on Albert Street, so I was headed there. Then I heard footsteps behind me but I couldn't see who it was. Next fing I knows, a boy rushes out behind me from nowhere and nearly knocks me over in the dark and then someone grabs me by the collar and I find it's a cop—I mean, policeman, sir.'

The two men began to whisper to one another. Griff tried to make out what they were saying but only caught the odd word here and there, namely 'give a chance' and 'destitute'. He didn't know what the latter meant and hoped, whatever it was, it would go in his favour. The younger man stood. 'Can anyone from the theatre vouch for you?'

'Yes, Mr Gittings, sir. He's the stage manager.'

'Then I think the sensible thing to do would be for us to speak to him so as he can act as a character witness for you in front of the judge this morning and also prove you performed last night on stage. You will be on in court as a suspect in a case where a lot of jewellery and silver were stolen from a house on Manor Way. Do you understand me?'

Griff nodded. 'I do, sir. The policeman who collared me

told me that, but I ain't been near anyone's house. I swear it on Mrs Hollings's life.' He licked his index finger and made the sign of a cross on his chest.

'Very well then,' the elder man said, and noted it down in the ledger. 'You are to return to your cell while we send a policeman to locate Mr Gittings. Would he be at the theatre this morning, do you think?'

'Yes, sir. He's in early every morning to go through rehearsals. I should be there myself this morning.' He frowned. He'd much rather be working than have to attend court to prove something he hadn't been involved in in the first place.

Griff was led away by a policeman and given a crust of bread and butter with a mug of tea. The tea was very weak compared to the strong tea Mrs Hollings brewed, but he was grateful for anything given to him.

One hour later, the cell door was opened again and he was led to the courthouse next door.

Following Megan's altercation with Elsie, and Kathleen's intervention, Megan had no further trouble with the girl at all. As if realising the error of her ways, she went out of her way to help Megan instead. Nothing was too much trouble for her and she took orders from Megan well, though Megan still did not entirely trust the girl. She'd need to prove herself in the future. It took more than an offer to 'Let me clear the tables whilst you put up your feet!' for Megan to forgive and forget.

Kathleen called into the tea room regularly that week to check all was well, but she needn't have worried at all. She was home on a visit to see her husband, Dafydd, and Megan had even been able to meet him when she brought him into the tea room once.

One day, when they were sitting having a jam-and-cream scone and a pot of tea whilst the shop was quiet and Elsie was tidying up in the background, Kathleen said, 'I did make enquiries about Griff in London, Megan, but I couldn't find him anywhere. There are so many music halls and theatres and no one I know in the industry has heard of him. Maybe he never went back on stage . . .'

Megan shook her head sadly. 'Maybe he never even went to London in the first place . . .'

'That's a possibility, but you must never give up hope. Maybe Griff will return here some day in the future.'

Megan nodded and stared down into her cup of tea. It was in a pretty, flowered china cup with matching saucer. How she had gone up in the world since her workhouse days, she thought, but she could take no pleasure in it today as all she could think about was knowing how Griff was doing.

As if to change the subject, Kathleen asked, 'And how are Eli and Mrs Mathias these days?'

'Eli is much stronger now, Peggy says. I only talk to her

through the window, as she doesn't want me to go down with consumption too, but he's stopped coughing up blood and she says he's put on a little weight, but it's doubtful he'll ever return to the bakery. People in the area know that he's got the disease and they wouldn't want to buy any baked goods from someone who's had that.'

Kathleen nodded. 'That's understandable, I suppose.' She lifted her teacup with her pristine white glove.

Some day, I'll be a lady like Kathleen, Megan thought. She added a spoonful of sugar to her tea and stirred. 'Mrs Mathias thought at first it might affect business, people knowing about how one of the bakers had got ill with consumption, but she's only lost a handful of customers over it.'

'Thank goodness for that,' Kathleen said, then took a bite of her scone. She dabbed the jam and cream from her lips with a white cotton napkin. 'These cakes are delicious.'

Megan had to agree. Peggy Mathias's tea room was classed as one of the best in all of Merthyr Tydfil. When she was older she wanted a tea room of her own, too. Peggy said it could well happen one day. The boys were only interested in the bakery, apparently, but Megan knew that with three sons, that might well change when the chance presented itself. Plus, she knew deep down she could never inherit the shop – it just wouldn't be fair.

'How's your brother Tom?' Kathleen asked.

Megan giggled. 'He's courting now. A nice young girl from

Twynyrodyn. She works as a maid at the Court House, and when she gets an afternoon off, he takes her for a walk. She's even been to Mrs Evans's home for tea. Her name is Amy.'

'That's nice. He's a hard worker, your brother, just like you.'

Megan felt her cheeks burn with embarrassment. 'Oh, I don't know about that, I just do what I can to help Peggy.'

'You don't give yourself enough credit, Megan Hopkins. You're a very special young lady.'

Megan looked away shyly. Since leaving the workhouse, people were so nice to her it took some getting used to.

'Thank you,' was all she managed to say.

Chapter Seventeen

Griff stood in the dock, his legs trembling and teeth chattering. He wished now he hadn't eaten that crust as he felt he might vomit with all those stern eyes upon him. The judge in his long curly wig sat on a podium with a gavel in his hand.

'With regard to the case of a burglary at the house known as Marlborough House at a quarter to ten last night, how do you plead?'

'N–not guilty, sir.'

From the corner of his eye Griff could see Mr Gittings and yet even though he knew he hadn't been guilty of such a crime, he could not bring himself to make eye contact with the man. He'd already let him down once, thanks to his uncle. He couldn't do it a second time.

'I now call upon my first witness, Mr Marlborough, who owns the house in question.'

Griff caught his breath. He had never seen the well-dressed

man before in his life, even though the man was staring at him intently with curiosity. The judge asked a series of questions and then finally said, 'Is the boy you see before you the one you saw running down your path, Mr Marlborough?'

'I . . . I can't honestly say for certain, your honour. It was dark, but he's about the same size, I would say.'

After further questioning, the man was dismissed and the constable gave his evidence of apprehending him, certain it was him he had seen running from the house.

The lawyer who was to represent Griff asked, 'But did you catch Griff Rhys Morgan with a sack of valuable goods in his possession, PC Simes?'

Simes's face flushed red. 'Well, er, no. But he could have thrown it away in the hedgerow.'

'And were the hedgerows searched and was any such sack discovered?'

'Er, no. But that doesn't mean—'

The judge then dismissed the constable. Finally, Mr Gittings was brought to give a character witness and evidence on behalf of Griff.

'How long have you known the boy, Griff Rhys Morgan?' the judge asked.

'Only just this past month, your honour. It's from my understanding that the boy had trouble with that uncle of his who I think was making him perform on stage to get money. The lad escaped and found me again and I've put him back on stage at his own request. In all the time I've known him I haven't had a moment's trouble with the boy. Last night he performed on stage and took an encore with the rest of the cast at half past nine, hardly time for him to have broken into some house down the road, taken a sack of valuables and hotfooted it far enough to hide away the stash, is it? He's worked hard for me and I've never found him to be dishonest. I feel this orphan deserves a chance in life.'

Something was being discussed between the lawyer and Mr Gittings, then the lawyer stood before the judge who halted proceedings to summon the lawyer to his chambers.

There was a long thrum around the court room and Griff feared what would happen next. All he could see in his mind's eye was a large sailing ship taking him to Australia with a load of petty criminals. Oh no, he'd die if that ever happened.

Finally the judge and lawyer returned to the court, then the judge announced: 'Mr Gittings says that he had already been in talks with his cousin and wife with a view to adopting Griff Rhys Morgan, and they are agreeable to it. So as the lad will now, in the future, have a stable environment to grow up in, and a good education, I see no sense in pursuing this matter any further. Case dismissed!'

He banged his gavel down hard on the small wooden block before him.

Griff's mouth popped open in surprise. He thought Mr Gittings had forgotten all about his promise as he hadn't said a single word about it of late. He caught his employer's eye as the man smiled at him from the gallery.

Griff had a lot of explaining to do to Mrs Hollings when the stage manager dropped him off in his carriage outside the shop.

'Cor, Griff, I 'ardly slept a wink all night worrying that uncle of yours had nabbed you.'

He gave her a big hug and she kissed the top of his head. 'I'm sorry for putting you through all that, Mrs Hollings. But I honestly didn't do nuffink!'

'Of course I know that, Griff, I never doubted you for a second.' She ruffled his hair. 'Now, tomorrow we'll go and see Mr Gittings to check out the details about you going to live with his family. But for the time being, I'm going to make you a nice toad-in-the-hole and a glass of milk!' Griff pulled a face, and Kitty, realising that Griff thought she meant a real toad, chuckled. 'You daft thing, it's only a sausage cooked in something similar to a Yorkshire pud. You'll like it.'

'All right, Mrs Hollings, whatever you say . . .' He was fast asleep as soon as he laid his head down on her old horsehair couch.

Kitty sighed as she went to fetch a blanket to place over him. The toad-in-the-hole could wait a while longer yet.

Early next morning, Mrs Hollings and Griff were in the stage manager's office and had been there talking animatedly for the past quarter of an hour. Kitty waved her brolly in Mr Gittings's face. 'However, there's just one condition if you wish to send the boy to live with your relatives, Mr Gittings,' she said.

The stage manager looked at her curiously. 'And what might that be, madam, pray tell?'

She stopped waving her brolly in his face and said, 'That I get to meet these people. I don't want the lad taken away for ill-gotten gains again!'

'I can assure you, madam' – Mr Gittings loosened his cravat as if it had been tied too tightly – 'that my cousin and his wife are perfectly respectable people. If taken on, and they like Griff, I think they would pay for his schooling and upkeep.' He shot a sideways glance at Griff. 'I like the lad and can see he's a good sort who maybe hasn't had the best start in life. He was at a disadvantage being orphaned and having to live with someone who wanted to leech off him. I didn't care for his Uncle Berwyn on first making his acquaintance. I had a strange feeling about him as soon as I laid eyes on him. He's the sort who has ambitions above his station, and on more than one occasion in his presence, I detected the strong odour of alcohol.'

Mrs Hollings cackled, throwing back her head. 'Cor, and all of that coming from a stage manager. It's well known that people in music halls like a little snifter now and again, isn't that so?'

Mr Gittings's chin jutted out as if appalled by the woman's suggestion. Oh dear: was this going to scupper Griff's final hope of getting away from London? If he could get away from here, he figured maybe after a while he could find his own way back to Merthyr Tydfil and to Megan. Mrs Mathias would take him in for sure. He'd work hard for her, he would. Chopping wood, helping in the bakery, anything she wanted in fact. He held his breath as he waited to hear what Mr Gittings had to say.

Then the stage manager relaxed and laughed also. 'You're not too far wrong there, Mrs Hollings. How do you know these things?'

'Ah well, I was a performer meself as a young girl. "Burlington Bessie" they called me. Me act drew in crowds from near and far, till a few years later I got knocked up and in the family way. It were another performer at the theatre, but he made an honest woman of me.'

Mr Gittings smiled and nodded and extended a hand for a handshake with 'Bessie'.

'Come along, Griff, better get back to the shop. There's pies waiting to be sold!'

'Very well. I'll get a message sent over to you both when I've arranged things with my cousin and his wife.'

'Can't you move me today, though?' Griff pleaded. 'My uncle will find me for sure if I stay here much longer.'

'Don't worry yourself, Griff,' Mr Gittings reassured him.

'If he shows up, I'll send him away with a flea in his ear. In any case, he's probably got fed up by now and moved on, and will have found some other way to make a bit of money.'

Griff knew he ought to have felt reassured but for some reason, he didn't. His uncle was like a bad penny and if he showed up he'd be trying to get something out of him, either a large share of his earnings or by trying to put him on the rob.

Megan had thought of a way she could keep Griff in her thoughts and that was to go to the Vulcan Inn and ask the landlord if she could maybe take Scamp out from time to time. After what happened the last time she went there, she took Tom with her, who immediately took to the little scruff. 'No wonder Griff loved this dog so much,' Tom enthused, as he helped her walk Scamp to Plymouth Street. 'He even knows the way. Look at him pulling on that old rope lead!'

'He ought to – Griff brought him to visit often enough!' Megan explained.

Mrs Mathias was happy to see the dog and insisted on giving him some of the leftovers from their dinner that evening.

'When does the landlord want the dog returned?' she asked as she patted Scamp on his head. The poor thing seemed to be missing his old friend as much as Megan did.

'He said we can borrow him whenever we want. We'd be doing him a favour as he doesn't get much time to exercise him. And, Mrs Mathias, it's cold at the back of that old pub. Please can we keep him here for a few days?'

Mrs Mathias nodded. 'Yes, I don't see why not, Megan, as long as he doesn't mess in the house. He can sleep in the old garden shed. Tom, you can make him a bed from one of the old wooden crates out in the garden. Megan, you can make some bedding from an old eiderdown I've got. I was wondering what to do with it.'

And so Scamp became a regular visitor at the Mathias house, and it made Megan feel a little more connected to Griff, knowing she was looking after his beloved dog.

Griff let out a long breath of relief. He was going to get away from here at last, as long as the Stanburys took to him. As he and Kitty walked out through the door and strolled down the street chattering happily to one another, Griff felt a heavy hand clamp down on his shoulder.

'Got you at last, you little beggar!' There was no mistaking that harsh, rasping voice and odour of stale beer on his breath.

Griff looked up in horror to see it was his uncle who was pushing down so hard on his shoulder. Mrs Hollings began to bash away at his uncle with her brolly. 'You leave that boy alone, you brute!' she shouted, as Bronwen cowered up against the wall.

'I can assure you, madam, that this boy should be coming with me. I am his legal guardian.'

'Poppycock!' she shouted at him, and bashed him some more. 'All you're doing is chastising him and using him to earn money. I've a good mind to call that policeman over there!'

At the mere mention of the word, his uncle let go of Griff's shoulder and moved away. 'You've not heard the last of this, Griff,' he sneered. 'I'll be back and I'll find you and next time I won't go so lightly on you.'

Griff shivered and Mrs Hollings drew him to her and cuddled him. When his uncle and Bronwen were out of earshot she whispered, 'Believe me, Griff, he won't get within a hair's breadth of you ever again.'

Chapter Eighteen

Mr Gittings called Griff into his office after his performance the following night.

'Sit down, Griff,' he said.

Oh, no! Is he going to give me bad news that the Stanburys have changed their minds?

He looks so serious.

'Sir, have I done anything wrong?'

'No, not at all, quite the reverse in fact. It is I who should be apologising to you. I knew your uncle was an old cadger of a man, but I had no idea he would accost you again in the street. Mrs Hollings came and told me whilst you were on stage earlier this evening. So, what I've decided to do is to send you to another theatre called the Royal Music Hall. It's in a different location, and hopefully that man shan't find you there.'

'Thanks so much, Mr Gittings.' Griff let out a long breath of relief. 'I feel like a weight has lifted off my shoulders.'

The stage manager smiled. 'You'll also be given a new name so your uncle won't know it's you on the bill.'

Mrs Hollings loaned Griff a small trunk to pack the few belongings he already had. He'd earned enough from his performances at the theatre, as well as working for her, to buy himself a new tweed jacket, three shirts, two pairs of long trousers instead of his usual short breeches, and some badly-needed new underwear. He'd also bought a strong pair of leather boots as his old ones were letting in rainwater. He stood in the hallway of her house waiting for the cab to arrive.

'Yer've done well for yerself, Griff! Come 'ere, lad!' Kitty said, planting a kiss on both his cheeks. 'I've packed you a couple of pies an' I hope that landlady will take care of you as good as I 'ave . . .' She wiped away a tear with her cotton hanky.

'I'll never be able to repay you for your kindness, Mrs Hollings.' He felt quite overwhelmed at leaving her behind, but it had to be done. It just wasn't safe, him staying in this part of the city. His eyes watered, but he didn't want to act like a baby so he swallowed his sadness down.

A sharp rap on the door indicated the horse-drawn cab had arrived. Griff looked around him one last time as he opened the door for the cabbie to take the trunk, then followed behind him.

Mrs Hollings stood on the doorstep as the cab pulled away, with Griff sticking his head out of the window, waving all the way until she became a little dot in the distance. He was moving on in life and leaving the past behind.

Within the month, Griff had performed at the new theatre and had enjoyed every performance. The stage manager had been as good as his word, giving the act a new name: 'Little Lorrie'. It went down a storm, just as it had at the previous theatre and, before that, the Temperance Hall, which now felt many moons ago. Now there was no dog performing alongside him, as Molly, who had taken over from Scamp, had got herself in the family way by a scruffy mongrel who had been sniffing around the stage door, and was put out of action. So now there was just himself, as he developed a different style of act where he didn't just sing but now told jokes, too. He seemed to have a natural aptitude for looking on the humorous side of life. The name Lorrie was a short form of 'Laurence', as that's what the family who were to adopt him thought sounded a good name.

He was going from rags to riches, and they wanted a name to suit. He would also be expected to take something that sounded like 'L-O-Coosh-Un lessons' to learn how to speak properly, and he'd be having a home tutor. He'd never gone to school in his life, though he could read a little, thanks to Megan.

He liked William and Arabella Stanbury, warming to them immediately. They were due to take him home after his final performance at the Royal on Friday evening. Mrs Hollings had been given a ticket to see his last show and there were plans for him to have a chance to say goodbye to her and to thank her for her kindness before he left. He'd kept some of his money to buy her a pretty, pink mother-of-pearl brooch to remember him by.

He couldn't wait for Friday, to begin his new life, but he was sorry to say goodbye to Mrs Hollings. He promised he'd write to her regularly. He figured he'd have to get someone to help him to begin with, until he became a proper scholar. His heart still yearned to be with Megan, but he feared she'd have forgotten all about him by now. How he missed her funny little ways and how she tried her best to be a lady like Kathleen. If she could only see him now, and know the new life he would soon lead. Mrs Hollings had said that from now on he was going to be a proper little gentleman.

The Stanburys had told him he would have his own quarters at their home. *Quarters?* He didn't even understand the meaning of the word. Didn't that mean chopping something into bits? He'd heard the saying, 'hung, drawn and quartered' . . . It didn't make sense – until Mrs Stanbury told him it meant he'd have a very large bedroom all to himself, with his own bathroom, and another small room called a 'drawing room'. He had no idea what the drawing room was for, but he'd find out soon enough. The Stanburys were very kind to him indeed.

Arabella Stanbury had the kindest face he'd ever seen on a lady of her stature and means, barring, of course, his two favourite ladies back in Merthyr Tydfil, Megan and Kathleen. Arabella took her time to nurture him, taking him to see the horses they owned at the stables. She got him fully kitted out and they went riding together. As fast as the wind they flew across green fields and into the woods, where they stopped for picnics. William took him fishing and taught him about all the countries he'd visited, showing him everywhere on a large, colourful map he kept in his study.

The Stanburys bought him new clothes from a proper gentlemen's outfitters in the area. And soon, after a period of study with a home tutor to enable him to catch up with the other boys he'd encounter, he started in public school – something, he realised, that Megan in Merthyr would find astonishing. He thought of writing to her often – he could write properly now – but feared how he would explain his disappearance and lack of writing for so long. The Stanburys had advised him to lose touch with all the people he'd known back home if he wished to remain safe. If word got out where he was, he was scared that his uncle could discover his whereabouts and try to reclaim him. There were many young lads like him in Merthyr Tydfil. It was probably best Megan forgot all about him anyhow.

Megan did well at the tea room and Mrs Mathias was pleased with her progress. One day she called her to the house to speak about something. She could now visit the house again as Eli was up and about, and the doctor said he no longer posed a danger to others.

'Megan, I am very pleased with your work, but I think it's time we took care of your schooling, *cariad*,' Peggy said kindly. 'Now that the baby is due any time at Morris's home, you can help out there whenever you can, but I really think we need to focus on your education. You've saved enough money to afford to attend school.'

Megan frowned. 'But I had some education at the workhouse,' she said. 'I can read and write, and I can add up sums. I don't need any more education to work in the tea room and that's all I want to do.'

Why was Peggy being like this? It would only give her more to do on top of everything she was already doing. She didn't have time to sit down and take lessons when she didn't need to.

Peggy smiled warmly. 'I know all of that, and you are streets ahead of most your age, but it will stand you in good stead. I'm telling you this because I think you are an intelligent girl who could go far. I wish I'd been better educated. Some people would bite off your hand to have your chances in life. It's not often many young women from Merthyr who get the chance of a good education; most end up in menial jobs if they're not stuck at home bringing up children and serving their husband.'

Thinking about it, Megan realised she had it better than

many in Merthyr and definitely those she had left behind at the workhouse. 'But I don't see how it could help me as I know what I want to do already.'

'Which is?' Peggy blinked.

'One day run my own tea room just like yours.'

Peggy chuckled. 'There's nothing wrong with that, and I told you, when I pass away from this life, I want you to take it over.'

'But how can I? You have three sons.'

'They'll have the bakery business and this house between them. They won't need my shop too.'

Somehow Megan doubted it. Although she got on well with Jed and Morris, the two eldest sons had wives and she could see that decision causing trouble.

'I'll tell you what then,' Peggy said. 'Seeing as how you're so stubborn, with some of your savings we'll pay for a tutor to come to this house a couple of evenings a week.'

Megan let out a long sigh.

Peggy wagged a finger. 'You'll thank me for it some day.'

Megan knew she was talking sense, but she felt a little overwhelmed with the responsibility of the tea room as well as being expected to help out when Morris's new baby was born. It was something she felt she could do without right now, but Peggy insisted she pay six pennies a week to the tutor. It wasn't that she was ungrateful or anything, far from it, but she wanted to concentrate solely on her work at the tea room. One day she'd have a shop of her own – she sensed it – so why did she need to have school lessons to achieve what she was already doing so well? But Peggy was so insistent that she have them and Megan didn't want to hurt the woman's pride as she had been so kind to her, so she found herself reluctantly agreeing to them.

Miss Marsh, her new tutor, had never married, and had a very prim and proper manner about her, but she did her job well, and Megan found herself enjoying her lessons. Miss Marsh taught her interesting things like the proper etiquette to use with customers, how to balance the books, keep ledgers and even about customs in other countries, some of which Megan found very strange indeed.

With things going well, all she wanted was to tell Griff about it all. She knew he'd be so proud of her and all the hardships in life she had overcome. She wondered what he was doing right now. Her mind flipped back to that day in the market when he'd brought Scamp along and both had performed in the street for passers-by. She knew he was clever and talented and he could live off his wits if needs be, but she hated the thought he might still be being beaten up by a big bully like that uncle of his. She dearly wished that he might also have a break in the same way she had. She knew that she could not get in touch with him, but satisfied herself with the fact that she could keep an eye on Scamp for him.

1877: Ten Years Later

Chapter Nineteen

Megan was tidying up the tea room. It had been damn hard work ever since Peggy had passed away – thankfully peacefully in her sleep a couple of months ago – and running the business now took all of her time. She took such pride in her work and she wanted to keep Peggy's spirit alive in the tea room she had spent so many years building. When Megan had got to the age of twenty-one, she had insisted that Peggy leave the tea room to her sons in her will, knowing that they'd allow her to rent it from them. When the time came and she could afford it, she would offer to buy it herself. It was something she felt strongly about, and Peggy, knowing how stubborn Megan could be, finally agreed to her wishes.

The brothers, though, to be fair to them, had agreed to only charge Megan a peppercorn rent for the place. But the way things were going – with very slow business and fewer and fewer customers by the day – she thought it would be years until she could afford to buy them out, if ever. But at least it salved her conscience; she'd have felt guilty taking part of their inheritance. So one day, she'd either buy the shop from them, so they could share the money equally, or failing that, she would continue renting from them so they received a profit and she'd receive a nominal wage. It was looking increasingly probable that the latter option would be the more likely.

She had employed her two younger sisters, Lizzie and May, at the shop. They were such good workers and becoming proper little ladies. Tom had married Amy and they were living on the Tram Road. He now had his own carpentry business and still popped back and forth to see his brothers, and Mr and Mrs Evans, at the shop. They were quite elderly now, but Harry and Alfie did most of the work and were more than happy to do so.

It was nice to see all her brothers and sisters getting on so well in life. Kathleen and her husband, Dafydd, often called into the shop – they now had a little girl called Rebecca. She was the sweetest little thing, all curls and dark brown eyes. Kathleen had done well on the London stage, to much acclamation, but circumstances had forced her to return to Merthyr, a fact that Megan couldn't help but take some selfish delight in.

Aside from money troubles, something else was concerning Megan. There were signs that someone had tried to break into the tea room. Sometimes she kept the takings in the back room, locked away in a tin savings box – only when the bank was closed when she worked late, mind – but on one occasion she had felt she was being followed. It was as if someone were watching her movements.

She was ill at ease. In all the time she'd worked at the tea room, there had never really been any problems of that sort and it hadn't been something that Peggy had prepared her for. And, being situated in a more secluded part of town, it could feel quite unsettling when night fell early in winter time. She felt that it was safer to keep the takings in the back rather than risk being accosted on her way home. But now she wasn't so sure.

She still lived at Peggy's old home. Eli was still there. He had never married, which had never been an issue, but now Peggy had gone, she felt a little uncomfortable with them both being under the same roof. It wasn't so much what he said, but he sometimes gave her strange looks, almost as though he were undressing her with his eyes. She'd never had any time for boyfriends as she was so business-minded and cared more about the shop making a tidy profit.

Eli, to her knowledge, had not had a girlfriend, but there were times when she wondered whether it was something he yearned for. He didn't seem very satisfied with his life. He had taken to drinking again lately, and kept late hours. It had got to him that he hadn't been able to continue running the bakery and his lungs were too scarred and weakened for any kind of manual labour, so he had become a clerk in a solicitor's office in town. He'd already had more than one warning about lateness and turning up for work looking unkempt.

She always made him breakfast, as she woke up first in order to open up the tea room, but he was becoming increasingly irritable when she roused him. So she'd decided from now on, if he wasn't up for breakfast she'd leave it there. It was down to him whether he got to work or not. In her mind, the sooner she moved out the better. There was a small room above the tea room and the place, of course, had a privy and running water, so it was an option she was increasingly thinking about. Though as it was in such close proximity to the parish church, she realised the clock might well disturb her sleep during the night, for it chimed loudly every hour.

That day, after saying farewell to her sisters, she was just about to lock the shop door and count up that day's takings when all of a sudden the door burst open. A tall, broad-shouldered, thuggish man stood there towering over her.

'Takings!' he demanded.

Megan's bottom lip quivered. 'They've already been banked,' she said trying not to show just how frightened she was.

'Don't try to fool me, little lady. I've been watching this place for days. Now go and get them before I do something you might regret!'

'No!' she said firmly. 'You'll have to fight me for them first.'

He pushed her out of the way, and she fell up against a table, then he strode behind the counter, tossing around ledgers and stacks of small plates, which she feared might break.

'That's my best china!' she shouted, becoming angry.

'Oh, it is indeed, darling!' He picked up a pretty flowered saucer with gold edging and held it up ready to smash on the floor. 'If you don't tell me, I'll wreck this place!'

'No, please don't do that. I'll get you the money.' She could have wept. Today had been a wonderful day, takings wise, for the first time in a long time. She and her sisters had worked hard, and now she wouldn't have enough money to pay their wages. But what could she do? The man set the saucers back down gently on the counter.

'That's my girl. Now I think we'll come to an understanding, shall we?'

She nodded, naively believing that once she'd handed over the day's takings, she'd never see him again.

She walked behind the counter and pulled out the black tin box which she placed on the counter top, then with a silver key she kept in her pinafore pocket, she opened it up. He dipped his hands in the box with a leering smile on his face, stuffing his pockets with lots of coins and banknotes.

'Now, you've got what you want, please leave or else I'll—'

'Or else you'll what?'

'Or else I'll call to the police station and tell them what you did. I have a policeman friend.'

He threw back his head and laughed. 'I'm shivering in my shoes!' Then he glanced at her, his stare becoming penetrative as if warning her of what was to come. 'From now on you'll tip up once a week. That way you'll ensure no other brutes like me steal from you. I've left you a few pennies, taken a lot for the first week, but from next week I'll take just a regular wage from you, about half the day's takings like I do at other shops. In return you will be afforded protection from all the yobs in the area.'

Then he strode out the door as if he were just another customer. She ran to it and bolted it, then slumped down on the floor with her back against it. She put her head in her hands and wept bitter tears of pain and humiliation. How could she have been caught this way? She should have told Jed and Morris of her fears before now, then maybe it would never have happened if she'd had their presence around the shop.

All the way back to Plymouth Street, she kept looking behind her. It was dark by now and every echoing footstep scared her. There was a full moon that cast an eerie glow and caused flickering shadows to scare her; her heart thumped beneath her bodice. The walk home seemed long and laborious and when she finally arrived at the house, she was a bath of perspiration.

'What's the matter with you?' Eli asked, narrowing his gaze as she entered the hallway, immediately shutting and bolting the door behind her.

'I . . . I was attacked in the shop by a man who's taken almost all the day's takings and he says he'll be back next week for more.'

'Oh, will he now?' Eli said angrily. 'Well, if he tries it, he'll have me to contend with!'

Poor, fragile Eli – he could never beat someone like that, but she wasn't about to tell him so. 'That's reassuring,' she said. For once, he wasn't drunk but smartly dressed, as if he'd been at work all day. 'Have you had anything to eat yet?'

He shook his head. 'No, I was waiting for you, but now I think you've had such a nasty shock, I can't expect you to make the supper.'

'Well, I shall do,' she said wearily, removing her cape and hanging it on a peg behind the door.

'Not yet, you won't,' he insisted. 'I'm going to make you a cup of tea for a change, and you don't have to cook – there's some leftover stew from last night. I didn't have mine as I was out, at Morris's house. His wife made me a cup of tea and a small bite to eat.'

'I wondered where you were, I thought—'

'I know what you thought – that I was out drinking some-place. I've had a good think about my behaviour of late, and now I need to pull up my bootstraps, Meg.' He sounded so humble that her heart went out to him.

'Come on, I'll make us both a cup of tea,' she said, with warmth in her voice.

'No, please sit down and I'll do it. Then later, you can put the stew on to warm.'

'But you wouldn't want to do woman's work now, would you?' she said, in more of a jest than in all seriousness.

'Well, I used to bake bread and cakes for a living.' He laughed and filled the kettle with water to make a brew. It was nice to see him smiling again. How could she possibly think about moving out right now?

They drank their cups of tea and chatted for a while, and later, following the beef stew, sat in companionable silence by the fireplace. She was going to have to have a word with Jed and Morris about the new-found threat at the tea room.

Chapter Twenty

Griff, or Laurence, as he was now known, had done well at college, eventually graduating with honours from Oxford. It had taken him a while to get used to having a private tutor at home and learning to speak properly. Eventually, he'd deliberately lost his Welsh accent so none of the boys at his new school would tease him. It took some considerable time to fit it there, though, but after a long spell, he became well accepted as he was good at sport and something of a scholar, which surprised even him, becoming one of the most popular boys at the school. He had come to gain the respect of his peers.

Oxford had been hard going and many times he had felt like giving up, but he'd studied Law, and eventually took all the examinations to qualify him as a lawyer. He was set up for life, but there was only one thing that preoccupied his mind these days, and that was to return to Merthyr Tydfil, to find Megan. He had never forgotten her. He'd had girlfriends he'd stepped out with, but none had taken his heart. So far, that remained beating for one girl back in his old life. He wondered what she was doing right now and if she was married. He wondered if she ever thought of him.

He planned a trip to return home next month. He'd take the train. He looked at himself in the long mirror of his walnut wardrobe – with his silver-grey silk cravat, crisp white shirt and long grey tailcoat with matching trousers, he didn't scrub up too badly for someone who had once been a street urchin.

One evening when she was in the house with Eli, Megan noticed that he was acting strangely. Every so often she caught him gazing at her, then turning away.

'Is everything all right?' she asked. She was beginning to wonder if she had a dirty mark on her cheek, or a tear in her dress, the way he was staring so intensely.

'Yes,' he said as his face flushed bright red. What was the matter with the man? Was something wrong?

'Fancy a cup of tea, then?' she asked brightly, trying to break the awkward silence between them. He'd hardly said a word to her since she'd arrived home from the tea room.

'Er . . . no, thanks. Sit down a moment, Megan, will you?'

A feeling of dread came over her. Had his illness returned? Were the brothers about to sell the tea room? Or maybe he wanted her out of the house?

She took a seat in the armchair near the fire and was surprised as he knelt before her. What was happening here?

'Megan,' he said, gazing up into her eyes, 'I've been thinking this through for some time. We've known one another a long time now and I feel we get on well, don't we?'

'Y–yes.' She nodded.

'So, how about we get together properly, then?'

'Get together?' Did he mean what she thought he meant? He wanted them to live together? What would the neighbours think about that?

'Oh, I don't think it would be right for us to live in sin with one another, Eli. I just couldn't do that – it goes against my moral grain.'

'No, silly.' He chuckled. 'I want much more than that. I want us to get married, if you'll take me as your husband?'

'Married?' Megan blinked several times. She and Eli had grown close lately since Peggy had died. He'd cleaned up his act and she'd found he was actually quite pleasant to be around.

'Yes, why not. We get along nicely don't we?'

'We do indeed, but—'

'But what? Now you can't say we don't know one another well – we've lived under the same roof for the past ten years or so.'

'I know, it's just I've never thought of you that way before. You've been more like an older brother – or young uncle – to me.'

He chuckled. 'Well, you're a beautiful young woman who is free to make her own choices in life. And thankfully I am neither brother nor uncle to you. Will you tell me you'll think about it, at least?' He gazed into her eyes as if trying to gauge her response.

She nodded. She really wasn't sure. She did have some kind of love for Eli, but it wasn't passion she felt at all, yet how many Merthyr women had been left on the shelf as they'd taken too long to make up their minds? She should be thankful she had a man who had his own home and a job; many of her former contemporaries at the workhouse did not.

So she'd promised she'd think about it as it gave her some breathing space.

There was no more trouble at the tea room for the time being as Jed and Morris took turns to watch the place in the evenings and escort Megan safely home. And when they couldn't do it, Megan stayed on at the shop, ensuring the door was locked, sitting out in the back room reading a book until Eli showed up an hour later after he'd finished work at the solicitor's office to walk her home. He had been so kind and caring lately that she was beginning to come around to the idea of marrying him. He was a good ten years older, but that didn't matter to her. He hadn't mentioned having children and she wondered if his health was good enough for him to perform his husbandly duties.

Could she survive a marriage, though, where there were no

marital relations at all? Could she survive a marriage without passion? Yet she felt it unseemly to ask him about such things. She had even wondered if that was why he had never married. Maybe he felt more comfortable with her, as she knew him so well and cared for him.

One thing she told herself was that Peggy would have been happy with the union. That woman had done so much for her. She owed her old friend.

And so the wedding was arranged for May. Mrs Evans had made the dress for her from some light blue French silk she'd purchased at Merthyr market at cost price. She was going to look so beautiful, Mrs Evans said, and Megan trusted her. But there was something missing and she didn't know what it was. She should be excited, like all new brides, but she wasn't. There was a deep yearning for something inside her. But what it was for, she didn't know.

Laurence arrived in Merthyr Tydfil just as darkness began to fall. The outdoor market was being packed away and as he passed a fruit and veg stall with its rosy-cheeked apples, he remembered that day so long ago when he'd made off with an armful of them, chased by a pretty little girl who was kindness itself; the day he'd first met Megan – and how much had changed for him since then.

He needed to find a hotel for the night, but first he was on a mission: he was going to see if she still, by some slim chance, worked at the tea room near the parish church.

As he passed on by, he heard people muttering things like 'Who's he?' and 'Looks like a toff to me!' He realised he must look so out of place in this working-class area, where the best-dressed men were the ironmasters, pit owners and businessmen. Not a lot had changed, except that now he had grown into an adult; things appeared a little smaller than how he remembered.

As he neared the lower end of the High Street, he heard the clock of the church chime seven times. It was too much to hope that even if Megan still worked at the shop, she would still be there. The shop would no doubt have closed by six o'clock.

He let out a long breath as he approached, to find the shop was in darkness. He couldn't resist peeping in through the window, the bay one that he remembered so well, with its leaded glass and pristine white lace curtains. Beneath the gaslight, he could just make out some tables and chairs. It looked just the same as the day he left, and memories came flooding back as if it were yesterday. He was just about to turn and leave when he thought he saw movement inside. In fact, he was sure he had. There was a thin sliver of light emanating from the back room. On a whim, he called out: 'Hello!'

From inside he heard a woman's voice cry out, 'Please go away. My brother will be here soon to walk me home!'

He called out, 'Please let me in. I will not harm you. I'm looking for Megan Hopkins.' And with that, the light went on in the shop and the front door slowly opened.

Megan realised by the man's well-spoken voice that he wasn't her attacker. In fact, that man had not been back since, but she continued to keep her routine of being walked home just in case. Tentatively she opened the door and blinked at the man who stood in front of her. He was tall; that was the first thing she noticed. He wore a top hat and was very well dressed.

'May I come in?' he asked. His accent did not sound Welsh at all. He lowered his head as he entered the shop.

'Very well, but you can't stop for long . . .'

'You do not recognise me, Megan, do you?'

She studied him carefully. Was this some kind of trick? Had Morris or Jed, or even Tom, sent the man here to poke fun at her, as a ruse maybe? But no, she didn't think either one would do that.

He stood firm, staring at her. His shoulders broad, he fitted his long grey tailcoat well; his shirt so crisp and dazzling white and his silver-grey cravat, pinned in place with a small diamond pin. She didn't know anyone of a class such as the type his clothes indicated.

She breathed in slowly and let the breath out again. This man was astonishingly handsome.

'Forgive me,' he said, then he removed his top hat and gloves, placed the gloves inside the hat, and set it down on a table.

Still, she was puzzled – what would a toff like this gentleman want with the likes of her? Then it dawned on her. Morris had said there was a gentleman interested in purchasing the tea room. Maybe it was him.

'No, I'm sorry I do not recognise you. Are you here to view this place?'

He chuckled, which threw her off guard. 'Well, in a way, maybe I am, but I have really come to see you, Megan.'

How did he know her name? 'I'm sorry, sir, but if this is some game you're playing—'

He smiled broadly, a smile that made his eyes glitter with amusement. 'Do you remember that little boy whom you chased after that day so very long ago? The one who stole the apples? The one who could have been caught and transported to Australia if you had not come to his aid?'

Megan was robbed of all breath. He had come about Griff. Was he all right? She had not heard from him in all the years he had been gone. Composing herself, she said, 'I do indeed. You know where he is? Griff Rhys?'

The stranger nodded. 'The little boy is right here, Megan. Beneath your very nose.'

Megan studied him carefully. Surely not? But then again the man would be around the age Griff would be now. The more she stared, the more she noticed familiar features: the curly dark hair, the sparkling eyes, the sense of humour.

'Yes, if I had Scamp here with me right now, he'd be rolling on a barrel!' Then he started to sing the song he'd sang that night at the Temperance Hall and she knew without a shadow of a doubt it was him, her Griff.

'Griff, is it really you . . . ?' Tears ran down her cheeks.

He stepped forward. 'Yes, it is really me, Megan—'

And she was in his arms and she was eleven years old once again. It felt so good to be held by him, the person she had always loved, the missing piece of her heart.

He drew away to look at her. 'Of course, I look so different now, and sound it, too. I was Oxford educated, you know.'

She smiled. 'I'm so pleased for you, but what happened? Where are my manners! Please sit down.'

He did as requested and he talked; he talked about his uncle making him go against his will to London; he talked about how he ended up on the stage there, and eventually, his escape to live with the Stanbury family, who had taken great care of him and turned him into the gentleman that sat before her today.

'That's wonderful, Griff,' she said, feeling that she wanted to hug him again. But somehow his well-tailored clothing and new voice seemed like some sort of armour between them, the difference between working class and middle class.

'My name is Laurence Stanbury now.' He chuckled. 'No one has called me "Griff" in years, but it feels so good for you to say it, Megan. It's you who drew me back here. I have never been able to forget you and I hoped . . .'

She wondered what he was about to say. Her breath caught momentarily in her throat, then after a pause, she said, 'You will always be Griff to me, even if you don't much look like that scruffy street urchin any more.' Her eyes began to fill with tears, and she turned away. 'But why did you never get in touch with me this past ten years? I never, ever forgot about you. I even planned on going to look for you. You never said goodbye to me, that's what hurt the most. We were such good friends, too. I've cried a river for that little boy over the years, the only real friend I ever had . . .'

He took her hand across the table. 'Oh, Megan, I never wished to upset you . . . I was forced to leave Merthyr by my uncle who saw my success at the talent show at the Temperance Hall and thought we could make money in London. Believe me, I wanted to get in touch the whole time I was there. But we were so scared my uncle would find me I didn't dare risk it. I managed to get away from him and met a lovely lady called Kitty, who put me up for a while in her pie shop. I even got work on the stage and, eventually, was adopted by a lovely couple who gave me a good education. I couldn't have wished for better.

'But I'm here now, Megan, and that's all that matters. We are reunited at last. I never forgot you, even if you don't believe that. I put off writing to you as it was so painful to think of you in Merthyr and knowing I might never see you again. The Stanburys, my adoptive parents, advised me to break all ties with this town. I figured you'd be better off forgetting all about me. I kept telling myself I'd write tomorrow, but tomorrow never came. Until now. Now we can finally be together, if it's what you want, too?'

She turned towards him through a haze of tears. 'It's not that, Griff. I am so very pleased to see you again, but now I am betrothed to someone. We are due to marry next month.'

His dark green eyes clouded over. 'I left it too late . . .' He shook his head and turned away. 'Please tell me it's not too late? Who is this fellow?'

'It's Eli, Mrs Mathias's son. We've grown close to one another since her death.'

'I remember him well. He's a lot older than you . . . But if you love him, you must do what your heart tells you. I will not stand in your way, but if it's me you love' – his voice cracked as he said this – 'you need to do the right thing by him. And me.'

Megan put her head in her hands.

'Look at me, Megan . . .' She lifted her head. 'What do you see?'

'I see a very handsome man, a man I don't know. But when you smile, I see that little boy Griff once again . . .' She sniffed. 'The boy I fell in love with many years ago.'

He smiled broadly. 'I knew it.' He squeezed her hand in reassurance. 'And I fell in love the moment you caught me that day, as you ran like the wind to catch up with me and we hid in the graveyard. I love you too, Megan. You captured my heart that very day. I've always loved you and never forgotten you in all these years. For me, there were others, but none were you . . .' He gazed at her intently and lifted her hand to lay a kiss upon it.

Megan felt herself tingle from top to toe. She didn't get that feeling with Eli. 'Oh, what shall I do about this? I don't want to break Eli's heart.'

Still holding her hand across the table, he said, 'But you must, Megan. Or your own heart will be broken in the process; mine, too. It is better to break just one heart that will mend than two who are destined to be together.'

She nodded as the tears coursed down her cheeks. He put his hand in his pocket and extracted a silver-grey silk handkerchief and dabbed at her tears. Although they were now adults whose lives had gone off in different directions, they knew one another, oh so well.

'I'll tell him tonight,' she said finally. 'Where are you staying?'

'I'm going to book into a hotel on the High Street, hopefully. How about if I call here first thing in the morning to see how the land is lying?'

She nodded, feeling better now. 'Yes, that sounds good to me.'

'Shall I walk you home, like I used to?'

She shook her head vehemently. 'You'd better not. Jed will

be calling here to walk me home soon. I had trouble with a man accosting me here. He robbed me of the day's takings,' she said by way of explanation. 'Though Dafydd, Kathleen's husband, thinks that the man is probably in jail now from the description I gave him. He said that's why he hasn't been back here to pester me for more money – a gang of men were detained by the police just one week after my experience. That was several months ago. But anyway, for the time being, I feel better being escorted home, so now either Tom or Eli or one of his brothers escorts me home from work. Tonight, it's Jed's turn – you'd better leave before he shows up and asks too many questions.' She chewed her bottom lip, then stood, and Griff followed suit. He took her in his arms and gazed into her eyes.

'I so long to kiss you, Megan, but it wouldn't be right until you have broken off your engagement . . .'

She nodded, then he pulled away, lifted up his top hat and gloves from the table, smiled, then left the shop, leaving her standing there with a quickened heartbeat and the emotional pain of seeing him go. Now they were reunited, she wanted to be by his side, always.

Laurence found a hotel on the High Street. The room wasn't what he was used to – these days he'd become accustomed to grand living and could afford to stay at first-class establishments – but there didn't appear to be any hotels of that calibre in the area. It was flooded with migrants from places like Ireland, Spain and even Eastern Europe, to work in the ironworks. He'd rubbed shoulders with many of those when he'd lived in the China district of town with his uncle. *Uncle Berwyn*: now there was a blast from the past. He hadn't thought of him in years; maybe by now he had even passed away. For one fleeting moment, he thought of the good times they'd had, but they had been few and far between. But in some respects he had a lot to thank him for, putting a roof over his head and taking him off to London, else he'd never have met the Stanburys. Once the initial fear that he would be recaptured by his uncle had faded, and he realised he was perfectly safe living with the Stanburys, he'd relaxed and put him to the back of his mind. Merthyr and his uncle were relegated to just a bad dream. If it wasn't for Megan, the only good part he remembered of his life here, he wouldn't have returned at all.

The room he was staying in was far pokier than what he was used to, but it was clean. He hung up his tailcoat in the wardrobe and lay on the bed staring at the ceiling. It was another hour until it was time to dine there, so plenty of time to think of the one woman who meant the world to him.

When Megan arrived back at Plymouth Street, she felt breathless with anxiety. The walk home with Jed was difficult. She had been so absorbed in her own thoughts that he'd actually said to her, 'Did you hear what I just said, Megan?'

She'd had to pretend she was worried about the takings at the shop being poor that day, which was a barefaced lie. She felt guilty that she was about to upset so many people by calling off the wedding to Jed's brother. Arrangements were in progress; she would be a coward if she went through with it, and an even bigger coward for ditching Eli. It seemed she just couldn't win.

'Never mind, gal,' Jed said as he escorted her to the door. 'This time next month, my brother will make an honest woman of you. You know what the gossips are like around here – you two living under the same roof without my mother being there to supervise any more.'

Her cheeks blazed under the gaslight outside the house and she hoped he would not notice. *Is that what people were thinking? Now that Mrs Mathias had passed away, she was living tally with the woman's son?* But then Jed chuckled heartily and she realised it was just a joke.

But maybe people *were* thinking that. As soon as she broke things off with him, she would need to move into the room over the shop, for a little while at least.

She thanked Jed, then closing the door behind her, prepared to face Eli, but the house was cold and in complete darkness. That was odd. He should have been home by now.

Chapter Twenty-One

Megan lit the oil lamps in the living room and kitchen, then set about banking up the coal fire. Where on earth was Eli? He was usually home from work by now. The house was freezing cold and there was no sign whatsoever that he'd returned and gone back out again. What if he'd collapsed or something? After getting the fire started in the living room, she began to prepare the evening meal of beef stew with dumplings, which was a favourite of his.

Why couldn't he have been home tonight, of all nights? The very night she'd decided to sit him down after supper and explain about Griff's return to Merthyr. There would be no easy way of telling him, of course, and he would be hurt, she realised that, but as Griff had said himself, it was far better to break one heart than two. *Two hearts that were destined to beat together.*

Eli would eventually get over it. He had his brothers and their families, and his work as a clerk, to keep him going. If she were being honest, she was only marrying him as she felt pity for him anyhow. She liked him but she was not in love with him.

She sat and ate her stew in silence in the kitchen, watching as the mantel clock moved its hands to nine. There was still no sign of him. She pulled her shawl off the peg on the back of the kitchen door and wrapped it around herself; she'd call to Jed's house to see if he was there or if he'd heard anything.

But when she got there, Jed said he hadn't set eyes on Eli for several days and after consulting with his other brother, neither had Morris.

She chewed her bottom lip. What was she to do? Then she realised – beyond a shadow of a doubt – that he'd hit the bottle again and had gone to a pub after work that day. He had been sober for such a long time, too.

She must have drifted off to sleep in the armchair in front of the fire, as the next thing she knew, she heard a door slam and sensed a presence hovering over. She tried not to cough as she ingested the strong fumes of alcohol.

'Ah, so this is my lovely wife-to-be!' Eli chanted. 'Get my dinner on, woman!'

She stood, fearing to say anything. Then he slapped her hard on the backside. She was instantly repelled. Maybe if she gave him something to eat, it would soak up the alcohol, then he'd fall asleep and she could talk to him when he was sober tomorrow.

'I'll just warm your supper up . . .' she said quietly, heading for the kitchen.

He threw himself down in the armchair and closed his eyes. He was fast asleep before the stew had even warmed up. She knew better than to wake him – it might disturb him and change his mood, making it even worse.

She removed the pan of stew on the hob from the heat, then brought a thick Welsh blanket down from his bed upstairs and draped it over him. At least the fire was lit and would keep him warm. She ensured the fireguard was in place. It would probably be out by morning.

Sighing, she turned off the oil lamp and made for her bed.

By the time she awoke the following morning, Eli had already got ready for work and was out of the house. Normally, he'd be there at the breakfast table, but she guessed he was probably ashamed of last night's behaviour. Now she had a dilemma: she hadn't told him she was leaving, and Griff would be calling to the shop to see her first thing.

Before anyone had arrived, even her sisters for work, Griff was knocking at the tea-room door gently. She allowed him in.

'I couldn't sleep for thoughts of you last night . . .' he said quite breathlessly. He looked even more dashingly handsome in the daylight. 'I've been thinking things over in my mind, and I'd like to move my law firm here to Merthyr Tydfil. Oh, Megan, then we can be married . . .'

He picked her up in his arms and swung her around, but she felt stiff and wooden. Somehow she couldn't match her joy with his and she felt bad about that.

'Oh, Griff, I don't know how to tell you this . . .'

His eyes widened. 'What? Please don't tell me you've changed your mind, Megan?'

'No, no, it's not that at all, but I was ready last night to tell Eli when I realised he hadn't come home. He didn't return until almost midnight and he was drunk, so I couldn't possibly tell him and he'd left for work early this morning, so he still doesn't know.'

'Oh, Megan, you can't stay with a man who tempers his lips with strong liquor. Please, I implore you, pack a bag and get out of there whilst you can, or he might become abusive. I saw enough of it with my uncle – he battered me black and blue and it never got any better. It was the main reason Mrs Hollings and Mr Gittings got me to a safe haven with the Stanburys.'

She nodded, recognising the names from their talking the previous day. 'I agree with all you say and I'm truly sorry for all you suffered, Griff . . .' She looked into his eyes and realised she could never let him down. 'So far, Eli hasn't really laid a finger on me, apart from last night when he slapped me hard on the behind when I was slow to get him his supper. By the time it was ready he was fast asleep in the armchair . . .' She raised an eyebrow.

'Then, Megan, I think you should go back home whilst he's at work and pack a bag and get out of there. Leave him a letter telling him you've changed your mind about marrying him.'

She nodded, though felt it was the coward's way out. 'I'll get my sisters to mind the shop whilst I return to Plymouth Street, though you must not accompany me, Griff. There are too many gossips about, and Jed and Morris live nearby.'

Griff nodded. 'Very well, Megan. If you wish, I could book you into my hotel?'

'No, thank you all the same, there is no need for any of that. I can stay in the room above the tea room for the time being. There's a couch I can sleep on and there's running water and a privy, and of course, a stove, so all my needs shall be met until I find something better.'

'Oh, and we will have something better, Megan. I'll buy you a beautiful home to live in after we're married.' He stepped forward and kissed her on the forehead. 'As soon as your sisters arrive, go back home and pack that bag and leave a letter.'

She nodded. 'You'd better leave before Lizzie and May get here. I need to explain it all to them first.'

'Very well, but I shall be back later, dearest Megan.' He flashed a smile at her that melted her heart once again. It was the same endearing smile she'd loved so much when he was a young lad.

And now she loved Griff the man, too.

Griff left the tea room bitterly disappointed that Megan hadn't had the opportunity to break off her engagement to

Eli. He felt desperately sorry for the man. Even if it were him that Megan loved more, he still felt it would be a bad thing for her to live with a man who put the bottle before his wife.

Still, hopefully things would be better soon.

He'd made an appointment to see someone about the purchase of chambers for his new law firm. The rooms were above a large shop on the High Street and he was pleased to see they were in good condition and would only require a lick of paint, and some new furnishings. Maybe some small touches that Megan could procure, like eye-catching artwork and ornaments and thick velvet drapes. She had an eye for these kinds of things. He wanted to attract a good class of clientele if possible, but he also felt it important to take on those less fortunate than himself. After all, he once walked in their shoes and would never forget where he came from. He was lucky to be given a second chance in life.

Megan had left her sisters in charge of the tea room. She ran as fast as her feet would carry her back home, stopping every so often to draw a breath. Time was of the essence. It was bitterly cold and she'd left her coat at the tea room and now wished she hadn't. She approached the front door, possibly entering it for the very last time. That made her feel so sad and she stood staring around at the house, filled with so many memories of Peggy and Eli.

A voice inside her warned her to act quickly, so she began to fill a couple of carpet bags with her clothing and anything else she needed. Her heartbeat increased at the thought of Eli coming back early. He was never usually home at this time of the day, but her ears pricked up at every small sound that the old house made, just in case it was him. When she'd packed all the belongings she wanted to take with her, she sat down at the table to pen a letter to Eli. The words didn't come easily and there were many cumpled up pieces of paper thrown in the fire. She decided to keep it brief, without bringing Griff into it, or Laurence, as she realised she should now address him.

My Dearest Eli,

I have decided that it is in both our best interests if we were to break off our engagement to one another. I think we have both been so laden down with grief that our feelings became confused. We were both hurting inside and sought solace where we could find it.

I have decided to move out of the house but shall remain working at the tea room. I hope in time you will comprehend this decision.

Yours truly,
Megan

There, she'd done it, and she hadn't accused him of being a drunk, nor had she said she'd be leaving him for someone else. A shard of guilt pierced her heart nevertheless as she realised she should not have agreed to marry him in the first place. She also felt guilty for Mrs Evans and all the hard work she had put into making her wedding dress for her, and Jed and Morris too, for the wedding cake they planned to make. But still, even so, not too much damage had been done, and she would pay Mrs Evans for the dress.

She took one last look around the room, realising she would be saying goodbye to it forever.

Just as she was about to leave, she heard the back door unlock. It was Eli. And he was drunk. He staggered into the room looking slovenly, almost as if he hadn't worn the pristine shirt she'd left out for him that morning.

'I've been dismissed,' was all he managed to say as tears coursed down his cheeks. 'And it's my own fault. I was told I'd turned up for work smelling like a brewery and it just wasn't good enough. Now what am I to do?'

He slumped down in an armchair, not noticing the two carpet bags near the front door, nor the note on the table. Eli sounded so downcast and dispirited – how could she possibly tell him she was leaving right now? She sidled over towards the dining table and stood with her back to the letter. As she spoke softly to him, she skilfully reached behind her and slipped it into the pocket of her dress. He was distracted, talking into the flames of the fire, and she managed to kick the two carpet bags under the table, where they would be hidden by the long, red chenille tablecloth. It gave her some breathing space.

'Anyhow, enough about me,' he said. 'How come you're home this time of the day?'

She felt her face flush red hot and hoped he wouldn't notice. 'I . . . er . . . came to change my frock as I spilled a jug of cream on it. I tried to wipe the mess up and get it off my dress but it was soaked, so the girls said they'd cover for me. Anyhow, I've changed it now.'

'Come over here and sit down a while. Lizzie and May can manage without you. I need some comfort right now.'

Although they had shared no more than a long kiss, suddenly Megan felt very uncomfortable. It was then she noticed the bottle of whisky peeking out from his trouser pocket. She shivered involuntarily. Letter or no letter, she needed to get away and fast.

'I . . . h–have to get back to the shop. It will become busy soon. It's the time of day when we get lots of customers . . .' She began to back away, but Eli was on his feet and approached her, suddenly a lustful glint in his eyes.

'I don't think we need wait for the wedding night,' he said, and looked at her suggestively. She stumbled backwards in her haste to back away from him and tripped over one of the carpet bags that she hadn't managed to push far enough under the table. And then he was on top of her, the smell of the whisky on his breath and the scent of stale perspiration emanating from his body. It made her nauseous. This wasn't what she wanted at all.

If only Griff were here to save her – why hadn't she got out sooner? Eli was pinning her arms down above her head. For someone who had been so fragile with his illness, now he seemed strong as his lustful urge drove him on. He removed one hand and used the other to hike up her skirts as he found the place he wanted to go. She felt him drag at her drawers. She was a virgin and this wasn't how she wanted things to be.

'No!' she cried. 'No. Please. We can wait for the wedding night. I would not want to do this without being wed first. It's wrong.'

As if her words had somehow got through to him, the look in his eyes changed and he let her arms go. He knelt beside her and wept, his shoulders convulsing heavily at the horror of what he had been about to do to her. She looked at him and pitied him for the weak man he was. He was truly broken, and no marriage would be able to fix it.

'I'm so sorry, Megan,' he said. 'When you said that to me it reminded me of what my mother used to say – that sexual relations outside marriage were wrong and sinful.' He rocked back and forth and she pulled herself up on her haunches. Even though he'd just tried to do a bad thing, it made her mind up for her.

She stood, then brushed down her skirts and tidied up her hair. Then in a calm and clear voice, which belied her inner feelings of upset at what had almost occurred, she said, 'I'm sorry, Eli. It's over. I was about to leave you. That's why I was home. I was packing my bags. I already felt our union was wrong, but I could never stay with you after what you just tried to do to me.' She pulled off an old shawl from a hook in the kitchen and draped it around her shoulders. Then she dragged both carpet bags out from under the table and lifted them. She paused at the door, watching him crying, still kneeling on the rug in front of the fire. She couldn't save him from himself – she had to think now what was in her own best interests. As she closed the door behind her, she said a silent goodbye to Plymouth Street, knowing that she was ending a chapter of her life for good.

Chapter Twenty-Two

Megan walked back towards the tea room with determination. Tears were streaming down her face, not just because of how she was almost raped back there but because she now realised she was helpless to do anything for Eli. She felt like she was letting Peggy down. She had no intentions of telling her sisters – nor anyone else for that matter – about what had just occurred, and so entered the tea room by the back door, took her carpet bags upstairs and sat down on the old couch to console herself. She had a good cry, and then, when she felt a little better, she went over to the bosh and swilled her face, wiping it on a clean towel. Griff would be calling later and she wanted him to see her at her best.

She took a deep, composing breath and descended the stairs to enter the tea room where Lizzie and May were busy serving customers. Lizzie was taking orders and May was slicing up cake. They had the silver tea urn boiling and it puffed out a cloud of steam, in readiness to make copious pots of tea.

They both stopped what they were doing to look at her with wide-eyed expectation. She donned her pinafore. 'All is well,' she said firmly. 'You can carry on with your tasks. Thanks for keeping this place ticking over.'

Then she went behind the counter and checked the takings, which looked nice and healthy. It seemed that this time of the day, just before lunch, was the most popular, with people dropping in for elevenses.

However hard she tried, though, she couldn't stop thinking about the incident with Eli. The only brief respite she got was serving customers, when she could distract herself. She was looking forward to the next time she might see Griff, as she knew he would know the right thing to say. He'd promised to come and visit her at the tea room and every time the door opened, she'd look up to see if it was him, but each time her heart sank a little in her chest when it was someone else. Where was he?

Eventually, as the afternoon wore on, she gave up all hope of him turning up. She'd sent the girls home, and now she didn't have to worry about being walked home. It was still risky walking to the bank on her own, though, so she decided she'd lock the money in the tin and take it first thing in the morning. As she saw the last of her customers off the premises, she sighed deeply. Griff wasn't coming and now she had the evening and night to spend all on her own. It was deadly quiet inside the tea room, save for the hourly chiming of the bells from the parish church. She somehow managed to find a comfort in this.

Deciding to keep herself busy, she filled a metal pail with hot soapy water and took it, along with a scrubbing brush, to clean the window frame and floor upstairs. Once satisfied it was clean enough, she went back downstairs and made herself a cup of tea whilst she waited for it all to dry. Then she set about unpacking her clothing from both carpet bags. She didn't have any clothes hangers – or even a wardrobe – but figured she'd buy herself everything she needed when she got the chance. She ended up draping her best dresses over a chair, and neatly folded her nightgowns and undergarments. The only thing she hadn't thought of was blankets – she'd intended to take the old Welsh wool one from home – but in amongst all the upheaval it had skipped her mind. She'd just have to cover herself with her woollen shawl and coat. It was better than nothing and the couch was comfy enough. She kept a small fire going in the upstairs room anyhow, so she shouldn't be too cold.

She debated whether she should call at Griff's hotel to check what was going on. She felt so weary and it was dark outside but she didn't think she could sleep without calling there to check.

She slipped on her coat and made her way from the tea room to the hotel, which was only a short walk way. When she got there she asked at the main desk, 'Is Griff Rhys Morgan around, please?'

The receptionist, who was a young woman in a long black dress with her blonde hair neatly pinned up in a chignon fashion, frowned. What was wrong? Didn't they know him here? Was this the wrong hotel? Then it dawned on her: he would have registered as Laurence Stanbury. The woman's face immediately lit up at the sound of his name, which made Megan wonder if Griff had been charming her, too. A sudden flash of jealousy hit her.

'Instead of standing there preening, could you please tell me Mr Stanbury's whereabouts?'

The receptionist's cheeks reddened. 'He went out on business early this afternoon and has yet to return. If you would care to leave a message . . .' The young woman's chin jutted out as if Megan had slighted her, and maybe in a way she had.

'Would you please tell him he can find me, Miss Megan Hopkins, at the tea room? I shall be there all night.'

The young woman raised an eyebrow in disbelief that anyone should spend an entire night at a tea room, but said nothing more. She nodded, then wrote something down in a big leather-bound ledger. 'Yes, ma'am,' she said, as if to get a rise out of Megan – as everyone knew young unmarried ladies were addressed as 'miss'.

Megan tossed back her curls and took a breath. She needed to leave in case she became much less of a lady than she already was.

She'd left an oil lamp burning in the tea room and entered as quickly as she could, looking both left and right for fear that the man who had accosted her should return. But there was no one around. All was quiet except for the rustle of the branches of the trees in the graveyard. She shivered as she turned the key in the lock and immediately shut herself inside, bolting the door as well as locking it. She was taking absolutely no chances.

Once inside, she went to the kitchen and put on a pan of milk to boil. It had been a hard, emotional day for her and a cup of cocoa might just do the trick. Even though Eli had intended on doing a bad thing, until his conscience had got the better of him, she didn't want him to suffer. She planned to call around to see his brothers at the bakery early in the morning before their shift ended. She wouldn't tell them what had happened, just that she was concerned about Eli's drinking and had left him as a result of it.

She would have to see the minister of the High Street chapel, who no doubt might try to get her to reconcile with him. But there was no going back now. Even without Griff on the scene she knew it was the right thing to do.

She waited downstairs in the shop but by nine o'clock Griff still hadn't shown up, so she went upstairs to bed. It was hard for her to get to sleep as the couch wasn't the most comfortable. She used a rolled-up dress as a makeshift pillow and tried to snuggle beneath her woollen shawl and coat, but it just wasn't the same. Her bed at Mrs Mathias's house had a feather mattress, and it was always comfy and warm in winter.

Eventually she drifted off to sleep, only to be woken on the hour by the sound of the parish church clock chiming; it was something she was going to have to get used to. In the morning she woke at half past six and her neck ached so much she knew she couldn't take another night on that couch. She was going to have to either move out or make her living arrangements more comfortable.

She tried to eat a leftover scone from yesterday but it was like eating sawdust; she just didn't have the appetite for it. So, after getting herself ready, she threw her shawl around her shoulders, tied up her bonnet and made her way to the Plymouth Street bakery.

As she locked up the shop behind her, a male voice called out her name. Relief flooded through her as she recognised it to be Griff's. Of course, his accent was new, which made it all the more recognisable.

She turned towards him. 'I was worried about you yesterday . . .'

He closed the space between them. 'I know. And I'm sorry about that. I received your message this morning. I didn't get back until the early hours. I went to view a property in the Brecon area and one of the horses pulling the stagecoach became lame. Something sharp had got wedged in its hoof. It was a simple thing really. But there was no way to let you know.'

'Brecon?' she furrowed a brow.

'Yes, I'd heard from someone about a new solicitor's practice that will be coming to Merthyr. Goldstein's. I was going to ask him if he'd consider a partnership as he has by all accounts an excellent reputation and I'm not known in these parts. He said he would consider it, but then I thought, no, I shall go it alone.'

'But that will make you rivals if Mr Goldstein should set up on the High Street too.'

'Oh he is, and he will be.' He chuckled. 'By the way, where are you off to?'

Her thoughts clouded over. 'I have to get to the bakery at Plymouth Street before Jed and Morris knock off. I need to speak to them about something very important.'

He looked at her intently. 'About leaving Eli?'

'Yes, that's what I came to tell you about. Yesterday he was drunk again, and got fired from his job. I felt bad leaving him that way, but he tried to accost me.'

'Accost you?' Griff's green eyes darkened.

She turned away. 'It was nothing, honestly, Griff.'

'Look at me, Megan. I've known you a long time and even when you were a little girl I could tell if you were trying to cover up for somebody.'

To her horror, her shoulders began to wrack with grief as she broke down sobbing. 'You're right, Griff. He tried . . . h–he tried to rape me.'

In an instant, she was in his arms and he was comforting

her. 'The monster. I shall have words with him. He shall not go unpunished.'

She drew away and through glassy eyes, she said firmly, 'No, please don't. He eventually realised that what he was doing was wrong and he broke down crying. No harm was really done other than to my dignity. He's struggling. He's grieving the loss of his mother.'

'But didn't we lose our mothers too, Megan?' Griff spat out the words in disgust. 'And neither of us did anything as deplorable as that.'

He looked at her. What could she say? She realised he spoke the truth. There had been no excuse for Eli's bad behaviour, none at all. He was a grown man who should have known better.

So she stood for the longest time staring at the pavement beneath her feet, not even noticing the people who passed them by. They all became a sea of faces; she was fixated on how it felt, as if she might drown in her sorrow.

'I'll walk you there,' Griff said gently.

'No, please don't. It would look bad if you arrive with me. They could say that Eli had taken to drink because of you, and our relationship, but of course nothing has even happened between us. But they don't know that.'

He nodded. 'As you wish, but under no circumstances turn up at the house to see the man, will you?'

She shook her head. 'I shall be giving him a wide berth from now on. No fear.'

'Good. Then I shall call to the shop to see you later this afternoon.'

She smiled and nodded, then turned to walk off purposefully in the direction of Plymouth Street, her blue-ribboned bonnet bouncing on her head as she marched away. This was something she needed to do for herself.

Chapter Twenty-Three

Jed looked up from the wooden pallet he was packing with bread as Megan approached. When she told him what she had to say his eyes clouded over. Then, wiping the sweat away from his flour encrusted brow, he said, 'Well, it's been coming for a long time. Eli can't cope with Mam's death. She just did too much for him.'

Morris stood there in silence behind his brother. His expression, too, looked as if he did not quite believe his ears.

'Obviously I can't stay there any longer, so I've moved in above the shop,' she said.

'Aye, kick a man while he's down,' Morris mumbled.

Jed glared at him. 'Perhaps you want to try living under the same roof as our Megan has done all these years. Pampered, that's what he is. Got himself some sissy clerical job and can't even hold on to that!'

Morris walked away, muttering.

'I'm sorry, Jed. I'm afraid the wedding is off.'

'That's understandable. I never thought he was right for you in the first place . . .' It seemed as if he were about to say something else, but then Morris called him over.

Morris, she feared, now hated her. She felt bad about that as she had lived with him and his wife at his house for a few months, back when Eli had consumption. Maybe he'd never forgive her. But Jed on the other hand seemed very understanding about the situation.

'I'd better leave you to it,' she said.

Jed reached out and touched her shoulder. 'Pay no heed to Morris,' he whispered. 'Deep down he realises the truth.'

Megan arrived back at the tea room and put the urn on to boil. Lizzie and May showed up shortly after, fresh-faced from their walk from Abercanaid.

'Take your coats off and sit down,' she told them. They both exchanged glances. 'I didn't tell you this yesterday, but I've moved into the room above the shop,' she said, then paused to draw a breath. 'I won't be returning to Plymouth Street.'

'But I don't understand,' Lizzie said, her eyes glinting as if it were a shock revelation, which maybe, to her, it was.

'I know what it is,' May began. 'You moved in here as it's customary for the bride and groom to be under separate roofs before the wedding!' She smiled as if pleased with herself.

Megan shook her head. 'Something happened which I won't go into right now, but Eli and I shall no longer be getting wed.'

There was silence, until Lizzie broke it. 'But why ever not? Have you fallen out?'

Megan clasped her hands, her palms were perspiring. 'Not exactly . . . sort of, I suppose. He's taken to the drink again and got a bit, how shall I say, abusive yesterday. I decided I can't marry someone who would put the bottle before me.' Both girls nodded. 'How do you feel about it, both of you?' She realised how they'd looked forward to being bridesmaids and wearing the new dresses Mrs Evans had laboriously stitched.

'Well, I'd rather see you happy, Megan,' May said, standing and embracing her sister. Then Lizzie did the same thing. She'd have to tell Tom, of course, but she knew he'd understand, as would Harry and Alfie.

Later that afternoon, Griff arrived at the tea room and Megan called both sisters over to meet him. 'This is Laurence Stanbury, a very dear friend of mine. He used to be known as Griff, if you remember him.'

Lizzie's jaw almost hit the floor with surprise, and May just stood there blinking. As with most of the town of Merthyr, they weren't used to seeing distinguished gentlemen such as Griff. It also didn't hurt that he was very handsome indeed, she thought proudly.

'You can close your mouth now, Lizzie. Don't want to be catching flies now, do we?' Megan chuckled.

When the girls had got over the surprise, the four of them sat with a tray of tea and some cucumber sandwiches, and fancy cakes for afters.

'Do you both remember me then?' Griff asked the girls.

'Only vaguely,' May said. 'I was very young back then. But Megan often spoke about you over the years – she could never forget her special friend who went to London to seek his fortune.'

Griff quirked an eyebrow and gazed intently at Megan as if to say, *What on earth did you tell the girls that story for?* But then he relaxed as he realised she could hardly tell the truth to the two young girls at the time. Maybe one day they'd all sit down like this in the future and he could tell them the real story; they were old enough now and had grown into beautiful young ladies, just like their elder sister.

After a very pleasant time, Griff stood and said, 'Well, ladies, I have to be on my way. I have to sign a contract this afternoon for the chambers I shall be taking over for my new law firm.'

Megan smiled proudly as the girls became excited.

'So, you're stopping in the town, are you?' Lizzie said, her brown almond eyes shining brightly.

'Yes, I plan to stay around for a very long time' – he glanced at Megan – 'if a certain someone should like me to?'

Megan felt a flush rise up from her neck towards her face as her sisters stared at her, putting two and two together.

And as she watched Griff leave the shop with a spring in his step and his cane beneath his arm, she realised that there was someone else that she must take Griff to meet.

After closing up the shop for the day she made her way up the High Street towards the Vulcan Inn. It was a long time since she'd visited Scamp and she wondered if the dog was even still alive – it had a been quite a few years since she'd last set eyes on him. At first, her intentions of regularly walking and taking care of the dog had been good, but all the work at the tea room and other family duties had worn her out, and over time, her visits had got fewer and fewer.

When she arrived at the pub it was busy as usual. There was no sign of Florrie – perhaps she'd already moved. There was another young barmaid in her place, who was shamelessly flirting with the men, handing out foaming tankards. They teased her and she slapped their hands away good-naturedly.

Feeling downhearted that nothing seemed the same any more – now that she was an adult she was no longer petrified of the pub – she suddenly realised how stupid her idea had been. Of course the dog still wouldn't be here. What a silly thought!

She was about to turn to leave when a well-dressed woman with her hair swept up elegantly into a bun emerged from behind the bar. They stared at one another for a moment before Megan found her voice. 'F–Florrie? Is that you?'

The woman, who had up until now appeared quite calm

and in control, began to grin broadly. 'Well I never, if it isn't young Megan! I haven't seen you in years, *cariad*. You used to come around regularly to walk old Scamp.' She hugged Megan warmly.

'I'm sorry I kept away. You know I often thought of coming to see you all but eventually I got so busy at the tea room. I'm running it now, you know.'

'Well I never!' Florrie arched an eyebrow. 'That's Mrs Mathias's place?'

Megan nodded. 'She passed away, sadly. And what about you, don't you look the lady these days?'

Florrie chuckled. 'Well I'm now the honourable wife of Fred Harper, the landlord.'

'That's wonderful. I'm so pleased for you, Florrie. Fred's a good man. And I've got some news for you, too: Griff is back in Merthyr!'

Florrie's eyes rounded like two saucers. 'I can't believe it. Whatever happened to him? You wondered for years, didn't you?'

'His uncle had taken him to London like we thought but he managed to escape and ended up being looked after by a wealthy couple and educated at Oxford. He's quite the gent now and hopes to open a legal practice in the town.'

'Well, well,' Florrie said with hands on hips, just like she did back when she was a simple barmaid.

'So I wanted to surprise him and I wondered . . . is Scamp

still alive?' She didn't want to get her hopes up but at the mention of the little mutt's name, Florrie's face warmed.

'He is, an' all. I'll take you to see him. Doesn't get walked much these days, with his old bones being so stiff and all.'

She led Megan out through the bar and into the backyard where, in the corner sleeping on his rag bed, was Scamp. His fur had greyed, and he was a little thinner, but there was no denying that it was the same dog that she used to spend so much time with. He opened one eye when he saw Megan, then the other, and wagged his tail. He stood and slowly made his way over to her. It was obvious his hips were playing him up, but it didn't stop him coming over.

'Oh, Scamp,' she cried. 'You remember me! I've got such a surprise for you. Your Griff is back! It'll be our little secret!' Crouching, she snuggled into the dog's wiry fur and felt his heart beat against her skin.

'Anything Fred and I can do to help with your surprise for Griff, let us know,' Florrie said. 'Now, how would you like a nice cup of tea? We have a lot to catch up on . . .'

'That would be lovely,' said Megan, as she brushed away a tear with the back of her hand.

Chapter Twenty-Four

'Lizzie and May, you'll be in the carriage with Harry and Alfie, oh and you do look a treat in your bridesmaid dresses,' Megan said, stooping to peck both girls on the cheek.

They were in Mrs Evans's living room, getting ready for the big day. Harry and Alfie both had matching suits and looked quite the young gentlemen, but it was Tom who stood out most. He was well over six feet tall and filled his suit so well. He was strong as an ox, just like their dad had been. He smiled proudly at his sister.

'Come on, Meg. It's time to go,' he said, holding out his arm so she could loop with his.

In the end, Mrs Evans had made Megan a new wedding dress, even more beautiful than the last. It was made of a very fine French white lace and had a long train and short veil. They'd decided that Lizzie and May should wear the original bridesmaid dresses as they'd been so excited about wearing them, and they really were very beautiful, with the blue ribbon and pearls. But Mrs Evans was very superstitious and said it would be bad luck for Megan to wear the first dress. She would sell that one; it wasn't meant for Megan. And if Megan were being honest, she preferred the second dress anyhow.

In her hands, she held a beautiful bouquet of white lilies and white roses. Garlands of green ivy trailed from it, creating a lovely effect against the white of her dress.

'Thank you for all you've done for me and the family,' she whispered to Mrs Evans, who was wiping a tear from her eyes. 'Now you'd better get in the carriage with Mr Evans – the one behind the one with the bridesmaids. Our carriage will be last of all, obviously.'

Mrs Evans chuckled. 'Oh yes, the bride cannot arrive before anyone else. You don't need to tell me that! And you've already had your fair share of bad luck over the years, haven't you? But I have a feeling your luck has changed. I always thought Griff – I mean Mr Stanbury' – at this she did a little mock curtsy – 'was a good lad who had a bad start in life.'

'Oh absolutely, Mrs Evans.'

Megan and Tom waited for everyone to leave for their respective carriages, before pausing to look at one another.

'Well your big day is finally here, sis.' Tom grinned. 'And I couldn't wish for you to marry a finer man.'

Megan nodded. She had never been more sure of herself in her life.

When they arrived at the parish church, the clouds parted and the sun shone through as if just for them. All was well and God was in His heaven.

As she walked down the aisle towards the man she loved, her mind shot back to that autumn afternoon so long ago, when she'd chased that little boy down the High Street and hidden in the graveyard of this very same church.

Griff turned and smiled at her, and as she reached him, he took her hand in his own. He had that same mischievous glint in his green eyes when they said their vows as the first time they'd met. What was he not telling her?

But when she gazed into his eyes, all her fears melted away as she said, 'I do.'

As they walked back up the aisle to Mendelssohn's Wedding March, she noticed Jed wink at Griff.

Outside the church, as people congratulated and wished them both well, Megan's eyes scanned the wedding guests for a clue as to what might be going on. Kathleen and Dafydd were there, beaming brightly and wishing the newly married couple a happy life together. That gladdened Megan's heart: she had been such an important part of their early lives together.

It was lovely to see Jed and his family despite what had happened, and even Morris had decided to make an appearance with his wife and daughter. There was no Eli, but that was to be expected. As Jed had explained, he was too raw after what had happened and was bitterly ashamed of himself. . Given time, though, Megan hoped things could go back to being how they used to be, when she'd just felt like he was simply an older brother to her. But nothing or no one could ruin today for her.

Megan had been on the lookout for Fred and Florrie, whom she'd spotted seated quietly at the back of the church without being noticed by Griff. Now they were walking towards them, and Scamp was at their heels. Megan tugged at Griff's sleeve. She couldn't wait to see his surprised face.

'There's a very special wedding guest I'd love you to meet,' she said.

He turned and only saw Florrie and Fred stood before him. 'But there are two of them, not one!' He grinned, though still pleased to see them both.

'No, Griff, look a little closer.'

'But I can't see anyone . . .' He shook his head.

Then Fred pulled on the rope lead and slowly Scamp emerged, shuffling towards him.

'Scamp!' Griff cried. 'I can't believe you're still here!'

'Aye, he is an' all,' Fred replied. 'He's an old dog now, mind, but he keeps going. He missed you like anything when you went away, Griff. Pined for you, he did, went right off his food an' all. From what Megan's been telling me, you've done well for yourself, lad?' He shook Griff's hand.

'I haven't done too badly, I suppose,' Griff replied modestly.

'And Florrie, aren't you the lady too!' He took Florrie's hand and kissed the back of it as she smiled.

'We all missed you so much, Griff, but maybe it's the best thing that ever happened, and that rogue uncle of yours did you a favour in the long run.'

'I've really missed you all,' Griff said, nodding.

'But apart from Megan, it's the dog you missed most, I expect?' said Fred.

Griff wiped away a tear, crouching down as Scamp sidled up to him and licked his face.

'Don't worry,' said Megan. 'He's not forgotten you.'

Griff hugged the dog to him as tears streamed down his cheeks. And he didn't care what people thought, either. He was that twelve-year-old boy again in the grounds of the parish church with Megan. He hadn't forgotten where he came from.

Scamp could no longer perform tricks and leap up into his arms, but Griff was so happy to have found his old chum again.

'Megan,' he said, when he'd finally found the strength to pull away from Scamp. 'I have a feeling you're behind this?'

'She is indeed,' said Fred. 'And you're welcome to visit him any time you like, Griff.' He patted his shoulder and then shook his hand. 'Well, thanks for inviting us to the service, Megan. Sorry we can't come to the wedding breakfast, but I have a pub to run. You'll always be welcome, the both of you.'

Florrie, Fred and Scamp, stood in the churchyard with the

other wedding guests who threw rice at the pair. Megan had never been so happy in all her life and guessed it was the same for Griff.

Finally, when they were settled in the carriage that was to carry them to their new four-bedroom home in Thomastown where the reception was to be held, she turned to look at her handsome new husband and asked, 'What's going on, Griff? You've been grinning like a Cheshire cat!'

He tapped the side of his nose with his index finger. 'All shall be revealed soon enough!' He chuckled.

Two minutes later he called to the carriage driver, 'Please can you stop here for a few minutes!' The carriage was drawing up outside the tea room.

'I don't understand. Why have you brought me here, Griff?'

The tea room had been the last thing on her mind for today. She'd closed especially for the wedding to take place.

He helped her down from the carriage and escorted her to the door with one arm around her waist. On the door itself was a 'Closed' sign and written underneath was *'For a very special occasion'*.

'Now what's going on here, Griff?' she demanded in a good-natured way.

He slipped his hand into his trouser pocket and extracted a heavy-looking silver key. 'I had this made especially for you. It's solid silver,' he said, and then chuckled.

'That was kind of you,' but she still didn't understand.

'Do I have to spell it out for you, Megan? I've bought this place for you from the brothers. From now on, it's all yours! You've got your very own tea room now. It's not rented, it doesn't have to be returned to anyone, it's all for you . . .'

Tears streamed down her face as he handed her the key and she unlocked the door. Then he took her arm, preventing her from going inside.

'One moment, if you please,' he said. She looked at him in a curious fashion as he swept her off her feet, carrying her in over the threshold as she clung on, with her arms wrapped around his neck. She laid her cheek against his, inhaling his raw male scent. 'Happy?'

'Thank you, Griff. I've longed for this day for so long, but I never thought it would happen . . .'

'The best is yet to come,' he said, setting her down and taking her into his arms. She tilted her head backwards and he kissed her with a fiery passion.

It was all she ever dreamed of and more, and now she was 'Mrs Stanbury', a woman of means with a man to match. Who could ask for more? she thought, as she melted into her husband's embrace.

Glossary

bach	term of endearment ('my dear', 'my friend')
bosh	sink, basin (Welsh dialect)
butty	a friend or mate
cariad	term of endearment ('my love', 'darling')
cwtch	cupboard or cubbyhole or cuddle
Oh fy ddaioni	'Oh my goodness' (Welsh)

Acknowledgements

The world is a better place thanks to people who wish to help others move up a rung on the ladder of life. One such person is Editorial Director at Quercus Books, Emily Yau, who discovered *The Workhouse Waif* on Amazon Kindle and offered me the chance of a traditional publishing contract for not just that book but *The Matchgirl* and two future books in the series. Emily is a delight to work with and she has the ability to make my stories sparkle and shine. Thank you for giving me a chance to reach for the stars and be over the moon about it! It's the start of an amazing journey for me!

The Matchgirl

Lynette Rees

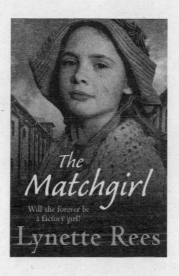

A heartwarming saga, from the ebook bestselling author
of *The Workhouse Waif.*

Sixteen-year-old Lottie Perkins has an important
decision to make . . .

Conditions at the match factory she works at are dire.
The girls get treated badly by the management and there is
a severe risk to their health. But then a young journalist,
Annie Besant, begins asking questions. Will Lottie and the
other girls welcome her help, even when it could cost them
their jobs – and their livelihoods . . . ?

A Daughter's Promise

Lynette Rees

A heartwarming saga, from the ebook bestselling author
of *The Workhouse Waif*.

Eighteen-year-old seamstress Kathryn Flynn lives in
Whitechapel, London, struggling to support her
widowed mother and younger siblings. But when her work
starts drying up and her mother falls ill, she is forced to
consider desperate measures . . .

Then she meets 'Squire', an older city gentleman, who falls
instantly in love with her and offers to take her under his wing.
'Squire' could give Kathryn the life she's always wanted . . . but
is there something darker lurking beneath his kindness?